Silver Darlings

LK Wilde

Prologue

All corners of the island heard the screams. New life, fighting its way into the world with force and ferocity equal to any gale which battered its shores. Souls teetered, and Bill prayed this would not be an exchange, one life for another.

Anna's face twisted in agony and sweat deadened her hair, leaving it tangled like seaweed against her pillow. With his hand clinging to hers, Bill forced his eyes away from the dark stain of blood beneath his wife and willed her to fight on.

An unearthly scream tore the air. As its echoes faded, a smaller cry filled the silence. Bill looked on as the nurse placed a bloodied, bruised parcel of flailing limbs onto his wife's breast. Anna lifted a protective arm around the bairn, and Bill's beard soaked with the happiest tears.

*

With one hand steadying herself against a wall, Rose lifted the other to her mouth and stifled a scream. A tide of pain ebbed and flowed like waves in the distance. Feet spread wide, she rocked her body, allowing it to follow its own well-trodden paths. She removed her shawl, her body hot against the crisp, cool, night, and looked towards the cottage. No one came, and she steeled herself to make it through alone.

A wave of pain coursed through her, and Rose let a wild cry escape into the night sky. Something slipped from between her legs.

She reached down and wrapped the creature in her shawl. Rose held the bairn close, offering him a breast onto which he latched. As she stroked him down, a tiny hand curled around her thumb. With the bairn content, she pulled the gutting knife from her waistband and hacked at the cord that held him to her.

Rose hobbled back to the cottage, the bairn in her arms. The older ones were sound asleep and Alex lay passed out by the fire, an empty ale jug kicked over by his feet. With the tiny boy placed in a basket, Rose eased her aching body into a chair and returned to the net she had been mending.

THE ISLAND

Chapter 1

January, 1900

In the cramped space beneath the table, Jimmy hugged his knees to his chest to stop them shaking.

"It'll be fun," Clara promised, as she dragged him through the legs of islanders and into their hiding place.

"I dinna like this."

"Don't be such a scaredy-cat, Jimmy Watson."

Jimmy stared at the booted feet of his da. Alex slumped lower in his chair, his legs inching close to Jimmy's face.

"That's me mam," Clara whispered, pointing to small, well-polished boots.

Jimmy's eyes bulged as Anna shifted in her seat and her skirt rose to show a pair of delicate ankles. Clara giggled.

"Shush," said Jimmy. His body shook, legs banging against Clara's back like sticks on a drum.

The tree trunk leg of his mam whipped across and kicked her husband's shin. If things were turning ugly, it didn't bode well for him.

"Ugh, what's that?"

A puddle of liquid crept to the edges of Clara's skirt. Face burning, Jimmy saw dampness spread across the front of his trousers.

Clara shrieked and bolted out from beneath the table. Light poured in as the cloth lifted and four grown-up faces stared. Dirty fingers reached for Jimmy, grabbing a handful of thick curls and yanking him out by the hair. He stumbled, sending glasses and plates spilling across the crisp white cloth. Before Jimmy could steady himself, Alex Watson hauled him towards the door. Children sniggered, men looked away, women tutted or smiled in sympathy.

Jimmy screeched as his feet lifted from the floor and hair ripped from his scalp. Their faces inches apart, the acrid stench of liquor filled the air between him and Alex. Flecks of saliva shot from Alex's curled lips as he spoke.

"Git yerself back home. I'll deal with ye once I'm back."

Jimmy hit the ground; gravel tore his skin, and the hall door slammed. From beyond it came sounds of celebration. He brushed himself off and crept to a window. Even on tiptoes, he couldn't see in. He dragged a creel from the nearest yard, climbed up and peered through the glass.

The hall was lit by a warm glow. Women busied themselves serving food, and the landlord of The Crown was doing a roaring trade from his barrel. Clara sat on her mam's lap, heads nestled together, their auburn hair a perfect match. A stab of jealousy hit Jimmy as he watched them. His own mam was chasing after his sisters, dragging them to sit beside her. After Jimmy's disgrace, she would keep a close eye on her bairns. On the makeshift stage stood Old John, readying himself for a song. In one corner, children huddled, comparing treats gathered from their earlier door-to-door Hogmanay.

Jimmy jumped down from the creel. His skin prickled beneath sodden trousers and the wind had a fair bite as it whistled through his thin shirt. He shuddered. Opaque cottages huddled against a dark sky. Nets hung like cobwebs, stacked creels like monsters guarding scuffed doors. The village streets filled with eerie wind's song and Jimmy remembered his sisters' tales of ghosts. They claimed they had seen a robed monk walking through the ruined priory and swore a Viking had called to them from the shore.

From the corner of his eye, Jimmy saw a lurking shadow and sprinted to his cottage. The fire had burnt out, the small room lay in darkness. Fear of Alex eclipsed any fear of the night, and he stepped out into the yard, removing his trousers and washing them in a bucket. He sniffed them to be certain they were clean, then hung them behind the privy, out of sight, and, he hoped, out of mind.

It was freezing in the cottage. Jimmy lay on a mattress and pulled rough blankets up tight. The shivering was incessant; no amount of blankets could still his trembling limbs. Like a caged animal, he stayed alert, jumping with every creak in fear that Alex had returned.

Joyful shouts filled the streets as islanders made their way to the watch night service. By midnight, he was still awake, welcoming the dawn of a new century with a deep sense of dread.

Chapter 2

February, 1905

Clara bent over a basket, placing the baited line down in neat rows to be sure it would not tangle. On a low wooden stool sat her mam, threading thousands of slippery mussels onto a line with speed and ease. Anna's complexion displayed none of the lines that exposure to the elements should have brought. With her back straight and waist slim, Clara thought she looked more like her sister. The only sign of the life she led was her hands, their skin chapped and raw. Years of working with a fish knife had left scars in patterned white lines that zigzagged her palms.

Mother and daughter hummed as they worked, only looking up when footsteps approached the cottage. Anna beamed as the wooden door creaked open and a large, bearded man ambled towards them. Clara jumped up, throwing her arms around his waist. He reached down and stroked her hair before tilting her face towards his.

"Bin a good lass for Mammy?" said Bill, smiling down at his daughter.

"She has... most of the time," said Anna, walking over to kiss her husband's cheek. "Good catch today?"

"Aye, was reet enough. A good few cod on the lines and lobsters in the pots."

Bill sat, pulling off his boots, then hanging his sou'wester on one of the many wall hooks. His enormous frame dwarfed the old chair, and it creaked as he lowered himself into it. Anna and Clara cleared away the lines and picked up their knitting. Bill threw another chunk of driftwood into the hearth. Its flames danced as the driftwood blackened, spreading a warmth through the cottage akin to that of the small family who lived within its walls.

Soon the cottage filled with the sounds of wood crackling and the clinking of thin metal. Anna's needles flew at twice the speed of her own, but Clara knew she was improving. Last year, she could only work on hems and cuffs, but this year she had begun work on her first gansey. Woven navy yarn spilled across the scuffed surface of the table, its patterns mirroring the nets and lines stored in the rafters above.

Anna glanced over at her daughter. "Keep it tight."

"Aye, I'm trying." Her hazel eyes squinted and concentration played across her brow. In contrast, Anna barely looked at the needles in her hands, her fingers sure and steady. Clara studied her mam's technique, hoping her efforts would pay off. She wanted her da to benefit the following winter as he braced himself against the freezing sea air.

Clara rubbed her tired eyes with the heels of her palms and gazed around the room. Rag rugs warmed the stone-flagged floors and a few precious ornaments littered the dresser beside her, hinting at a previous life Anna had left long ago.

Clara yawned, the warmth of the fire seeping into her tired bones.

"Time for bed," said Anna, glancing from her knitting while her slim hands worked.

"Aye."

Clara stretched her arms high, yawned again, then bent to kiss her parents goodnight. In the bedroom, she pulled back the heavy curtain which split the room in two. Her friends shared beds with at least four siblings, but as an only child, she had the space all to herself.

Beneath her patchwork quilt, Clara pulled blankets tight to ward off the chilly night. Not long after, her parents retired, causing Clara to stir from her slumber. From behind the curtain came Anna's quiet breathing and Bill's low rumbling snores. Clara closed her eyes and fell back into her dreams, a contented smile playing on her lips.

Chapter 3

March, 1905

Jimmy trudged through the village streets. Every front door he passed had cairns of shells, nets, and creels piled beside it. An icy wind whipped round him and he quickened his step. He kicked open the door of his cottage, dumping an armful of broken nets beside it. While his eyes adjusted to the gloom inside, the squalls and shouts of female voices reached his ears.

"Where's yer da?" said Rose.

"Where do ye think?"

Rose reached across the table and cuffed him round the ear. "That's enough of yer cheek, lad. Help me get the bairns settled, then go fetch him. If he drinks away today's earnings, we won't survive the week."

Rose heaved herself off a chair that squeaked in relief as her weight shifted from it. She wiped the slime of bait onto her filthy apron and set about gathering up hordes of bairns. The baby sat hitting driftwood against the floor, her cheeks red raw from wiping snot across them. Jimmy's stomach twisted as he watched. He pitied the poor bairn, not yet old enough to walk out of the door and far, far away.

Rose screeched at the feral bairns, and thin arms wrapped themselves round Jimmy's legs. A small face peered up at him. Even covered in grime, his sister shone with innocent beauty. He scooped the little girl up and kissed her filthy cheek.

"Hello, my little Marnie, how are ye doing today?"

Marnie snuggled into his neck, stuck a dirty thumb in her mouth, and began twirling his thick hair. Jimmy reached his hand round to her ribs and began tickling. His sister dissolved into giggles, squirming in his arms.

"Put the bairn down. I'll never git her to sleep with ye deeing that," said Rose, as one child became tangled in her long skirt and another tried to escape under the table. Jimmy winced as Rose pulled the little girl out by her foot, looking round for a slipper to give her a good hiding.

With coaxing from Jimmy and threatening from Rose, they rounded up the bairns. Girls lay crammed on a stained mattress, struggling for a piece of rough blanket, before huddling together for warmth. His elder sisters had put up a fight, indignant they should go to bed before Jimmy, but Rose would not entertain their raging.

When their breathing turned heavy, Jimmy crept over and looked at them. His sisters, all seven of them, lay in a tangle of limbs, slumber a brief respite from the harsh reality of their waking hours. The eldest, Sally, had outgrown the mattress, and her stockinged feet poked out from beyond its edge. Even in her sleep, her mouth turned down at the corners. Jimmy's eyes moved across to Marnie. Precious Marnie. He tried his best to shield her from the worst of family life, but those enormous eyes saw.

A harsh whisper snapped him from his thoughts.

"Jimmy, Jimmy."

"Aye?"

"Get yer da back here. Ye kna where he is."

"Aye," he said, pulling his coat back on and heading out into the dark night. He knew where Alex was, the same place he always was.

Inside the Fisherman's Arms, the smell of stale sweat, rotting fish, and tobacco hit Jimmy hard. Bile rose in his throat. He swallowed it down and pushed through the gaggle of fishermen. Alex was at the far side of the room. Jimmy wasn't sure how old his da was, but he couldn't be much over thirty. He looked like an old man.

Alex's head drooped forward, chin resting on his chest. A growing circle of saliva was forming on his gansey as he slumped unconscious against a barrel. The hair on his head was thinning and his cheekbones protruded like jagged fish knives.

Men jeered as Jimmy put his arms round his da and tried to heave him off the floor. Despite his thin frame, Alex was a dead weight. Try as he might, Jimmy struggled to shift him. Someone crouched beside him, and he turned to see Bill's large, bearded face looking at Alex in disgust.

"Dinna fret, Jim lad. I'll help ye," he said, adding under his breath, "ye shouldn't be needing to dee this, ye kna."

Bill lifted Alex to his feet. Together they dragged him from the bar, his feet scratching a smooth trail into the sand and dirt as he went. Once the frosty air hit, Alex came to, flailing around, cursing and hollering into the night. Jimmy's face flushed as his da stumbled towards home.

"Sorry. Ta."

Bill watched Jimmy melt away into the darkness. He gave a long sigh, before turning to make his own way home.

Jimmy drew closer to the cottage and saw Alex scratching at the door to find its handle. He reached across and opened it, Alex falling through and stumbling into a chair that crashed to the floor. Steadying himself against the upturned leg, Alex scowled at Jimmy, spat on the floor, then made his way to bed. Jimmy righted the chair as Alex lurched onto the bed and put a bony arm around his wife. Rose tried to bat it away with a rough, plump hand, to no avail.

After using the privy and fetching himself a drink, Jimmy sat down on a scruffy chair by the hearth. He rested his feet on a stool and pulled a thin blanket over him. A few embers still glowed deep orange, bursting with sparks that crackled as they burnt themselves out.

After a long day, Jimmy needed rest. He had long outgrown the cramped bed. It wasn't right sharing the floor with his sisters, who were turning from girls to women with every passing day. Besides, he enjoyed sleeping by the fire. He could sleep anywhere, and this was the only solitude he got.

From over in the bed came muffled voices and Rose's sharp whisper of, 'No.' But then it started up, the rhythmic creaking, the grunts of his da. Jimmy grabbed his woollen hat from the table and pulled it down over his face, praying it would muffle any noise that might otherwise reach his ears.

He was soon asleep, avoiding the thuds of a fist hitting Rose's soft flesh. He didn't hear the cries of the baby, shoved from the warmth of the bed into a box beside it, making room for the spindly man who didn't need the space.

Chapter 4

April, 1905

Clara stubbed the toe of her boot in the dirt, scattering earth and stones into the air. She hovered outside the schoolroom, contemplating whether the risk of playing truant would be worth the freedom. Mrs McKinnon appeared in the doorway; Clara had left it too late to escape. She met the teacher's frown with a scowl and shuffled inside to take her seat. A butterfly mind flitting through thoughts and ideas was not conducive to concentration. Her right hand still bore the bruises of a ruler against her skin.

White slipped across black as the teacher's chalk clicked and swirled against the board.

dough, gaunt, farce, serve, frame, mull, prune

Clara's mind soon drifted, soaring like the gulls she glimpsed through the tall windows. *Click, click, click.* Chalk in hand, the teacher rapped against her slate. *Click, click, click.* Clara gave a small jump and, looking down, realised her slate had filled with doodles; birds, flowers and boats. She looked up at Mrs McKinnon.

"Stand up, child." The teacher's lilting Scot's voice would have been pretty had it not housed such a hard edge.

Clara stood behind her wooden desk. The teacher marched across the schoolroom and reappeared with the dunce's hat. She ignored Clara's pleading eyes, pulling the hat down on her head and instructing her to stand in the corner. Clara turned puce, and tears stung her eyes. She would not cry. She would not cry. She would not... a fat tear slid down her cheek. With the sleeve of her dress, she scrubbed it away. Classmates sniggered. Time dragged on, minutes passing with agonising sedateness.

The dinner bell rang, and Clara walked out, head held high. Her composure lasted until she stepped into her cottage, where she unburdened her anger to the listening ear of her mam. Instead of offering comfort, Anna chided.

"You must pay attention at school, my love. It's important for your future."

"But it's so dull! And that Mrs McKinnon is as mean as a witch."

"I've met her a few times around the village and she's always seemed very pleasant to me. I think it's you that's in the wrong on this occasion."

Clara scraped her chair under the table and stormed outside. Too early to return to school, she paced the island paths, stomping out her anger, fuelled by hatred of both school and teacher. She often stole glances at Mrs McKinnon and concluded she was a miserable creature; dressed in black, hair pulled tight in an unflattering bun. She might have been pretty, were her mouth not set in a hard line.

Clara walked and walked. The sun tipped lower in the sky and she realised she was in danger of being late. By the time she reached the village, her breathing was ragged and sweat dampened her hair. Outside her cottage, she crossed the street, ashamed of how she had behaved but not yet ready to apologise.

She found Jimmy with his sisters, finishing up some bread and salted fish. Clara's stomach growled at the sight of the children eating and she realised she had missed dinner.

"All right?"

"Aye, I will be, as soon as I can leave the stupid school and evil Miss behind."

"You know she's only trying to help us? You could try listening in class, then maybe ye wouldn't get in trouble so often."

"I don't know why you stick up for her."

Jimmy sighed, threw his crumbs away for the birds and kissed his sister's cheeks. "Away with ye, Miss Troublemaker," he said, smiling at Clara. "We'd best be going or we'll be late and in even more trouble." With his arm linked in Clara's, he walked her back to school.

Clara kept her head down and avoided the teacher's eye. Jimmy sat straight-backed, hanging on Mrs McKinnon's every word. 'Teacher's pet,' Clara muttered, then regretted her unkind thoughts. It was hard to resent Jimmy, his dirty clothes disguising his too thin frame, the tangled mass of un-brushed curls perched on his head. She tried to emulate her friend; sitting still on the wooden seat, repeating her times tables, listening to the teacher. But the pull of the outdoors on her free spirit was strong, the view so tempting. By five o'clock, the effort of conforming had exhausted her.

Chapter 5

May, 1905

As Jimmy neared school, a spring entered his step. The first Watson bairn allowed an education, he didn't intend to waste the opportunity. Rose had announced on his seventh birthday that he would start school the next day. As he grew older, he realised it had been a calculated move on her part. As their only son, he would follow his da into fishing. But Alex Watson was unreliable. Drunk by the time he sold his catch, he often fetched a poorer price than if he had his wits about him. Rose was no fool; she needed someone to take over the finances, and for that, her son would need educating.

Jimmy always arrived early and found his teacher appreciated not just his promptness, but his attitude towards his studies. Mrs McKinnon was different with him. She looked into his eyes, willing him to absorb the knowledge she had to share. His teacher was aware, even if Jimmy wasn't, that he was a bright boy. 'Sponge Jimmy', she called him, on account of the fact he soaked up all the knowledge she could throw at him. Within weeks of starting school, she gave him his own work, leaving the other island children flailing behind.

This school day followed the pattern of every other. The time flew by, the end-of-day bell both a surprise and an unwelcome reminder of the reality lurking beyond the schoolroom walls. As Jimmy was leaving for the day, Mrs McKinnon stopped him. She placed a chilly hand on his arm and waited for the children to file out. When just the two of them remained, she looked at him.

"Jimmy, would you like to stay behind for extra classes at the end of each day?"

"Aye, Miss, that I would, but Mam will never allow it. She wants me home to help with the bairns."

"Let me see what I can do," said Mrs McKinnon. She winked, and Jimmy flushed at the uncharacteristic behaviour of his stern teacher.

That evening, Jimmy and Rose sat mending nets when a knock came on their door.

"Git that, Jim."

Mrs McKinnon stood in the doorway, her firm manner and steely eyes an equal match for Rose.

"Hello, Jimmy. Is your Mam home?"

"Uh... uh..."

Rose pushed past him in the doorway. "What dee ye want?"

Her rudeness left Jimmy mortified.

"I have a proposition for you," said Mrs McKinnon. "I need some help in the schoolroom. Could I borrow Jimmy for an hour at the end of each day, to help clean the place up, stack chairs and such like?"

"No ta," said Rose, moving to close the door on the teacher.

Mrs McKinnon stuck her booted foot in the doorway and poked her head into the gap, "I'll pay him a shilling a week,"

"A shilling?" said Rose. "Aye, alreet." With that, she closed the door once more. Mrs McKinnon knocked again. "What?" shouted Rose, loping back across the room. "Can ye not see we've work to do?"

"I wanted to say how well Jimmy is doing with his studies."

"Grand," said Rose, and turned away. Jimmy gave his teacher a shy smile and closed the door.

He turned to see Rose gazing at him. "Don't be getting any fancy ideas from Miss high and mighty. Yer place is here. Once ye can take care of the money, I want ye oot on the boat with yer da, reet?"

Jimmy nodded, his shoulders slumping down.

The following afternoon, as the school day drew to a close, Jimmy felt his palms grow sweaty and his heart begin a frantic thump in his chest. His classmates rushed out like freed prisoners, but Jimmy walked to the front of the room and cleared his throat.

"What job would ye like me to start with?"

Mrs McKinnon laughed. It was an alien sound coming from the fierce schoolmistress.

"No chores, Jimmy." She smiled at him and signalled for him to sit down. "Have you heard of Rabbie Burns?" He shook his head as she pulled a dog-eared book of poetry from her desk drawer.

Chapter 6

May, 1906

Thanks to the shilling a week, Jimmy enjoyed a year of extra studies. Rose made him hand over his coin on a Friday, and kept them hidden in a tin behind the privy, safe against Alex's wish to drink their money away.

One Friday, Jimmy returned to the cottage and handed over his shilling as usual.

"That'll be the last one," said Rose as she made her way outside.

Jimmy followed her. "What do ye mean, Mam?"

"Ha! Ye're the clever clogs, work it oot!" she said, brushing past her son.

"I thought ye were happy for me to be learning?"

"Aye, reet I was, but ye'll turn eleven tomorrow and it's time ye were oot helping yer da."

Jimmy was powerless. "Can I go tomorrow and say thanks to Mrs McKinnon?"

"Ye'll be oot on the boat tomorrow. Why thank her? Ye've been her skivvy for years, haven't ye?" Her eyes dared him to admit the unspoken truth between them.

Jimmy turned on his heel and fled the cottage. There school lay in darkness, but a yellow glow came from the rooms above. No pupil would dare venture into the teacher's living quarters. Mrs McKinnon appeared, framed within the lighted window, reaching across to close her curtains. She glanced down, holding his gaze for a moment before shutting out the night.

As he walked away, Jimmy heard his name being called.

"Jimmy? Jimmy?"

Mrs McKinnon stood outside the schoolroom, but she didn't look her fierce self. She was wrapped in a blanket and her hair, rather than pinned in a bun, hung below her waist. She beckoned to him and he walked towards her. Sharp eyes darted over him, taking in his flushed face.

"You'd better come in."

He followed her to a side door and up the flight of wooden stairs to her living quarters. Several oil lamps bathed the small room in light. Against the far wall stood piles of books reaching the ceiling. On another wall hung photographs and paintings of landscapes dominated by lakes and mountains.

"Sit," she said, and Jimmy sat himself on a wooden chair, adorned with coloured cushions. A small bed stood in the corner, covered in silks and cottons.

The room took Jimmy aback. It was so incongruous with the stern teacher that for a while he couldn't speak. Mrs McKinnon seemed not to mind, making tea, without asking why he had come.

Settling a steaming cup on a polished table, she pulled up a chair and looked at Jimmy with questioning eyes.

"I... I... I won't be at school tomorrow, or any other day. So, I wanted... to say ta."

"Well," she said, "they gave you longer than I expected. This moment was inevitable."

“I don’t want to leave,” said Jimmy, hands shaking as he picked up his cup.

“I know, but we don’t choose the life we’re born into. We have to do our best with the lot we’re dealt.”

Jimmy nodded and for a few moments they sat in silence, sadness hanging in the air, sucking the brightness from the room.

“Keep hold of your dreams, Jimmy. You’re a clever lad. Who knows where your path might lead? I never thought I’d be a schoolmistress on an island. Look at me now!” She gave a smile that didn’t reach her eyes, before moving across to the piled books.

Jimmy watched as she thumbed through the various titles. After squinting at the books for a while, she pulled out a volume with one hand, steadying the others on top so they didn’t fall. Mrs McKinnon handed him the book she had chosen. *The Complete Poems and Songs of Robert Burns.* Jimmy took it from her and stroked the worn book with his thumbs.

“Someone special gave that to me. Now I want you to have it.” She pushed his hands away as he tried to return the book, embarrassed by her generosity.

“Ta,” he said.

He opened the cover and noticed a handwritten message.

To my dearest Maggie,

My very own red, red rose

All my love, Christopher

Jimmy’s cheeks reddened, and he closed the book, abashed at this private world he had stumbled upon.

“It’s alright, Jimmy,” said Mrs McKinnon, noticing his embarrassment and smoothing over it. “Christopher was my fiancé. We were to marry when he returned from the Boer War, but he never came back.

Now you know why I've become the spinster school ma'am that I am. Please don't tell your friends. I'm not ashamed of my position in life, but I don't wish to be the subject of village gossip."

"I won't tell a soul."

Mrs McKinnon stood up, signalling it was time to say goodbye. She reached across and took his hand in hers. "Good luck, Jimmy, I hope life deals you a kind hand." As she was turning away, she said, "I've more books if you'd like them... but you'd need somewhere safe to keep them."

*

Jimmy stepped out into the dusk. The moon was three quarters full, the island bathed in a silvery glow. Not yet ready to return home, he passed the Presbyterian church, the parish church, and found himself by the ruined priory. Lit by moonlight, stone pillars and arches took on an ethereal quality. He could see the ancient monks walking through its grand halls and cloisters, hear the rustle of coarse robes and plaintive songs sung.

He strolled on and paused at a little sandy beach. Mrs McKinnon had told him of Cuthbert, and he wondered if he now stood in the footsteps of the saint. He thought of Cuthbert, wading out till neck deep in water, and shivered. Saint or not, standing in freezing water each night sounded like madness.

Jimmy stuck to dry land, leaving the beach and climbing up a grassy embankment. Halfway up he veered off, taking a path invisible unless standing on the beach below, his feet picking their way as the cliff descended inches to his left. He leaned into the rock, walking on until he reached a booth, cut into the cliff face. Nestled between the pebbled beach and cliff top, it hid him away from prying eyes. The remains of a fire sat in the centre of the cave. No doubt someone had been here wooing a lassie, he thought, and kicked the ashes to check they weren't fresh. Against a smooth rock, Jimmy took out the book of poems and read.

Chapter 7

March, 1907

Despite the winter fishing season nearing its end, there was plenty of work to do. Anna left soon after daybreak to fetch water from the well and sent Clara to collect mussels for baiting. Clara walked to the shoreline. She knew by heart the best places to find them and picked her way over loose rocks left exposed by the outgoing tide.

With no breeze, the rock pool lay still, acting as a mirror to the sky. Her bucket splintered its glassy surface, disturbing the life hidden on its sandy floor. Clara began removing mussels from their rocky home with an expert twist and flick of her wrist. Other women and girls were doing the same. The older women had creels on their backs and moved with a pace that Clara envied.

Clara walked to the Watson girls, working alongside them in companionable silence. When she straightened her aching back, she saw Rose stomping towards them.

"Get oot of there – that's our pickings."

"Oh, sorry," said Clara. "I wasn't trying to take what's yours. Here, take some of mine." She began transferring some of her haul into little Marnie's basket.

"Do ye think we need yer charity?" said Rose, grabbing a handful of mussels from Marnie and scattering them over rocks with force. Clara looked at her open-mouthed, but Rose stared until Clara moved away.

She glanced over at the family. Marnie looked up, caught her eye and smiled. She waved to Clara. Clara waved back. Rose noticed and Marnie got a smack that Clara felt the sting of from many feet away.

Clara returned home and sat with Anna, threading the mussels onto a line. She watched her mam, carefully trying to replicate her effortless movements, but try as she might, she couldn't match her pace. As they worked, Clara told her about the incident on the beach.

"How can someone be so unkind to their bairns?"

"Unkind people are unhappy people," said Anna.

As her mam reached over and squeezed her hand, Clara was aware how lucky she was.

*

Two small girls walked through the door of the cottage, followed by Jimmy. Their clothes were as grubby as their smiles were wide.

"Can Clara come play?" The youngest girl looked at Anna through a mass of untamed curls.

"Please, Mam. I'll take the bairns to search for fossils. I can help you with the bait once I'm home."

Anna smiled, put down the line she was working on, and knelt beside the two girls. "And who might you be?"

The younger of the two stuck a thumb in her mouth and hid behind her brother. "This wee one is Marnie, and this here is Ada," said Jimmy, trying to move Marnie from her hiding place. "Marnie the Monster," he said into the small girl's curls. She giggled, peeking out from beneath her mass of blonde hair and smiling at Anna.

"Ah, that's right. I've seen you girls around the village, but I get confused with the names. There are so many of you! Pleased to meet you, Ada." The girl shook Anna's outstretched hand. Turning to Marnie, she tried again. "Pleased to meet you, Marnie."

Marnie looked at her brother for reassurance. After getting his nod of approval, she removed the thumb from her mouth, wiped it on her dress, and offered an outstretched hand.

"I'm surprised to see you, Jimmy. Are you not out fishing today?"

"No, Miss Anna, my da's poorly in bed." Jimmy flushed deep red as he spoke. "Mam asked me to get the bairns out of the house so he can have some peace."

Anna nodded. "You'd best be off then. Bring me back a fossil and mind you're home in time for supper." She shooed the children out of the cottage.

The young girls took Clara's hands and Jimmy followed behind. Clara called over her shoulder, "What's up with yer da? Is he alright?"

Jimmy muttered a reply, but Marnie, shyness gone, was happy to give Clara information. "Mam said it's his own fault for getting paletic last night. He was heavin' in the night. Now he has a sore heed."

Clara didn't know Alex well, but she'd seen him staggering through the village and heard him yelling in the street when she was trying to sleep. She thought of Bill and once again recognised her own good fortune.

They walked through the village until they reached a cluster of small tin sheds. Creels spilled across the ground and a curtain of nets hung from poles. Old John Dunton perched on a box, pipe between his teeth, net between his legs.

"Back in a tick," said Jimmy, running to chat with the old man.

The little girls waited impatiently for their brother, Marnie jumping onto a wall and yelling, "Quit yer blethering!"

Old John waved to her as Jimmy obeyed and joined his sisters. Clara and Jimmy lifted the girls over a crumbling stone wall before climbing it themselves and following the edge of a farmer's field. Crops turned to grassy scrubland as the field sloped down to a pebble beach.

"Let's have a competition. Whoever finds the most Cuthie beads is the winner."

The two girls yelped with enthusiasm, searching among the stones for the small fossils.

"Look, Clara, look," said Marnie, holding out her palm. The grey fossil was as large as a shilling, the biggest Clara had seen. Neat lines rimmed its circular edge, as though someone had pressed a fork into dough. The lines smoothed out towards a round hole, gaping at its centre.

Clara ruffled Marnie's hair. "It'll be hard to beat that."

They continued their search and within half an hour, the pockets of Clara's skirt were bulging with small fossils. As Clara bent to pick a sixpence-sized fossil, something hard hit her head. She turned, and another object hit her on the forehead. Jimmy reached down to grab a handful of shells from his basket.

"Jimmy Watson, you stop doing that or I'll... I'll..."

"You'll what?" said Jimmy, pelting Clara with shells once more.

Clara bunched up her long skirt and ran, drawing fossils from her pockets and hurling them towards him. The girls joined in, and the four children ran screeching round the beach, shells and fossils flying like missiles through the clear air.

Clara grabbed another bead to throw, but her boot caught on a rock and she fell backwards into the icy March water. The cold acted as watery pins, piercing through layers of wool and stinging her skin. Splayed out on her back in a stunned silence, she could make out the shape of Jimmy blocking the sun.

"Hey, are you all right?" His face was full of concern, but seeing his solemn expression Clara laughed, and soon was laughing so hard she couldn't get herself back up. Marnie and Ada joined the laughter, jumping in the tiny waves that lapped the shore, flinging fossils high into the air, peppering ripples over the otherwise smooth surface of the water. Jimmy reached a hand to Clara and heaved her up. Her front was dry, but her back was sopping wet and she shivered with the bite of the cool March air.

"Here," said Jimmy, removing his gansey and placing it around her shoulders. They sat on the beach, watching the girls running in and out of waves.

"Jimmy? Can I ask you something?"

"Aye."

"How often is yer da... um... poorly?"

Jimmy stared at the ground. Clara wondered if he'd answer, but he lifted his head and said, "Most days."

The girls ran over, and the moment passed.

"I'd best get back," said Clara, pointing to her sodden back.

"Aye, ye don't want to catch a cold."

The girls protested, but Jimmy scooped one under each arm and they made their way towards the village.

Back at the cottage, Clara changed out of her wet clothes, hanging her dress to dry by the fire. She returned to her work and recounted what she'd heard about Alex Watson.

Anna sighed. "Aye well, I'm not surprised. Alex Watson should be careful. The sea's a dangerous place, but to be out there under the influence... well... that's madness."

Chapter 8

April, 1907

Jimmy leaned starboard and ran his palm across the hull of the *Mary Lou*. Sharp splinters scratched his skin, peels of paint jammed beneath his nails. The pads of his fingers pressed down, sinking into a soft patch of rot. He sighed. There was never enough money to fix her up. The *Mary Lou* was a shadow of her former self.

Men walked past, shaking their heads as they took in the peeling paint and bodged repairs. Jimmy kept his head down. Their footsteps receded, and he peered up through his curls. The *Mary Lou*'s crew were sauntering towards him and he vaulted out of the boat to greet them.

"Any sign of the skipper? I thought he might be with ye," said Jimmy. He scanned the shoreline but saw no sign of Alex.

The crew shook their heads. They leaned against the harbour wall, taking meagre pinches of baccy from rusty tins, rolling it tight, killing time. Jimmy wondered if they should begin preparing the boat, but until they knew whether Alex would appear, there was little point.

"I've got better things to dee than wait around all day," said Robert, self-appointed leader of their motley bunch. He sucked hard on his tab before jerking his head for the other men to follow. They looked from Robert to Jimmy.

"We should wait a little longer," said Jimmy.

"Na. Tide's heading out. If he's nae here by now, he's nae coming."

Jimmy knew Robert was right, but resented the weasel of a man questioning his authority. It was hard to find a crew for a boat barely seaworthy, whose skipper was unreliable paying wages. Jimmy was unsure where Alex had recruited his men from, but he guessed some of them had never fished before. Robert's smugness and swagger were unfounded, for he showed little aptitude out on the water.

"Get on with ye then," said Jimmy.

One lost day would not matter much, for the *Mary Lou* never matched the haul of other boats. Although Jimmy worked hard, no amount of work could reverse the fortunes of his da's enterprise.

Knowledge passed down to Jimmy by his da was scant. A less able lad would have missed the titbits flung out during sober episodes. Information crucial for navigating the waters and steering the boat away from hazardous rocks that lurked beneath its waves. Relief came when Alex passed out, and Jimmy could guide the men in their endeavours. Fishing was in his blood. With another crew on a different boat, he might have even enjoyed it.

Further along the harbour, Bill was readying his boat, and Jimmy strolled over to watch. The *Annabelle* was a beauty, flat-bottomed and high bowed, painted in crisp blue, red and white.

"Ye nae oot today?" said Bill.

"Nah. Da's not shown up."

"Want a trip on *Annabelle*?"

"Aye," said Jimmy, grinning as he jumped down beside Bill.

The crew shuffled to make room for Jimmy and picked up their oars. Beyond the harbour, they raised the lugsail and were soon sprinting over curling waves. A vast sea spread before them. The world opened up, and Jimmy dreamed of sailing to new lands. From Bill, Jimmy filled in the blanks left by patchy knowledge handed down by his own da.

Bill would have Jimmy as a permanent member of his crew given the chance. Although young, Jimmy was tall and strong and kept pace with the best of them. Bill remembered Clara telling him Jimmy hated fishing. Watching him mucking in with the rest of the crew, Bill didn't believe it was fishing Jimmy hated. It was his fisherman da.

*

The following day Alex graced them with his presence and the *Mary Lou* creaked her way out of harbour. Jimmy looked across at the *Annabelle*, the crew nodding to him as he passed. Alex couldn't go out as far as the other boats, given the condition of his vessel, and Jimmy couldn't decide if he preferred the days they came home with a good haul or the days they didn't.

After successful trips, the joy of a good catch would be short-lived. Coming from the Fisherman's Arms, whose landlord acted as banker, Alex would be drunk. Jimmy curled in embarrassment as he slurred out lies, cursing the stingy banker, the stench of ale on his breath exposing the true miser among them.

Today would not be one of those days. Alex sat grim-faced and stony-eyed as the *Mary Lou* sailed home, nothing to show for their day at sea. He was the first to leave the boat when they moored up, striding along the harbourside, fists clenched. There was still work to do, but Jimmy recognised the signs and threw apologies at the crew as he ran to catch Alex.

Jimmy kept a few paces behind, waiting to see the direction Alex would take, praying he would head to the pub and not the cottage. Alex stood in the middle of the street, feeling in his pockets. He pulled them inside out, but they were bare. Jimmy knew what was coming. He jumped in front of the cottage door.

"How about we go for a walk, Da?"

"Let me pass."

"Come on, Da, yer upset. Let's leave the bairns a while and come back later."

"Let me pass."

"Da..."

Alex put his shoulder to Jimmy's side and shoved him out of the way. He pushed past, standing in the middle of the room glaring. Rose sat still at the table, holding her breath. The bairns ran and cowered in a corner.

"I need coins."

"We dinna have no coins," said Rose.

Alex took a step forward and bent down, nose to Rose's cheek.

"I said, I need coins."

"We dinna have none."

In one swift movement, Alex grabbed Rose's hair, slamming her head into the table.

"Where are they?"

Rose tried to speak, but he had squashed her head down so hard her lips couldn't move. Alex yanked her hair, whipping her head back before smashing it back down. Pinned to the table, Rose's eyes sought Jimmy's. Blood was pooling on the wood beside her. In three strides, Jimmy reached Alex, pulling him backwards. Alex kept hold of Rose's hair and she let out a scream.

"Let go of her," said Jimmy. "Let go!"

Alex laughed, released Rose from his grip, and turned to Jimmy. Experience taught Jimmy it was best not to fight back. If he did, the beating would last longer and his sisters would be more frightened. Jimmy stood and waited for Alex to do his worst.

The next few minutes blurred into a series of fists and feet. Slumped beside the table leg, Jimmy's fingers felt around his body. There was an egg on the back of his head. Sticky blood clung to his eyebrow, a stream of blood poured from his nose. He tried to stand, but pain ripped through his chest. Below his gansey, he saw the first blue tint of bruises forming.

Alex turned his attention to the cottage, turning over the mattress, chairs, blankets. Beneath the store of driftwood, he found a shilling. After holding it to Rose's face, he stormed from the cottage, slamming the door behind him.

However hard he hit her, however much damaged he caused, Rose never once mentioned the tin of shillings in the privy, and Jimmy admired her for it. He wondered what she would be like had she married a man like Bill. She worked as hard as any woman on the island, but did it with bruises and broken bones, knowing her hard-earned money would go into the pocket of a pub landlord.

She fed her children on scraps; rejected fish from her husband's catch, potatoes, and the odd loaf of bread. Her size was thanks to nature, not nurture, for Jimmy often noticed her skipping meals so her children ate. She was harsh, brash and often unkind, but Jimmy was astute enough to realise she loved her bairns.

Chapter 9

April, 1907

On Easter Day Clara woke to the soft thud of a mug being placed beside her on the dresser, and the weather-beaten face of Bill smiling down at her. Steam danced in the air and her own breath mixed with it as she reached to pick up the cup. Back against her pillow, she shivered as the cold of the room hit and slunk further down under the coarse woollen blanket.

"What time is it, Da?"

"Five," he said. "We need to git gannin' if we're to make sunrise."

Clara slipped from the warmth of her bed and wrapped the blanket around her shoulders, following the sounds coming from the small kitchen. The hearth had been lit and Clara hung the blanket on the back of her chair as she sat down.

"Happy Easter, Mam."

"Happy Easter, love."

Anna placed down two boiled eggs in front of her daughter. She cleared the broken nets and fishing hooks Bill had been tinkering with, and in their place put a jug of wild flowers.

"Eat up, Clara, the sun will come up soon."

Once they finished their eggs, the small family pulled on their warmest garments and headed off down the dark village streets. Just visible was a small light on the Heugh, the highest point on the island.

They climbed towards it, joining other local families gathering for the ritual of seeing in the Easter dawn. Someone propped a large wooden cross against a stone shelter, and they waited with anticipation for the sun to ascend.

They had witnessed countless sunrises, but none compared with the Easter dawn. The weather blessed them with a clear sky, and it wasn't long before a vast array of pastel pinks replaced the solid darkness. As the first sliver of sun slid above the distant castle, a band of orange burnt above the sea like flames. Their collective voices welcomed its coming with a hearty rendition of 'Christ the Lord is Risen Today'.

The sun continued its ascent, throwing shards of light onto the ripples of the harbour. Many would've thought their life hard; all their time devoted to the rhythms and tasks of fishing life for little reward. But standing on that hill, island life felt magical.

The family took their time greeting neighbours. Bill shook the hands of his fellow fishermen, even nodding to Alex Watson. Anna huddled with the womenfolk, sharing any gossip from the few hours since they last spoke. Clara smiled as she watched them. No stranger could pick Anna out as an interloper. She looked as at home among the fishing community as any other woman there.

The disquiet caused when Bill had announced Anna as his bride was long forgotten. There had been an expectation he would marry his own kind, and many questioned whether his young lass would keep up with the work of a fisherman's wife. Within a few short months, Anna had not only proved the islanders wrong, but had captured the hearts of men and women alike. Island men respected the way she carried out her duties and envied her husband for finding someone with such beauty. The women of the island warmed to her amiable smile and conversation. A year after they married, the islanders thought her one of their own.

Anna left her friends and stood beside Clara, wrapping an arm across her shoulder as they stared out at the sea. "This is the most beautiful place on earth. I thought so the first day I set foot on this island and nothing's happened in the intervening years to change my mind."

"Tell me again how you came to marry Da."

Anna laughed. "Again? Really?"

Clara grinned and gave an enthusiastic nod of her head.

"Well, I was living down in North Shields with my parents when I met your Da. He was in town dealing with some fishing business. The first time I saw him was when my mother sent me out to run some errands for her. I was carrying a basket full of bits and pieces, walking through Fish Quay minding my business, when the heel of my boot caught the hem of my skirt. Everything from my basket spilled over the path, and a man bent down to put the items back. The most handsome man I ever saw. He made sure I got home, and I had butterflies in my stomach long after he'd left. After that, every time he came to North Shields, he would call on me. Before long, we were stepping out. My father was not best pleased about it, I can tell you. He shouted and cursed when I told him we were to be married, and none of my family came to the wedding. I've not seen any of them since I left that house, and I don't regret it for a moment. It was the best decision I ever made." A smile played on her lips as she spoke, a mischievous glint in her eye.

"It's so romantic," said Clara with a sigh.

"Aye, it is, but you've got plenty of years before you need to think about romance. Now, why don't you join that rabble?" Anna pointed to the beach where the Watson children were playing.

Clara ran down to the harbour and joined Jimmy and his sisters. Soon they were skimming stones, squealing with delight as they skipped along the surface of the calm water. It was a rare opportunity to play by the harbourside, for they knew the upset it would cause if they were here while the fishermen were working.

Bill told Clara many times of the occasion when, innocent of their ways, his new bride brought him supper before he ventured out to sea. Her appearance at the water's edge caused terror among his crew. They abandoned fishing for the day, convinced some terrible fate would befall them. He laughed as he told the tale, but Clara was careful to keep her distance when she knew the men were working.

As the islanders began to disperse and climb down from the Heugh, Clara left her playmates and ran over to her parents. She took her da's hand, the familiar roughness of his skin worn hard from hauling ropes and lines.

"Clara, why don't you have a quick tidy of the lobster pots? There's something there you'll like," said Anna.

Clara rushed to the strewn debris by their front door. Amidst the lines, nets, pots and mussel shells lay a small package wrapped in newspaper and tied with string.

"Is this for me?" she asked.

"Yes, love. Bring it inside and you can open it."

Clara rushed inside and put the package down on the table. Fighting back her impatience, she pulled back the paper, taking care not to damage whatever was inside. A small toy rabbit sat amongst the paper. Clara picked it up and turned it around in her hands. It was beautiful, made from patchwork fabric and sewn delicately with invisible seams.

"I thought it would be nice to have a sign of spring," said Anna.

"Did you make it?" Clara asked.

"Aye."

Clara hugged her. She knew how hard Anna worked, how little free time she had. "You're the best mam in the world," said Clara, hugging Anna again.

Chapter 10

May, 1910

A thick mist hung over the island for the entire month of May, clinging to the rocks along the shoreline and cloaking the village in murky half-light.

On the eve of her fifteenth birthday, Clara rubbed at the small window of the cottage, as if by clearing the inside of the glass she would banish the ghostly fingers that swirled beyond it. To walk out in clear air, gulls above and seals basking on rocks, would be the best birthday gift. It didn't look promising.

"Staring at it won't make it go away," called Anna.

Clara sighed and joined her parents at the old wooden table. Bill chuckled upon seeing her deep frown and covered her small hand with his.

"Tomorrow will be a fine day, even without fine weather," he said.

Clara looked up at him and smiled into his big, kind eyes, creased in amusement at her frustration. She jumped at a loud banging on the door.

"There's a ship in trouble," yelled the voice from outside as the sound of heavy boots thundered past the cottage.

Bill stood and his chair fell with a crash against the stone floor. Without stopping to pick it up, he grabbed his sou'wester from its hook, pulled on his boots, gave his wife and child a kiss, then ran out of the door.

*

Jimmy sat fighting with a tangled piece of line when a hammering came on the cottage door.

"Alex," said a gruff voice. "ALEX." The man's voice was urgent. Jimmy rushed across to open the door. Old John stood outside in his wet weather gear, face flushed and an anxious look in his eyes.

"Where's yer da, lad? We need to launch the lifeboat."

Jimmy glanced over his shoulder in embarrassment. Old John looked through the gloom, to the pathetic figure of Alex by the fire. Slumped backwards, his arms hung by his sides, head tilted back, cheeks puce.

Old John swore and kicked a lobster pot in anger, causing Alex to stir before resuming both his position and his snoring.

"I guess ye must dee then, lad. Grab yer gear."

Jimmy hesitated only briefly, for he knew there would be no waking Alex, and besides, Jimmy wouldn't dare say no to Old John Dunton. He grabbed his sou'wester, boots and followed the burly old man through the village. They met Bill coming out of his cottage, and Jimmy listened as the two men discussed the situation.

"It's a steamer, likely run aground. They saw the rockets at Longstone, but Seahouses lifeboat is in for repairs, so we got the shout."

The beach teemed with island men. Old John led Jimmy to the lifeboat house. Trepidation mingled with awe as Jimmy stared at the thirty-four-foot vessel, her low middle sweeping to high air-cases at either end. He got straight to work, attaching horses to the trailer that would launch the lifeboat into swirling mist-strewn waters. She was a heavy beast, and it took six horses to help her slip into the water. Jimmy climbed aboard and took up his oar. As he gripped the wood, his knuckles clenched white, aware that as the smallest of the crew he would need to hold his own.

It seemed as if the entire island were holding its breath, then exhaling in a plume of misty smoke that hung just above the waterline. The crowd on the shore was silent but for quiet prayers muttered under their breath. *Grace Darling* slipped her way into the water and the men began their perilous journey into the dense fog.

Jimmy had been out in rough seas, where waves rose like ancient monsters, threatening to consume you beneath their aching jaws. Tonight, he was more frightened than he ever had been at sea. There was an eerie stillness. The sea was flat and calm, but the surrounding air nightmarish. Tendrils of fog swirled around the boat in a slow, ghostly dance. The silence chilled him. He was used to sea that played out a rowdy song of crashing waves and screaming gulls. Now, all he heard was the plopping of oars cutting through the black water beneath, and the patter of droplets as the oars rotated through the air.

The coxswain signalled to put down their oars. The men pulled them up and caught their breath. The lifeboat was heavy, and Jimmy cursed the sting of blisters on the pads of his fingers. A sticky trickle of sweat ran down the back of his shirt.

"What's deein', John?" asked one of the crew.

"Ah dammit, I canna see a thing oot there," said their coxswain, scanning the horizon to no avail.

The men looked around them. A shudder of fear flowed through the boat. The usual landmarks that guided their way had vanished; Heiferlaw, Swingle Trees, Beal Muck Midden, The Beanstacks. All had melted away beneath the blanket of fog.

The men sat in silence, twisting themselves round to glimpse anything that might give them a clue where they were. Nothing. The boat sat bobbing on the oily, ebony surface of the water, the cloying dense fog showing no sign of abating. They knew these waters like the backs of their hands, knowledge passed through generations like a treasured heirloom. This damn fog had rendered all that prized knowledge worthless.

Jimmy's body prickled with panic. He was taking many breaths but getting no air into his lungs. His head spun, his palms were sweaty. Jimmy pressed his hand to his chest to still his heart, but it beat rapidly, banging against its bony cage. He spun his head round, trying to spot signs of hope in the other men's faces, but the frowning foreheads, wide eyes and silent mouths betrayed their fear. Jimmy's small body shook. He wrapped his arms around himself to control it, but to no avail.

A large hand came down with some force on his shoulder and squeezed it. Bill leant in close and began speaking into Jimmy's ear.

"Deep breaths, Jim lad, deep breaths. Ye'll be reet. We will git oot of here, dinna ye fret."

The pounding in his chest let up, his breathing became slower and the prickling around his body ceased. "Ta," he said over his shoulder.

"Nae bother," said Bill, giving Jimmy's shoulder one last squeeze before resuming his position in the boat.

"Lads," called the coxswain, and twelve heads spun around. "We canna sit here all night. I say we press on. We kna we're heading north-east but easy does it. We will na see the rocks in this bloody fog, and we dinna want the rescuers to end up needing rescue!"

On his command, the men gripped their oars and continued to row, parting the curtain of grey that closed behind them as the boat inched its way through.

A shout pierced the ghostly silence. "Ahoy there, over here!"

The crew paused their rowing, listening out for the voice. Old John barked orders, and with some effort they swung the vessel round and followed the sound of the call.

Out of the gloom appeared the silhouette of a ship. As the lifeboat edged towards it, the crew knew something was amiss. Its hull was at a strange angle, the starboard side jutting out too high. It reminded Jimmy of when he'd fallen from a tree and broken his arm, leaving the bone straining at the skin.

The lifeboat pulled up alongside the ship. As they drew closer, Jimmy rubbed his eyes, convinced he must be hallucinating. Other men exclaimed at the sight, and Jimmy knew the image was real. Over the side of the ship leaned a young boy with a fishing line. Jimmy's mouth gaped open. It reminded him of the Tweed, where children gathered with crabbing pots and fishing lines. But this was no summer's day.

On seeing the lifeboat approach, the boy raised an arm and waved at the crew on board.

"Ahoy there! Have you come to rescue us?"

"Aye, that we have, lad," Old John called back, tugging at his beard in bewilderment. "Where's the rest of yer crew?"

"Oh, they're down below trying to patch the hole. We got lost in the fog and found ourselves caught on these here rocks."

"So I see. Um, will ye fetch the captain fer me?"

"Yes, sir, that I can. He's my father."

The boy propped his fishing rod against the side of the ship and disappeared, returning a few moments later with the captain.

"Good evening, gentlemen. I see you've met my son."

Old John shouted instructions to the captain and soon the crew of the distressed steamer assembled on the deck, ready to make their way into the lifeboat. It was a slow process getting the men across, but at least the sea lay docile beneath them. The captain's son came across first and settled himself next to Jimmy. The boy chatted away, oblivious to the danger he had been in, and thrilled at the rescue. Jimmy warmed to the boy, drawing comfort from his laissez-faire attitude. His clenched muscles loosened as the boy wittered on.

Once the last of the crew reached the safety of the lifeboat, Old John issued the order to pull away and the *Grace Darling* slipped back through the water to the relative safety of the open sea. The men briefly paused their rowing as the steamer let out a groan, before keeling over, the sea eating it up into its depths.

Relief was temporary, for the next challenge was to navigate to Seahouses further down the coast. Once again, they slipped through the fog, but they were in safer waters, the dangerous rocks that were the downfall of so many ships now behind them.

They reached Seahouses at first light. A night on the water had exhausted the men. Jimmy's oar had turned a reddish brown as the blisters on his hands burst, leaving a stain upon the wood. The village greeted them with a heroes' welcome. The King's Arms opened its doors, and the men gathered by the fire, blankets around them, sipping sweet tea.

"Got anything stronger?" called out Old John, raising his cup as a signal to the landlord.

"Bit early, isn't it?"

"Not if ye haven't bin to bed," said Old John to guffaws from the crew.

Soon, the men each had a pint of ale in their hands, jovial despite their tiredness. The rescue had been a success, all lives spared. The captain's son lay sleeping across three stools and only woke as jugs of ale slammed down on tables as men laughed and bantered with each other.

Bill clinked a knife against his jug, and the men paused in their merriment. "Lads, I've just recalled that today is my daughter's birthday, which means it's also Jimmy's."

The crew cheered, clinking glasses with Jimmy, and causing him to blush with pleasure.

"A fine way to begin yer special day," said Old John, and everyone cheered.

A cart arrived to take the crew home, and they piled into the back, ready to begin the slow trudge up the coastline back to the island. The men were soon dozing, lulled to their slumbers by the rocking of the cart and the rhythmic clacking of the horse's hooves.

Chapter 11

May, 1910

As dawn broke, Bill was yet to return. From Anna's uneven breathing, Clara knew she was awake. She tiptoed round the curtain and sat down on top of Anna's blankets.

"Can we go to the harbour?"

"Aye, alright, but I'll put the kettle on first."

Clara was impatient to scan the horizon for signs of the lifeboat and its precious cargo. But seeing her mam's red-rimmed eyes, dark purple half-moons beneath them, she complied and went to fill the kettle herself.

Anna was pulling on her underskirts as Clara appeared with a cup of steaming tea. She gave a weak smile, took the offered cup and wished Clara a happy birthday.

In all the worry, Clara had forgotten that today she turned fifteen. Despite herself, she rushed to the window. The fog had cleared. One birthday wish granted. If only Bill would walk through that door.

By the time the women had dressed, there was still no sign of the lifeboat crew. They walked through glorious spring sunshine to the harbour where they met several women from other families. None had news, but no news was good news, and all clung to that hope. The women shielded their eyes from the bright sunlight as they stared towards the horizon. Other than the few small fishing boats bobbing gently on the early morning tide, there was nothing but a calm, flat expanse of blue, stretching out for miles, broken only by the dark mass of the Farne Islands in the distance.

Clara and Anna turned themselves away from the harbour and back towards their cottage. They walked in silence, neither wanting to burden the other with the dark thoughts filling their minds.

A familiar figure sat at the kitchen table.

"Da," said Clara, running to Bill and flinging her arms round his giant frame. Anna followed suit and only released him when he began laughing and spluttering.

"I'm alreet, or I will be as long as ye let me git some air," he chuckled, wrapping an arm round Clara's waist and pulling Anna onto his lap.

The relief that flooded the cottage was palpable. Clara and Anna settled themselves at the table as Bill sipped from a jug of ale thrust into his hand by a publican on his return. They listened as he recounted his story of the struggle through the fog. Clara's eyes widened as he told how they had found a small boy leaning over the side fishing, while the men below worked in a frenzied panic.

"We reached them just in time, five minutes after we'd got them all on the lifeboat their own ship keeled over. If they'd still been on board, we'd have lost them to the sea."

"What about the lad?" Clara asked.

Bill gave a deep guffaw and took another swig of his beer. "Oh, he was reet enough. He reckoned it was the most exciting voyage his da had ever taken him on. I'll eat my hat if the boy's story dinna appear in the *Advertiser* this week."

*

His head already fuzzy from the ale in Seahouses, Jimmy refused the offer of another on his return and left the other men behind to their revelry. The island was looking beautiful in the spring sunshine. As Jimmy walked along the grassy track, he stopped and bent to gather wildflowers. Satisfied with the blaze of colour that filled his palm, Jimmy carried the posy down to his shed by the harbour. Among the disorganised shelves, he found a roll of twine and secured the stems together.

As he walked through the village, Jimmy paused at Clara's door, unsure whether to knock or leave the flowers for her to find. He told himself he didn't want to disturb the reunion taking place inside, but truth be told, he felt shy, his heart hammering inside his chest. He settled on a middle ground, placing a quiet knock on the door, hoping they wouldn't hear.

*

Clara looked up from her sewing as she heard a gentle knocking on the door. She found Jimmy bending down, leaving a neat little posy on the doorstep.

"Jimmy? What are you doing?"

Jimmy straightened up, colour flushing his cheeks. He held the flowers out in front of him.

"Happy birthday," he said, going redder still.

"Thank you," said Clara, her face turning a similar shade to his. "Happy birthday to you, too."

A voice called out from inside the cottage. "Is that you, Jimmy? Come on in."

Clara stepped aside and Jimmy walked past her, head down, neither of them wanting to catch the other's eye. Bill slapped Jimmy hard on the back. "This lad's a hero," he told his wife and daughter. By now Jimmy was sweating, desperate to escape into the air outside.

"I'm no hero. I did no more than the rest of ye."

"Ye did, lad, had to listen to that wee boy blethering away fer hours. If it were me, I'd have shoved him overboard." He let out a loud guffaw that splintered the tension and left Jimmy more at ease.

"Aye, he was a chatterbox, that one. Didn't seem afraid of being on a sinking ship, just wanted to catch his fish." Jimmy started laughing. He laughed and laughed till his sides hurt.

Clara watched Jimmy, and Anna watched Clara. She had seen them in the doorway and smiled to herself. Oh, to be young again.

Bill poured some of his ale into a cup for Jimmy, and this time, Jimmy didn't refuse. He sat with the family for a while before deciding he must return home. He thanked Anna for her hospitality and nodded at Clara, who blushed again.

When he walked through the door of his cottage, Jimmy was almost knocked off his feet by the gaggle of girls who flung themselves at him. Several of his sisters had red-rimmed eyes, and it startled Jimmy that Rose's were the same.

"Glad yer back, lad." As Rose moved past him, she squeezed his arm.

Alex didn't get up from his seat, his mouth set in a hard line of resentment. "Git off the lad," he said. "He's back from sea, nae war."

Jimmy's sisters took no notice, and Marnie gripped his hand all day.

Chapter 12

June, 1910

The days were drawing out, and the air turning warmer. So far, June had been unusually warm and as Clara lay in bed, the mix of heat and anticipation made it impossible to sleep. With the herring season only a few weeks away, the island was abuzz with excitement. Everyone had more spring in their step, and island life teemed with colour and drama. Soon the population would swell, not just with crew but also with herring girls.

Bill's snoring was grating, making sleep more elusive. Layers of blankets lay strewn on the floor. Clara counted sheep, worked on her knitting, then gave up and climbed out of bed. She grabbed a shawl from the dresser and crept through the cottage. Her foot caught on a wooden stool, sending a loud scrape against the stone floor. She paused, listening for sounds of her parents stirring. Nothing. She clicked the iron door fastening up, and stepped into the night air.

Clara filled her lungs with a big gulp of sweet summer air and strolled through the village. Her legs guided her, following the paths they knew by heart. At the harbour, the air filled with sounds of small waves washing against fishing boats, then licking the pebbles as they lapped against the shore. Stones crunched beneath her feet. Below the Heugh, she hoisted up her skirt and climbed the rocky outcrop. Surrounded by inky darkness, she paused just a few seconds before moving on.

It was cooler on the Heugh, and Clara pulled her shawl closer to her as she walked. On the descent towards the priory, she hesitated, then turned to a thin path that hugged the rugged cliff. It was only wide enough for one foot at a time, and Clara questioned the sanity of walking it shrouded by darkness. A faint glow of light emanated from within the cave nearby. Unnerved, Clara considered heading back and retracing her steps, but there was no room to turn, and navigating the meagre path backwards was foolish in the dark.

As she edged her way to the cave, relief flooded her when she poked her head around the jutting rocks and realised the light belonged to Jimmy. She watched him. He was reading by lamplight, his face shifting with emotion as his eyes moved down the page. An uninvited onlooker, she gave a quiet cough to make Jimmy aware of her presence. His head whipped up from the page he was reading. Her form unrecognisable against the night sky, Jimmy jumped backwards, kicking over the lamp, and snuffing out the flame.

"Who's there?" he called.

"Jimmy, it's me, Clara."

"Clara? What are ye doing here?"

Clara moved around the cold rock and flopped with relief in the small cave. Jimmy pulled a match from his pocket, struck it against the cave wall and held it to the lamp.

"Couldn't sleep, so I went walking. What are ye doing here?"

Jimmy waved the book in front of him. "Here's the only place I can read. I'd be struck if they caught me at home."

Clara nodded, then a thought occurred to her; "Jimmy, where did you get the book?"

Jimmy looked at her. "Can ye keep a secret?"

Clara nodded, and he moved further back into the cave. She watched as he removed several large rocks that Clara had assumed were part of the cave wall. From beneath them, he pulled out a large cloth bag and handed it to Clara. Inside lay a pile of books. Clara gazed across at Jimmy.

In answer to her unspoken question, he explained they were from Mrs McKinnon, given on the condition he kept them somewhere safe. Clara knew that this meant away from Alex. Even if people found the secret caves, it would be dark enough for them not to notice the carefully placed rocks at its farthest recess.

Clara reached into the bag and pulled out a copy of *Oliver Twist*. "Can I?"

Jimmy nodded, picking up his own book and resuming where he had left off. Clara shifted to a more comfortable position, turning the book in her hands before settling down to read in companionable silence. She stole glances across at her friend, so unlike any other boys and men she knew. His blond curls glowed in the lamplight, and thick lashes framed eyes the colour of the green flash at sunset. His book engrossed Jimmy, but Clara couldn't focus on the words on the page, reading the same sentence over and over. She dropped the book into her lap in frustration.

"Jimmy?"

"Mmm," he said, not looking up.

"Why do you like these books?"

"'Cause they take me to different places, other lives," he murmured, turning the page and continuing to read.

"But why would you want to? Our island's the best place on earth."

Jimmy looked up. "Is that what ye really think? There's an entire world out there, Clara, so much more than, than this." He gestured with his book to the beach, the sky, the island.

"Nowhere's as beautiful as here."

"How would ye know? Have ye ever left the island?"

"You know I haven't, Jimmy Watson, but I can read too, and I listen to stories me mam tells of where she's from."

"There's more places than just the island and North Shields," he laughed.

Clara felt stung. "Well, if you hate it so much, you'd better go."

Jimmy stood up, slamming his book shut and dropping it down to the floor. "Don't ye think I would if I could? It's alright for ye. Perfect family, perfect life. Ye dinna understand what it's like for me, ye're just a spoilt little girl!"

The walls of the cave amplified his raised voice, and tears sprang to Clara's eyes. She wanted to run, but the dangerous path prevented her. Instead, she crept along the cliff, Jimmy's eyes burning into her with every step.

Back on firm ground, Clara ran all the way home. Angry with Jimmy, but also frustrated at herself for not understanding. She'd seen enough of his life to know it wasn't a bed of roses. Back at the cottage, Clara crept into bed, pulled a cushion over her face and groaned.

Chapter 13

June, 1910

It was the end of June and all the fishermen were out landing their creels. They piled them high on the harbour shore and outside their cottages. The excitement in the air was palpable, and at supper that night, Bill was both jovial and restless.

He went to bed early, but lay tossing and turning, nervous energy keeping sleep at bay. When Clara woke the next morning, Bill had already left. After fetching water from the well, Clara wandered down to the harbour. Ahead of her were Jimmy and Alex. She hadn't seen or spoken to Jimmy since the night in the cave. Her cheeks flushed as she remembered that he'd called her a little girl. She did her best to dawdle, but Alex shuffled along, and it wasn't long before she had caught them up.

"Morning," she said, flushing again as she strode past. She marched on, determined to put some distance between herself and the Watsons. To her dismay, she heard footsteps behind her as Jimmy caught her up. A large piece of rope hung from his shoulder, and the cap on his head couldn't quite contain his mass of golden curls.

"Clara, I wanted to say sorry about our disagreement. I was unkind."

"Well, you were, aye, but I was also rude and insensitive. I understand there's more world out there than this island, Jimmy, but the island is all I need." She looked at him in the hope he understood. He caught her eye, but looked away.

"If the island were a patchwork quilt, ye'd be one square," he said with a smile that didn't quite reach his eyes.

The area around the harbour was a hive of activity. All the fishermen were out, dragging nets from sheds and rolling barrels up above the Ouse, ready for barking ropes, nets, and sails. Despite the hard work that lay ahead, the harbour had a festive feel. Sullen fishermen were grinning and laughing with one another. Several greeted Clara and Jimmy as they passed.

"What jobs are you doing today?" Clara asked as they neared the sheds.

"Need to get the ropes barked. Want to come?"

"Aye," said Clara, keen to be amidst the action.

They entered the dusty wooden shed and Jimmy bent down, fumbling around beneath a cluttered workbench and rifling through boxes. There was a small glass window facing the harbour and Clara stepped over boxes and creels to look out. It was thick with grime and she doodled the outline of birds into its filmy surface.

"Hey, come give me a hand, will ye?" called Jimmy, his voice muffled by various debris.

Clara bent down and grabbed the long length of rope Jimmy was holding out behind him.

"I know there's more in here somewhere, but it's hard to see amongst all this junk." He sat back on his heels and stretched his arms out above him. "Didn't feel such a small space when I looked there last year."

Clara laughed. His blond curls were grey with dust and cobwebs. A small spider was crawling down his back. "Stay still," she said and put her hands to his back. "I think ye've disturbed this poor creature's slumber." Clara cupped her hands around its small body and showed it to Jimmy. He yelped and leaped back further into the shed. Clara looked at him in surprise, then burst out laughing. "Jimmy Watson, are you scared of spiders?"

"Na," he replied, a blush creeping from his neck to his cheeks. Clara folded her arms and stared at him. He squirmed and looked at his feet. "Well... aye... maybe a little."

"You'd best come here then. You've probably got a fair few more in that mop on yer head."

She walked over to brush the cobwebs from his hair. Jimmy had to bend down for her to reach and Clara ran her fingers through his curls, pulling out bits of sticky web.

Despite the grit and tangled spider's silk, Jimmy's hair was soft, and curls twined round her fingers. A strange sensation crept through Clara's stomach, as if a kaleidoscope of butterflies were dancing around in there. Her hands paused their movement and Jimmy looked up at her from beneath his hair. Clara pulled her hands away, causing Jimmy to cry out as a curl caught around her finger.

"Careful, ye'll pull it all out."

Clara twisted away. For now, it was her turn to blush. Not at the pain she had caused him, but at the butterflies whose dance had intensified as she looked into his clear green eyes. She threw herself under the bench so he wouldn't notice her pink cheeks and called behind her.

"Tell me what ye need and I'll get it. It's easier for me. I'm not a lanky bean pole like ye."

"Hey," he said, grateful to avoid both small space and spiders.

Jimmy instructed her to look for the thick rope in need of barking. Clara slithered backwards and lifted a large piece of rope over her shoulder.

"This is all you need?"

"Aye, it will do for now. Da can get the rest... if he can see straight."

Jimmy opened the door for Clara, who stepped blinking into the bright summer sunshine. Her butterflies had ceased their frantic dance, but for occasional quivers of wings deep inside her. Oblivious, Jimmy spoke of the preparations ahead. The silver darlings would arrive any day now.

At the Ouse, they threw down their ropes and watched steam bubble up from the large iron tanks.

"Clara, what are ye deein here?" She turned and saw Bill carrying a large net, which was spilling over his muscular forearms.

"I was helping Jimmy and wanted to come and watch."

"Alreet, lass, but dinna stay long. Yer mam needs ye back at home. Here, come with me."

Clara smiled at Jimmy as she followed Bill to one of the large vats teeming with murky liquid. Nets and ropes lay along the grass, turning deep brown and left to dry in the warm sun.

Jimmy spotted Alex amongst the group of fishermen and carried the ropes over to him.

"Where's the nets?"

"I got the ropes like ye asked."

"Stupid lad, I asked fer nets and ropes."

"No, ye didn't," said Jimmy, holding his ground.

Without warning, Alex lunged at him. Jimmy, taken by surprise, fell to the ground. Several pairs of hands, stained brown from the barking, reached down to help him up. Jimmy stared at Alex, then turned to fetch the nets.

Clara looked on as Jimmy trudged back to the sheds, head hung low, shoulders slumped. She wanted to run after him and offer comfort, but knew she couldn't. That would be the last thing he wanted. It was an unspoken truth on the island that Alex Watson beat his family, but family business is private and therefore no one thought to intervene. Instead, the islanders tried to help in other ways. Women left cast-off clothes at Rose's door. Mrs Guthrey at the post office gave Sally a few shifts a week to make up their income.

Jimmy closed the shed door, pulled out an old wooden chest and sat down. It was bad enough Alex treated his family like dirt behind closed doors, but to do it in front of the other men? That was a step too far. The fishermen witnessing the swiftness of Alex's fists, left Jimmy mortified. He must return soon with the nets or face another public humiliation. He allowed a moment to collect himself; pull on the calm face that he displayed to everyone while boiling inside.

Head in hands, he ran his fingers through his curls. He thought of Clara's delicate hands moving through his hair, and how happy he had been just a short while ago. *Happiness*, he thought, *is fleeting.*

Chapter 14

June, 1910

Clara didn't go straight back to the cottage after leaving the Ouse. Instead, she walked the long way through the village, keen to take in all the excitement. Nets hung from poles and hooks outside most of the small dwellings, and families moved in and out of their homes with a sense of urgent purpose. Every spare patch of grass on the outskirts of the village was strewn with nets and ropes, stretched out to dry from barking. Children ran squealing through the streets, caught in the flurry of activity around them.

Fishermen wandered back to their homes for lunch, hands covered in a brown stain that spread to their elbows. Anna sat in the sun outside their cottage, a large net spread across her knees.

"Clara, come help me, this needs barking tomorrow and there are still some tears to mend."

Pulling her wooden stool from inside, Clara positioned it close to Anna so they could share the net across their laps. Their hands worked skilfully, finding any tear or tangle, their delicate fingers mending with speed. Both looked up as Bill strode towards them.

"Oh, Bill, look at you!" Anna said, shaking her head at the sight of him.

His hands and forearms had turned a deep brown and his rolled shirt sleeves had not escaped the sticky liquid. There were splashes on his trousers and boots. Even his greying hair had turned rusty brown in places.

"Wash yourself in the yard. I'm not having you in my cottage in that state."

"Your cottage, is it?" he said and reached down to kiss his wife. She batted him away, screeching and giggling as he threatened to caress her with his dirty hands.

The sound of splashing water came from the yard. They stored the finished net carefully in a basket. Clara sat back in her chair and closed her eyes, the sun warming her lids. She opened them as Anna returned and sighed at the huge armful of nets she carried.

Anna chuckled. "You didn't think we were done yet, did you?" She smoothed out a corner of the old net and they resumed their work.

By the following morning, with most of the nets and ropes barked, the men had moved on to the sails. Clara snuck down to the Ouse before Anna could find her more jobs. She loved to watch the men work, finding the camaraderie between them delightful. She perched herself on a stone wall and watched as men laid out sails on emerald green grass, the boiling tanks of bubbling brown liquid beside them. They grabbed buckets, ladles, anything they could lay their hands on, and filled them to the brim with thick, oozing goo. Liquid flew against the backdrop of a clear summer sky, covering the fabric of the sails with a satisfying thud. The men returned to the boiling tank, filled their containers, and threw another load over the sails. Thuds and splats filled the air as the sails turned a deep shade of brown.

Jimmy appeared with a brush and began working the liquid into the fabric, rubbing hard against its seams. He moved fast, his face red with the effort, his shirt sleeves tightening over his muscles as he left no patch untouched.

Clara jumped off the wall, not wanting to impede the men or their work. She would return the following day to watch the brown sails lying on the grass, turning a deep shade of red as they dried.

Over the next few days, the barking continued until everything was dry and ready for tarring. What a fine sight they would be when they sailed off in search of silver.

Chapter 15

June, 1910

Jimmy returned from the day's barking, exhausted. It hadn't gone unnoticed by any man that Alex had slunk off earlier that afternoon. By the time Jimmy finished work for the day, Alex was already asleep in a drunken stupor, the younger bairns sleeping too. Soft light flickered as Rose sat mending nets by candlelight.

"Alreet?" she asked him, glancing up from her work as Jimmy walked in.

"Aye, not bad." Rose pushed a plate of food across the table. "Ta," he said.

"Yer a good lad, Jimmy," she said, eyeing the snoring figure of her husband before sighing and turning back to the net she was mending.

Jimmy watched her working. He often wondered what had led her to this life. His grandparents had been long dead by the time he was born, and he knew nothing of her life growing up on the island. It couldn't have been easy, or she wouldn't have married a man like Alex Watson. As if reading his mind, Rose looked up at him.

"He wasn't always like this, ye kna." She cocked her head towards the sleeping figure of her husband.

"Aye, right," said Jimmy, embarrassed by his mam's candour.

"Not when I married him anyhow. He was handsome and clever. All the island girls wanted to marry Alex Watson. I was the lucky one he chose." She let out a laugh that held no mirth.

Lucky. For the first time, Jimmy looked past the bitterness and discontent. He saw a hopeful young girl, wooed by a handsome fisherman, dreaming of a life so different from her own. Rose set down her net and muttered that it was time for bed. As she hauled her heavy body onto the wooden frame, Jimmy heard her whisper softly, "Ye're a good lad, Jimmy. A good lad."

*

Jimmy woke at first light and headed for the beach. Several men had gathered, and the tar pots were already bubbling away. Men nodded a greeting and didn't bother to ask whether Alex would make an appearance. Jimmy had gathered up his barked ropes the previous evening and now he laid them beside the tarring pots, ready to get to work.

Tarring was a mucky business and Jimmy's least favourite part of the herring preparations. He was keen to get it over with. To protect his hands, he rubbed them with butter, then began the slow process of dipping long lengths of rope into boiling tar. Taking care not to burn himself, he couldn't avoid the splattering of tar as he dipped and removed miles of rope.

By the time he finished, he had been at it for hours, and black splodges covered his body and clothes. He walked down to the shoreline and began rubbing salty water over his hands and arms, but the damn stuff clung to his skin like limpets to rock. The sight of tar-splattered men became a familiar sight over the next few days as the preparations rolled on. Men prepared their equipment and began painting the keelboats, which had lain idle all winter.

From the herring yard came hammering and sawing. The coopers had arrived, crafting mountains of barrels for storing and exporting fish. Ships appeared, bobbing lazily on the calm water of the harbour, their crews unloading large quantities of salt and barrel staves. Strangers arrived, incomers, some of whom the locals recognised from previous years, others for whom this was their first time following the silver darlings.

Boat launching down day arrived. All the work had been leading to this moment. Villagers eagerly awaited this special day, which brimmed with anticipation, excitement and hope that a good season lay ahead.

As islanders gathered at the harbour, everyone lent a hand in getting the cumbersome keelboats down and into the water. There were over twenty boats and the work took all day. As the last boat slipped down, cutting through the still water and sending ripples across its surface, the assembled crowd let out a loud cheer and a cry went up; "Drink!"

Islanders scurried to the village, womenfolk to their homes, men and boys distributed between the many island pubs. Each skipper had contributed to the kitty, and the landlords were ready and waiting for their thirsty patrons.

"Why can't we have a drink too?" asked Clara.

"It's not the way of things here," Anna said, and handed Clara a small glass of gin. Clara swallowed it down, the liquid burning her throat and making her wince. Anna laughed. "You're supposed to sip it, Clara."

Anna topped up her daughter's glass, and although Clara didn't like the taste, she accepted the offering, more out of principle than anything else. If the lads got to have a drink, so would she.

Several hours later, the sounds of a fiddle and loud singing floated down through the night air and into their cottage. Anna got up and looked outside.

"I think they're down at the harbour. Want to go?"

Clara grinned and jumped up from her seat. The two women followed the sounds of music and voices, finding quite the gathering by the harbourside. There were other women down there that Clara didn't recognise, and she realised these must be the herring girls, all the way from the Scottish Highlands.

Bill spotted his wife and daughter in the crowd. "Come to join the party?" he slurred cheerfully and pulled them further into the throng. The air filled with shouts and raucous singing, the high spirits infectious. Clara smiled in amusement as Old John drew Anna into a dance.

Chapter 16

June, 1910

Jimmy was leaden with tiredness by the time he made it home. The incomers were a lot of fun, and several of the herring girls had persuaded him to dance. The memory of dancing with Clara made him smile. She had whooped and hollered as he'd galloped her round to the old fiddler's tune, hair flying behind her like a veil and eyes bright with joy.

As he'd pulled her closer, he caught the faint smell of liquor on her breath, and realised the child he had always known was becoming a woman. Their eyes locked, before her hands slipped from his and she swirled away into the arms of Bill, who twirled her round till she was giddy.

Jimmy settled down in his chair and pulled a blanket over himself. He fell into a deep sleep, the fiddler's tune still playing in his head.

Jimmy woke with a start as a heavy object landed in his lap. With one eye open, he saw Marnie bouncing around, determined to wake him from his slumber. He grunted and closed his eyes, but she had her hands on his shoulders, shaking him.

"Are ye going to catch the silver darlings today? Jimmy? Jimmy? Wake up!"

Jimmy stretched his arms above him and yawned, pulling Marnie closer and resting his head on hers. "I hope we catch some, aye, but not till tonight, so I was hoping for a longer rest." He shut his eyes, the warmth of his sister lulling him back to his dreams.

"Why are ye going tonight? Are the fish sleeping now?"

There would be no peace, so he lifted his sister off his lap and stood up. He buttered himself a hunk of bread and stood out in the fresh sea air, hoping it might rid him of his drowsiness. The island streets were quiet. Jimmy envied the fortunate souls still tucked up in their beds.

The day passed, crawling through the seconds, minutes and hours with a frustrating lethargy. By lunchtime, Jimmy wondered if the evening would never come. But come it did, the sun slinking down, scattering hues like rose petals on the water of the harbour. As the pink water turned black, the fishermen gathered atop the Heugh. There was a reverence, a pause in the excitement which had characterised the previous weeks.

They faced out to sea, eyes trained on the horizon, searching for clues that the silver darlings were nearing their shores. Jimmy yawned, drowsiness shrouding him. He longed to lie on the mossy grass and close his eyes. A yell pierced the quiet night. Jimmy's eyes flung open as he snapped alert, sleep banished till the morning.

"There," said Bill, aiming his large hand at a point on the horizon.

The other men followed the line of his arm with their eyes, hoping that Bill's assertion was correct. Jimmy held his breath, squinting out at the water. A smattering of silver, like the Milky Way, glittered on the dark water.

Men scrambled down the rocky bank, lured by the glimmering silver. With a half-drunk skipper and an inexperienced crew, Alex's boat was last to leave. They hoisted the red sail and followed the line of drifters disappearing toward the horizon.

The island was nothing more than a small dark speck on a vast expanse of navy water by the time they brought the sails down.

"Shoot the nets, lads," said Alex. The men began flinging nets overboard until they hung like curtains over the murky depths below. The corked edges bobbed on the undulating waves, and the boat drifted over the water. Alex pulled out a hip flask and took a glug. It seemed they would be a man down by the next morning.

The crew settled down in the hull and alternated between sleep and look-out duty. Jimmy stirred as his back caught on a hard piece of wood, and opened his eyes to a fluorescent dawn sky, shades of pinks and oranges splintering as they hit the choppy sea below. He looked around at the sleeping crew and pulled himself up on the gunwale, peering over its side.

"Lads," he called. "Lads, stir yersels."

One by one, the crew joined Jimmy. With no sign of the nets, a ripple of excitement passed through the crew.

"Skipper!" called Robert. He picked his way across the boat and shook Alex. All he received in return was a loud snore in his ear. Robert tried again, but this time he received a sharp left hook before Alex slumped back down and resumed his snoring. Jimmy took charge.

"Let's get the nets in, lads."

It took all their strength as they heaved the nets from their sunken position. *A good omen*, thought Jimmy to himself. As the waters parted, the men could see a squirming mass of scales appearing like an apparition below. Hollers and cheers went up as the men took in their bumper catch.

The noise woke Alex from his slumber and he staggered over to see what was happening. He slapped his crew on their backs and slurred congratulations before slinking back into his drunken stupor. They drew the nets over the roller on deck and the crew shook them out, spilling hundreds of silver fish onto the deck. Their muscles strained with exertion as the dead weight of the net inched up and over. It was back-breaking work and the crew barely had time to wipe their brows. But spirits were high, the sounds of singing and chatter filling the air.

Hours passed before the catch was in the boat. When the last fish were in, they collapsed, exhausted, taking in the abundance of silver darlings with awe. Jimmy took a swig of water and lifted one fish above his face. He gave it a good smack on its lips, causing the other men to roar with laughter. Once they had caught their breath, the men hoisted the sail and started for home. No man was idle. Those not attending to the sails or tiller were busy scooping their squirming treasure into baskets, ready to hand to the herring girls who were waiting on the shore.

They pulled into the harbour where most of the boats had already returned. It had been a good catch all round, and it was a jovial scene that greeted them. Baskets moved from the boat to the herring houses with no time to spare, for the gutting and salting could not wait.

Accepting the offer to join the crew, Jimmy headed to the Fisherman's Arms, where he settled himself on a stool and took a swig of ale. He smiled at the crew as Alex claimed credit for their successful outing. The men clinked their glasses with Jimmy's; they knew the true skipper that day.

Chapter 17

June, 1910

Clara hung back as the boats came in. She felt shy around the herring girls with their confident demeanours. The girls were as strong as any man, heaving creels on their backs and carrying them to the salting house with ease. Heads bobbed up and down with synchronicity as they reached for the herring, skilfully gutting them with their sharp knives before placing them in barrels. Hands blurred with speed, and the low rate of injury among them amazed Clara.

A girl spotted Clara and beckoned her over. Clara looked behind her, but she was alone. She jumped from the wall and made her way into the yard. The woman who had beckoned eyed her up, hands on her hips.

"Are ye going to sit watching, or will ye lend a hand?"

"Oh, I've never worked with herring before."

The women around the table laughed, and an older woman spoke up. "Ye have to start somewhere, lass. Come, stand by me and I'll show ye the ropes."

Clara moved to the far side of the table. The girls chatted in their native tongue, while the old woman grabbed a rag, bound Clara's fingers and handed her a knife. "Look," she instructed and gutted a small fish slowly, so Clara could grasp the technique. Clara held her knife with care and mirrored her mentor's actions.

"Good lass. Try another one."

Clara picked up a larger fish and repeated the motion. "Aye, yer ready," said the woman, and turned back to the table.

With slippery fish after slippery fish, Clara tried to keep pace with the other women. Their hands flew as hers stumbled, but they pretended not to notice. At one point confidence overtook her, and she sliced her hand rather than the fish, leaving a gash that oozed red, much like the guts she'd been handling.

"Come here, lass," said the old woman, bandaging her hand to stem the flow of blood. "Careful ye don't get salt in it or ye'll be screaming and howling the rest of the day."

The other women nodded agreement at her sage words, all the while continuing their work. The wound stung as though burnt by hot coals, but Clara suffered in silence, unwilling to lose face amongst these women she so admired. She kept her head down, working hard to earn the women's respect.

"Clara? Ye joining the herring lassies?" Jimmy was leaning against the wall of the yard, grinning in amusement.

"Aye, I am," Clara called back. Her face reddened as the other women gave sly glances across the table. Jimmy moved away, and one of the younger girls grinned at her.

"That yer young man?"

"No," said Clara, keeping her head down as her cheeks burned.

"That's grand."

"Why?"

"A handsome fellow like that, I fancy me chances at the next dance, that's why!"

All the women laughed, except Clara, who experienced a surprising stab of jealousy.

Within a few days, the herring girls had adopted Clara as one of their own. They offered to pay her a small share of their earnings and when Clara asked, Anna let her join them.

"I assumed you'd be starting work there next year anyway, so this will be good training for you," she said. "You're growing up fast, my love." Anna pulled Clara onto her lap, despite Clara now being as tall as she was.

During those sweet summer months, Clara learned to work hard and play hard. The herring girls were a cheerful bunch, always full of joy and song despite the hard nature of their work. With the final few fish packed away in the coopers' barrels, Clara would accompany them back to their dorms, delighting in their companionship.

They talked of their homes far away in the Highlands and islands, of men they had left behind, and freedom afforded them thanks to the silver darlings. Tales of romance left her blushing. She learned more in three months than she had in the previous fifteen years. Her new friends questioned her about Jimmy, but Clara kept quiet. He meant too much to her to be the subject of gossip, and besides, since they'd both been working the herring, there was nothing to tell.

On some occasions, the girls would forget themselves and revert to the languages of their homeland. Clara dismissed their apologies. She loved the lilting song-like way they spoke and knew it wasn't a deliberate exclusion.

*

The months flew by and soon the season would be over. Clara felt a pang of sadness at her friends' imminent departure.

"Ye should come with us, Clara," her friend Kitty suggested one day. "What an adventure we'd have!"

It was tempting, but as much fun as she knew it would be, Clara would not leave her island for anyone.

"Maybe next year," she offered, knowing she'd no more join them then.

"Aye right, whatever ye say," said Kitty, nudging her.

The day they left, Clara rushed to the yard to say goodbye. After hugs and kisses, she ran beside the cart until it reached the sands. Her new friends disappeared across to the mainland, waving until they were out of view. She would count the days until next season, and all would be well.

Chapter 18

September, 1910

Island life returned to normal, incomers a distant memory. News spread that Sally Watson was to marry Robert from the *Mary Lou*. Clara couldn't understand why anyone would marry Robert. On the few occasions they met, Clara thought Robert vulgar, arrogant and not at all clever. She read about love and marrying princes, but knew Robert was no prince. His thin greasy hair hung in a side-parting on his too small head. Pock marks covered his face, and his pot belly sat oddly on his otherwise thin physique. But Clara was as excited as the rest of the island. It was five years since the last island wedding and Clara remembered it as a wonderful celebration.

*

A floral scent and excited atmosphere replaced the depressing mood and stale air of Jimmy's cottage. Flowers lay on the scuffed wooden table. Sally stood in the middle of the room, surrounded by her sisters, some pinning her hair while others tried to squeeze her into Rose's old wedding dress. Sally had the same round figure as Rose, but there was no hiding her swollen breasts and distended belly. Rose was red in the face, fussing round her eldest daughter and shouting at the younger bairns to stop getting under her feet.

"Jimmy," she barked. "Take those flowers down to the church and tie them onto pews."

Jimmy, relieved to escape the gaggle of females, gathered up an armful of flowers, slipped a ball of string into his pocket and made his way to the church.

*

Clara and Anna entered through the church porch and found Jimmy struggling to tie flowers to the pews.

"Do you need some help?"

"Aye, that would be wonderful," said Jimmy, handing Anna both flowers and string.

Clara and Jimmy looked on as Anna selected flowers. She drew them into neat bundles and tied them to the pews, knotting bows in the string and putting Jimmy's attempts to shame.

"Why are ye here so early?"

"We're singing in the choir," said Clara. She motioned to the small group of islanders by the pulpit, scanning hymn sheets and talking in excited whispers. "How's Sally?"

"Aye, she's right enough, if she can ever fit that blooming bump into her dress." Jimmy winked, and Clara blushed.

Sally had been the subject of island gossip for months, ever since Old John interrupted her and Robert. The old man got quite the shock when he'd gone to put away some nets in his shed and found it occupied by two young lovers, naked and panting on his workbench. Island gossip claimed he had to lie down with chest pains for several hours after, and his wife had been none too pleased when she discovered why her husband had come over so queer.

In the Fisherman's Arms, Alex had beaten Robert black and blue. Clara had pitied Robert when she saw him limping through the village with an arm in a sling and two black eyes. Since then, prying eyes watched the seams of Sally's dress stretch, waiting for news of the inevitable wedding.

Once the couple was engaged, Alex accepted the situation. He let Robert resume his work on the *Mary Lou*, announcing to all who would listen how proud he was of his soon-to-be son-in-law. One night, blind drunk, he stood yelling into the night sky that Robert was the son he'd never had. *Rather him than me*, thought Jimmy. Perhaps he would no longer have to intercept the day's earnings or steer his da away from a pint of ale if there was a new son around.

"Where will they live?"

"With us to begin with." Jimmy shook his head at the thought of another two, soon to be three bodies filling up the tiny cottage. "I might sleep on the boat."

Clara opened her mouth to speak, but she couldn't tell if he was serious.

"I'd best get back to the madhouse. I'm sure there's some errand they'll want me for. See ye later?"

"Aye, can't wait."

Back at the cottage, Jimmy found a scene of utter chaos. His youngest sisters were running round, doing their best to avoid Rose, who was chasing them with a wet rag to get the grime off their faces. "Help me will ye, Jimmy," she called, catching Marnie by the hem of her skirt and pulling her towards the table.

Jimmy reached round and took both child and rag from Rose. With Marnie on his knee, he wiped the cloth over her round cheeks and smooth forehead.

"See, Marnie, being clean isn't that bad, is it?" She turned to him and pouted, but didn't disagree. "Ye'll look so bonny with flowers in yer hair. Do ye want me to put them in for ye?"

"Aye," she said, sitting still on Jimmy's lap as he combed his fingers through her thick golden curls. He tied a piece of ribbon around her head, and tucked flowers into it from ear to ear.

"Ye look beautiful," he said, kissing her on her cheek and lifting her off his lap. He turned her round, so she was looking at him.

"Marnie," he said in a voice so serious that his sister stood stock still. "Don't ye dare be getting dirty again."

She giggled and ran off, leaving Jimmy to wonder how many flowers would be in her hair by the time they reached the church.

Jimmy looked up as Alex walked in from the yard. He'd been smoking a pipe and doing his best to avoid the commotion inside the cottage. Jimmy did a double take. Alex had borrowed a suit from somewhere, his face shaven with clean hair combed in a side parting. His suit hung over his scrawny body, but he looked presentable. He could almost have passed for an average da rather than the monster Jimmy knew him to be.

Father and son nodded at one another and sat in the small room, each uncomfortable with their proximity to the other, but putting old battles aside just for one day. The crowd of females surrounding Sally parted, and she turned to face them. Alex let out a low whistle. She looked radiant. Excitement flushed her cheeks and the small lace veil brushed against her ivory-clad shoulders. The dress was straining at her rounded middle, but didn't detract from the overall effect.

"What are yous two gawping at? We need to git te the church," said Rose, but Jimmy noticed even she had to turn and dab her eyes with a hanky.

Alex offered his hooked arm to Sally, and they led the family outside. The island streets were quiet, all the villagers having gathered in the church. As they approached the Parish church, Sally and Alex hung back, allowing the rest of the family to find their seats.

St Mary's church was as full as a Midnight Mass. Jimmy nodded to the smiling faces as they made their way along the aisle. He shuddered at the sight of Robert standing puffed-chested near the altar. Even so, the atmosphere in the church was infectious and Jimmy smiled as he helped his youngest sisters up onto the old wooden pews.

*

Clara stood with the rest of the choir members and as they struck up in song, she had a first-class view of the bride walking down the long aisle. Sally was too much like Rose for Clara's liking, but she swelled with happiness at the sight of the young girl smiling as she stepped towards her new life. The choir took their seats and Clara watched the ceremony, daydreaming about her own wedding day, which she decided would not be to anyone like Robert.

As Reverend Barns declared the marriage, church bells rang out, and the congregation made their way into the churchyard to watch the ancient customs that every island bride and groom must adhere to.

Robert led his wife to the churchyard gates where Old John was waiting, hand outstretched. The groom reached into his pocket and handed the toll to Old John, who let the couple through. Beyond the churchyard, local men lined up, forming an arch with their rifles for the young couple to pass through. Robert and Sally clapped their hands over their ears as the sound of gunshots filled the still air and they ran laughing through to safety. After passing the men and their guns, Clara noticed Sally cup a protective hand around her swollen belly and wondered what it felt like to have a bairn growing inside you. Old John and Alex flanked Sally on either side, taking her hands and helping her jump over the petting stone. Raucous cheers came from the assembled crowd.

The islanders followed the young couple through the village and stopped outside the hall where two of Jimmy's sisters appeared from the crowd, carrying plates of wedding cake. They threw the cake, plate and all, over Sally's head, smashing it on the ground behind her. With a cheer, people scrambled to get inside the hall. Clara hung back with Anna and waited for the crowds to disperse a little.

"Was your wedding like this?"

"In some ways," said Anna, gazing into the distance. Anna took Clara's hand, and they sat down on the grass. "It was the happiest day of my life, also the most terrifying." She smiled at Clara, squeezing her hand.

"Why were you scared, Mam? Didn't you want to marry Da?"

Anna laughed. "I wanted to marry your da more than anything in the world, Clara. It was the islanders who scared me. They weren't keen on me living here, taking the place of a local girl, and goodness me, there were many your da could've chosen. Oh, and all those traditions. I thought I'd trip on the petting stone, or worse, get hit by a stray bullet!"

Clara leant into Anna, who wrapped an arm round her. "Did you have a big party after?"

"Oh no, we went to our cottage and people came round for tea and cake. Speaking of parties, shall we go in and enjoy ourselves?"

The small hall was abuzz with excitement. Each of the landlords from the nine village pubs had brought several barrels along, and the beer was flowing. In the corner, a small group of musicians were setting up their instruments, and colourful bunches of flowers and bunting adorned the walls. Clara and Anna joined Bill, and the three walked over to congratulate the Watsons.

Rose was far more jovial with a jug of ale in her hand, smiling and swaying to the music. Bill moved to shake hands with Alex, but already a few pints in, he struggled to attach his hand to Bill's.

Sally beamed at well-wishers. Robert slunk into a corner, a happy bystander to the festivities.

Clara scanned the room and saw Jimmy. He held Marnie in one hand and Ada in the other, swinging them round as the musicians played. The girls' shrieks of delight resounded above the chatter, and soon more people were joining them to dance. Jimmy caught Clara's eye and beckoned her over.

"Come and dance with us," he called as she approached their little group.

"Aye alright, I will," she said, removing her too tight shoes and throwing them into a corner. They joined hands and their little circle whirled and spun until they let go, staggering around dizzy.

The drinking and dancing continued long into the night. When Alex Watson threw up over the feet of his wife, Anna put a protective arm round Clara's shoulders, guiding her back to the sanctity of their cottage.

Chapter 19

December, 1911

In its quiet corner of the cold North Sea, the island and its people followed the familiar rhythms and seasons of life. In the spring of 1911, the Watson cottage had welcomed two new lives. Within weeks of each other, Sally birthed her first child and Rose her tenth. In the winter of 1911, another bairn arrived and the inhabitants of the cottage numbered sixteen.

For a man prone to temper, it was a terrible environment for Alex. There was no way of keeping the bairns from under his feet, and the cramped chaos amplified his anger. With no way to stop him from drinking, Rose encouraged it. His frequent blackouts were her only respite. Passed out by the fire, his fists were still, and his angry mouth quiet. His skin had turned yellow and his eyes bloodshot. He terrified the bairns, who considered him a real-life monster.

The table's wood became a bed, and Rose built a new shelf by which to sit and mend her nets. Whichever way they arranged the cottage, it left no room for Jimmy. He took to sleeping between the boat and the shed, depending on how hard the wind blew.

The winter of 1911 was a harsh one; storms were relentless, and it had been several weeks since the fishermen had taken their boats beyond the safety of the harbour.

The entire island felt the pinch. Food was becoming scarce, supplies were running low. Fear bounced off the village buildings and seeped into the homes within. The streets were quiet bar the howling winds that ripped through them. Even the hardiest of islanders hunkered down behind closed doors.

Jimmy shivered beneath his blankets as the wind threatened to tear the shed's tin roof clean off.

"Jimmy?"

He looked up as lamplight filled the small structure. "Hello?"

"It's me, Bill."

"Bill," said Jimmy, wriggling free of his blankets. "What are ye doing here?"

"Didn't like to think of ye oot in the storm. Come back to mine."

"Ta, but I'll be right." A gust of wind rattled the tin roof.

"Away with ye, Jim, this is nae time fer foolish pride. It's dangerous oot here alone. I have a fire gannin'..."

A fire, now that was tempting.

"Anna's cooked broth..."

Jimmy laughed. "Alright, alright, I can't turn that down."

"Good lad."

Jimmy made up his bed, ready for his return.

"Bring those with ye," said Bill, pointing to the blankets. "Nae point coming back here tonight."

Before Jimmy could argue, Bill retreated into the night, and Jimmy followed.

Jimmy thought Clara's cottage cosy by day, by night it was even more so. Anna and Clara sat knitting by the fire. Jimmy saw Clara blush as he entered the cottage. But it might have been the warmth of the flames.

"Sit here," said Anna, pulling up another chair. Jimmy sat down and held his hands to the flames, feeling returning to them for the first time that evening. His knee bumped against Clara's and she gave a small jolt.

"Sorry," he whispered, but she kept her head down, concentrating on her knitting.

"I know something that will warm you up," said Anna. She moved across to an old dresser and pulled out a bottle of gin, filling four glasses. Jimmy sipped, welcoming the warmth that spread through his body with each mouthful.

The alcohol relaxed Clara. She smiled at Jimmy as Anna thrust a bowl of broth his way. The smile he returned spread more warmth through Clara than any amount of gin.

*

Once she overcame her awkwardness, Clara welcomed Jimmy's company. The past few weeks had been monotonous. Anna made the best of things, filling Clara's time with sewing projects and mending tasks. But Clara hated being trapped indoors, longing to get out with fresh sea air on her skin. They were fortunate compared to most, with driftwood gathered during the warmer months and stores of smoked fish.

The small windows of the cottage rattled with ferocious winds, and Bill looked out for any signs of the storm abating. Anna frowned as the familiar patter of rain sounded against the roof tiles.

"How long have you been sleeping in the shed, Jimmy?" she asked.

"A while," he said, his cheeks turning pink.

"I suppose there's not much room in the cottage since the bairns arrived."

"There wasn't much room before," he laughed.

"No, I don't imagine there was."

"Yer lucky it's just the three of ye in here."

"Aye," said Anna.

Noticing her sad smile, Jimmy changed the subject. "When do ye reckon the boats will be out again?" he asked Bill.

"Dinna kna, but it canna come soon enough. Just need this damn wind to die down."

Anna was as keen as Bill for the winds to drop. He had been like a caged animal these past weeks, pacing the cottage floors. Eager to get back on the water, he wasn't much fun to have around the home.

It didn't look like the weather would clear soon. With no prospect of work the next day, the family stayed up later than usual. By the time they were ready for bed, the gin bottle was empty and all agreed it had been a most pleasant evening. Anna helped Jimmy lay out his blankets by the fire, and Clara appeared with her patchwork quilt.

"Here you go," she said. "This should keep you warm."

"Ta," said Jimmy.

She handed him the blanket, then reached her arms round him in a quick hug. "Goodnight."

"Sweet dreams," he called as she retreated to her bed.

Jimmy snuggled down beside the fire. When he wrapped himself in the quilt, it was as though Clara had her arms around him again.

The following morning, Jimmy packed up his blankets, ignoring the family's pleas to stay another night.

"He's too proud fer his own good," said Bill after Jimmy left.

"No, love, he's just had to fend for himself since he was a wee bairn. It's all he knows."

"Aye, well, he'll either starve or freeze to death if he stays living in that shed much longer."

"He won't accept charity. If you want to help him, think of another way."

Bill scratched at his beard and headed out into the yard.

It was Mother Nature who provided the answer. The following evening, a monstrous storm attacked the cottage, ripping tiles from the roof and the privy door from its hinges. Jimmy lived through every moment, the shed rattling in protest as howling winds fought against its walls.

When Bill appeared at the morning after, he found the shed still standing. "How's this old beast still upright when our cottage is torn to shreds?" he asked, stepping through the door.

"Reckon someone's looking down on me," said Jimmy, grinning despite his lack of sleep.

"Aye, reckon they are."

"Is the cottage in a bad way?"

"Nothing that canna mend, but I could dee with some help to fix it up."

"Nae bother, tell me what ye need doing and I'll be there."

Bill feigned embarrassment, pulling at his beard, not meeting Jimmy's eye. "Thing is, lad, I canna afford to pay ye fer yer trouble."

"I wouldn't take payment if ye offered it me," said Jimmy.

"And I would na take free labour if ye offered it me," laughed Bill. "Hows about we come to some arrangement?"

"Aye, and what's that?" said Jimmy, shrewd enough to know Bill was up to something.

"Well, we could pay ye in food and board. Once a week at ours?"

Jimmy shook his head. "I'll accept the occasional bowl of Anna's broth, but I'm no charity case. I was grateful for yer kindness the other night, but I don't expect it to become regular. I can take care of myself."

"Fine. But yer to come round once a week fer a hot meal. It's nae charity, it's family. Agreed?"

"Will there be gin?"

Bill laughed. "Ye drive a hard bargain, lad."

Chapter 20

September, 1912

Knee deep in fish guts, Clara wiped her brow, spreading silver scales across it.

"Done fer the day," cried Alice as the cooper came to seal the final barrel.

Clara set down her knife and gathered up her bag. "See ye tomorrow," she called, stepping out of the yard.

She didn't mind the work, but missed the company of Kitty and her crew, who had not returned to the island since Clara's first summer in the yard. She'd heard from Alice they had gone to North Shields. More work and more lads.

Down at the harbour, she knocked on the door of Jimmy's shed.

"I'm up," he called, and Clara let herself inside. Since he moved in, the shed had changed. Fishing gear lay in boxes, the floor was free of debris, and through the clean glass window came a spectacular view of harbour and castle.

"Here you go," Clara said, handing him the supper Anna had packed up for him.

"Ta." Jimmy had long since given up arguing against the generosity the family showed him. If he didn't accept, they would just leave the food outside the door and it would be the gulls who would benefit.

"You out tonight?"

"Aye, all signs are good."

"Your da coming with you?"

"Don't know. He's not shown up all week, so no reason tonight will be different."

"Hmm, must be hard being a man down."

Jimmy laughed. "It's a whole sight easier, I can tell ye."

In fact, Jimmy breathed a sigh of relief each time the *Mary Lou* set out from harbour without her skipper on board. It was only Robert who missed Alex, unwilling to take orders from Jimmy who became skipper by default in his da's absence.

To Jimmy's dismay, that evening Alex graced them with his presence. His face was the colour of fine sand.

"Nae natural," muttered one of the crew, shocked at the skipper's appearance.

Alex barked out instructions and the *Mary Lou* made her way out to sea. Not five miles out, Alex ordered them to shoot the nets. The choppy green water below showed no traces of silver, and gulls were absent from the sky above.

"Ye sure, Da?" asked Jimmy.

"Wat did ye say to me, lad?"

"I said, are ye sure? There's no signs silver darlings are about these waters. How about we go south of the Staples?"

"Who's skipper of the *Mary Lou*?" Alex asked Robert.

"Ye are, Da," said Robert.

So now Robert was calling Alex 'Da', was he? *Well*, thought Jimmy, *he's welcome to him*. Without further comment, Jimmy headed to the gunwale and began shooting the nets. The crew eyed Jimmy. His silence spoke volumes, and all regretted Alex's presence on board. Once they shot the nets, the men settled down for some scran.

"Wat yer git in that fancy tin of yers?" called Alex. Jimmy looked down at the food packed by Anna. He picked up an oat cake, held it up to his da, and popped it in his mouth.

"Someone's git themsel' a new mammy," laughed Alex. He looked around at the crew, but none joined in his laughter. Even Robert avoided Alex's eyes, as nervous as the next man at the tension between father and son.

Jimmy ate, then closed his eyes, eager to avoid the confrontation Alex was angling for. Before dawn, he woke to see Alex leaning over the edge of the boat, staring into the water below. When Alex looked up, there was a murderous look in his eyes. Jimmy crossed the boat to find the cause of his distress. Corks bobbed on the water, buffs sat on its surface. The crew joined them and glanced at Alex. The skipper straightened himself up and stared hard at Jimmy.

"Tis down to yer blethering that these lads'll gan hungry."

"What?" said Jimmy. "It was ye that told us to shoot the nets, ye that wouldn't go further."

Alex sauntered over to his son. The other men held their breath. "Think ye kna better, dee ye? Always thought yer above the rest of us. I'm skipper here."

"Aye, ye are when yer not holed up somewhere sleeping off the drink."

From the look in Alex's eyes, Jimmy knew he had gone too far. He didn't notice the fist as it flew, but felt it crunch against his nose. He staggered backwards, pinching hard to stem the flow of blood. Before he could get his balance, Alex was on him again, gripping him by the neck and pushing him hard against the gunwale. Of the two, Jimmy was stronger, but his foot had caught in a net and with Alex pushed against him, he couldn't free himself. Stars filled his vision as Alex squeezed his throat tighter. In an instant, Alex released his grip, grabbed Jimmy's leg, and heaved him overboard. As Jimmy fell, ten faces, white with shock, stared down at him. Before he hit the water, he heard Alex call, "Leave him."

*

Jimmy hit the water with such a force, he wondered if it had torn the skin from his back. The cold shocked him, and for a moment he fell motionless, deeper and deeper into the murky depths. Terrified by the ever-growing darkness around him, he kicked his foot free of the net and began pulling himself up through the water. His gansey and sou'wester weighed him down, but he drew on all the strength he had. As his head emerged, it met with the crest of a wave that sent him spinning within its frothy strength. His face met the sky, and he gasped in lungfuls of air. The *Mary Lou* had her sails up and was turning back to harbour.

"Help," he yelled. "Help."

Alex's face appeared above the stern. The boat didn't turn. Jimmy spun round in the water, legs kicking to stop him from sinking. In the distance were the red-brown sails of another vessel. Hope. He battled the water's angry peaks and troughs to stay afloat. The yellow sleeves of his sou'wester acted as a beacon, and the vessel made her way closer to Jimmy.

"Man overboard," someone shouted, the rope they threw slapping the water beside him. Jimmy gripped it and they winched him from the freezing sea. Strong arms grabbed him, and he collapsed into the hull, the eyes of a thousand silver darlings staring up at him. Bill's face appeared above him and soon he was being pulled out of his wet clothes. The crew were removing layers of their own clothes, and soon they'd bundled Jimmy up so tight he couldn't move. Despite the layers, he couldn't stop shivering. He curled up in a corner, shaking. The boat raced for harbour and on reaching land, four burly men heaved Jimmy ashore.

"Can ye stand?" asked Bill.

"Aye, I think so," said Jimmy, trying to get up. His head spun, and he collapsed against Bill, who put a large arm around him, holding him steady. Bill half carried Jimmy back to his own cottage. A stunned Anna made space by the fire.

As Clara came in from the yard, the sight of Jimmy, grey-faced, greeted her. He sat shivering despite the warmth of the flames. Bill shook his head as she went to speak.

"Some tea please, Clara," he said.

Once he was sure Jimmy was alright, Bill retreated from the cottage. He appeared several hours later, knuckles bruised and bleeding. Neither Anna nor Clara needed to ask where he had been.

Chapter 21

October, 1912

Clara was grateful for her woollen stockings and jacket as she set off towards the castle. It was rare for her to have a spare couple of hours. Autumn was slipping into winter. The few trees that dotted the barren landscape, bent with the relentless island winds, were shedding their leaves, and the nights were drawing in. For the first time in a week there had been a break in the weather.

Her irritability at being cooped up inside had not gone unnoticed by her parents. The sky was an ominous shade of grey, but Anna had insisted Clara get some fresh air in her lungs and she had been more than happy to escape the confines of the cottage. She skipped along the stone path, delighted to be out in the open air.

At the castle, she turned and headed toward the north shore. Her favourite place on the island, she could gaze out at nothingness, letting its peace wash over her. She made her way down onto the beach and followed the line of the tide as the coast curled around, like a piece of rope leading her towards her destination.

It wasn't the easiest route. Clara had to clamber over rocks and at some parts of the journey the beach disappeared, forcing her up onto grassy dunes. The closer she got to the north shore, the more even her path became, the rocky outcrops giving way to pebbles and fine grains of sand.

As her boots scuffed the sand, she noticed someone tumbling down the dunes, removing their shoes and running straight into the icy water. Clara hesitated, but as the figure let out a loud cry, she recognised the voice and increased her pace.

*

Jimmy walked through farmland until he reached the rolling dunes. Sand swirled around him, whipped up by the wind and stinging at his face. He tugged his collar up and his hat down round his ears. Here, he was free from the village, free from realities of life.

He reached the top of a large dune and stopped to take in the view. Before him lay a vast expanse of steely grey sea. The sky was watery blue with only the faintest wisps of cloud, gulls gliding on gusts of wind. Sharp-edged rocks jutted into the water, and seals of all shades of grey lay on ragged outcrops.

Jimmy let out a cry and hurled himself down the sand bank towards the beach. Halfway down, he lost his footing, landing in a sandy heap. He lay there for a few moments before standing up and dusting off the sand that now covered his clothes.

The inside of his boots were like sandcastles and as he emptied them, his feet sank into freezing sand. A chill swept through his body and he glanced at the water. It looked inviting, but Jimmy knew how cold it would be.

Before he could talk himself out of it, he was running to the water's edge. As his feet submerged beneath the water, he yelped, hopping from one foot to another. He stayed in the water for less than a minute before the pain became unbearable and he rushed to find his woolly socks. By the time he'd secured the laces of his boots, his feet were numb.

Jimmy caught sight of a figure looking at him across the beach. He squinted against the sun, but despite shielding the light with his hand, he could not make them out.

*

Clara waved her hand in a wide swoop across the sky, "Jimmy!" she called, "JIMMY!"

He was staring, hand to his forehead.

"JIMMY!" she called once more, moving closer. This time he heard and waved his arm in a mirror image of her own. He was grinning by the time she caught him up.

"What are you doing out here?"

"Escaping," he said.

"You heading back?"

"I was going to, but I can walk some more if ye like?"

"Aye, I would."

They walked along the north shore, conversation flowing as they followed the coastline round towards the Snook. Beyond the headland, the mainland came into view, shades of purple and brown sweeping the horizon like strokes from an artist's brush. Jimmy paused.

"You alright?"

"Aye," said Jimmy, but he continued to stare out across the water to the gentle curves of land beyond.

"Jimmy?"

He pulled his gaze from the view and shuffled towards to her. He took her hands in his and looked deep into her eyes, sending heat coursing through her body despite the cold of the day.

"Clara." He seemed to struggle for words, looking away from her but keeping her hands in his. "I have to go away."

"That's alright." She smiled. "I'll walk home with you."

"No. I need to go away from the island, just for a while, maybe for longer."

"No." The warmth of moments ago became smothered by a chill. "No."

Jimmy let go of her hands and turned away. "Ye don't understand."

Clara walked closer to him. "Help me understand." She took hold of his hand and pulled him down till they were sitting side by side on the cold, damp sand.

In Clara's presence, Jimmy found a sense of peace and certainty that left him clear-headed and sure-footed.

"Did yer da ever tell ye what happened that night?"

Clara knew what night he meant. It had cast an unspoken shadow that lurked between them every time they met. It showed on Anna's face when she met Rose in the street, and in the clenched fists of Bill every time he saw Alex.

"He never said a word, but I guessed there was some fight."

Jimmy laughed. "A fight I could handle. Clara, my da tried to kill me."

Clara stared at Jimmy. "You don't mean on purpose?"

"As good as. I don't think he planned it, but he was happy enough to leave me to drown. If it weren't for Bill, I'd be at the bottom of the sea by now."

"What about your mam?"

"She's not spoken to me since. Tried once, and he made her suffer for it. I don't think he wants her to know what happened out there."

"And Marnie?"

"Oh, I see Marnie plenty. She's a sneaky whatsit, comes down to the shed when Da's passed out. I don't see the other bairns."

Clara listened, trying her best to understand while her heart and mind mottled with sadness. "If you stayed, things might get better?"

Jimmy shook his head. "Na, Da won't let me on the boat again. The work Bill's thrown my way has helped, but I can't keep scrounging off him forever."

"There's no scrounging going on, Jimmy. He'd have you as a full crew member if he had the space. Says you're his best worker."

"It's not just fishing, though. The island's so small I can't avoid seeing Da. I'm afraid, Clara."

"Afraid of your da?"

"Aye. But worse than that, I'm afraid that I'll become like him, that if I stay here, I will turn hard, hateful."

"Oh, Jimmy, you could never be like him."

Jimmy gave a hard laugh. "Aye, I could."

"Jimmy..."

"Clara, the only way I can be better is if I get as far away as I can. Start a new life. When I'm set up, I can send for Marnie and the other bairns, give them a good life."

"But what about the *Mary Lou*? Yer da won't be around forever and it will be yours one day."

"The *Mary Lou* won't survive another winter, Clara. And besides, Da wants Robert to be skipper when he retires."

Clara sat for a moment, deep in thought, empty of any argument to make him stay. "Where will you go?"

"I'll follow the silver darlings. There's plenty of money in chasing them... if yer on the right boat."

A tear rolled down her cheek. Jimmy's hand reached across to brush it away.

"What about me?" she whispered, looking down and digging her fingers into the sand.

Jimmy cupped her chin and pulled her face up to meet his eyes. "Clara," he said. His face was inches from her own, twisted with grief, but his eyes were hard and certain. His rough, salty lips gently brushed hers. She whipped her head back and stared at him. Jimmy leaned forward and his lips met hers, harder and more urgent than before. This time she sank into him, her arms wrapping themselves around his strong slim body, his round hers, pulling her closer, closer.

The air around Clara became thick. Her senses dimmed until her whole being filled with him. Time stood still, their two bodies moving as one dark shape against the pale silver of the dunes. Their kisses slowed, and Jimmy's hands caressed her face, wiping away wet tears with his thumbs. Clara pulled him down beside her and they lay entwined against the mound of sand, her head resting on his shoulder, his fingers combing her wind-tangled hair.

"Clara?"

"Mmm," she said, nuzzling into his chest.

"Will ye wait for me?"

She lifted her head and looked down into his face, taut with hope.

"Aye, Jimmy, I'll wait for you." She placed her head back down, the beating of his heart against her cheek.

He kissed the top of her head, and she smiled. Jimmy began talking, growing quick and excited as he imagined their future.

"It will take a while to set myself up, but once I'm settled with some money behind me, I'll send fer ye."

"Send for me?" Clara propped herself up on her elbow, looking down into his eyes.

"Aye, I'll make a home for us somewhere new, away from Mam and Da and that dammed hovel of a cottage." He smiled at her, but she didn't return the hope in his eyes.

"You mean away from the island?"

"Aye," he laughed. But Clara wasn't laughing. Instead, icy fingers were trailing round her heart, tightening and squeezing out the joy that had filled it.

"Jimmy, I won't leave my home. I'm an islander." She looked down at him, begging him to understand. But her island was not his, her place within it the antithesis of his own.

Jimmy shook his head. "I can't stay here," he said, voice cracking as tears swam in his eyes. They broke apart and sat side by side on the sand, Clara hugging her knees to her chest.

"Are ye ready to walk home?" asked Jimmy, standing up and offering her a hand.

"No, I think I'll stay awhile." Clara gave him a weak smile. As Jimmy began walking away Clara called to him. "Jimmy? When will you go?"

"Not before the summer. I'll wait for the silver darlings." And with that, he turned and walked away.

Chapter 22

April, 1913

Clara flopped down onto her bed, exhausted. Anna had not been herself for months, and Clara had been trying her best to pick up the slack. At almost seventeen, the expectations placed on her had grown. In the mornings she would trawl the shoreline looking for driftwood to stoke the fire, then she would fetch water from the well. Mid-morning, she'd set about baiting the lines and attending to any mending. In the past few weeks, she'd been helping her mam with the cooking and cleaning too, and as spring wore on, she realised it had been weeks since she'd had any time to herself.

Clara was loading wood into the store when Anna came carrying a basket of washing to hang on the line. She put the basket down and grabbed a cloth from her pocket to wipe her brow. It worried Clara how pale she was, despite the hours she'd spent working on the nets in the sun.

Anna grabbed a sheet from her basket and reached up to peg it to the line. As she did so, her full skirt fell against her stomach. Clara gasped at the protruding round bump, hidden by swathes of cotton.

"Mam." Clara rushed over and placed her hand on her belly.

Anna looked at Clara with alarm and took her hand. "Come with me."

She led Clara back inside the cottage and poured them each a glass of water from the jug that stood on the table. Anna stared at the surface of the table, unable to speak.

"Mam, are you having a bairn?"

Anna looked at her daughter with tears in her eyes. "I don't know."

"But the bump?" said Clara, pointing at her belly as she spoke.

"Have you ever wondered why you don't have any brothers or sisters?"

It was something Clara often wondered and felt the stab of jealousy as her friends played with their siblings. But with her mam so fragile, she kept her thoughts to herself.

"No," Clara lied. "I've always been happy with you and Da."

"You're old enough now to understand the ways of the world, and it's time I told you the truth. There have been many times since we had you we thought we were going to bring another child into the world... but... but..." Tears began rolling down her cheeks. She took a deep breath and in a whisper added, "but nature had other ideas."

Clara understood what she was telling her, and a lump formed in her throat.

"But this baby? Is this one going to be alright?"

Anna reached down and began stroking her swollen stomach. "I hope so, but babies should wriggle and jiggle, that's what you did. This one, though... he's still. I haven't felt him move in two weeks." Her face fell, and she buried it in her hands, large sobs escaping from beneath them.

Clara got up and wrapped her arms around her. She had missed what was right under her nose and felt childish. Once Anna's sobs lessened, Clara got up, filled the kettle and hung it over the fire. She held her mam as she waited for the water to boil. The kettle whistled, and Clara made tea and set it down on the table. Anna lifted her head and took the cup, her hands shaking.

As Anna drank, Clara picked up a broken line and set about mending. She didn't want to tempt fate by admitting how excited she was at the prospect of a sibling, and they sat quietly, Anna picking up the line and working side by side with Clara.

Over the next few weeks, Clara cast furtive glances towards Anna whenever she could, checking for signs of colour returning to her cheeks or the movement of her belly. But she saw neither.

Clara woke one night to the sound of screaming. The noise ripped through the flimsy curtain separating the room, startling her into consciousness and action. She drew the curtain back and saw her da kneeling beside his wife, ashen-faced and gripping on to her hands. Anna was writhing in pain, sweat on her brow and her face twisted in agony.

"Clara, fetch Mrs Crow."

Clara pulled the blanket from her bed, wrapped it around herself, and slipped her feet into her boots. In less than a minute, she was out of the door and running down the lane to Mrs Crow's house. Mrs Crow had trained as a nurse in her youth and was the closest the islanders had to a doctor. Clara hammered on Mrs Crow's door for an age before slow shuffling footsteps made their way towards her. The door opened a crack and Mrs Crow peered out. One look at Clara's face told her all she needed. She turned, calling over her shoulder, "I'll git me bag, pet."

She returned with a leather bag in hand and pulled on her coat with one hand, closing the door behind her with the other.

Clara wanted to run, but Mrs Crow was old, and her steps slow. As they neared the cottage Clara ran ahead, bursting through the door and rushing to her mam's side.

"She's coming," Clara said, and Bill nodded his reply.

She saw her mam turn from ashen white to grey, her breathing laboured, the silence of the cottage punctured by the piercing cries that came every couple of minutes.

Mrs Crow arrived panting at the cottage door. "Put some water on to boil, pet." She went to Anna, touching her forehead and holding her wrist to check her pulse.

Clara turned to fill the kettle, but as she looked back, Mrs Crow lifted the blanket that was covering Anna. She wished she hadn't looked. The sheets below Anna were deep red, and alarm crossed Mrs Crow's face as she took in the scene before her.

"I'm going to need sheets, blankets, towels, everything ye've got," Mrs Crow ordered. Clara began taking items out of the chest near her parents' bed.

"Come on, pet, hold on in there. It will be over soon." Mrs Crow was stroking Anna's hair, but her eyes were glazed, and she appeared not to hear. A scream ripped through the cottage and Mrs Crow was lifting the blanket again.

"All right, pet. The bairn's coming now. Ye need to push."

Clara looked at her mam's fragile frame and wondered if she would have the strength required, but in that moment something primal took over. Her eyes cleared, and she grunted, pushing down against the edge of the bed and letting out another piercing scream.

Something slimy and grey slipped into the arms of Mrs Crow. For the first time, Bill spoke.

"Is that the bairn? Is he alreet?" His eyes switched from hope to devastation, as Mrs Crow shook her head and wrapped the body of the baby in a blanket, laying him gently against Anna's chest.

Anna made no move to hold the baby. Her eyes glazed over once more, and Mrs Crow shook her shoulder.

"Come on, pet, yer bairn's here. He needs his mammy to hold him before ye say goodbye."

But Anna didn't reach for the baby; instead her arms flopped down, hanging listlessly beside the bed. Her head rolled to the side. Anna's eyes were open, but there was none of the usual light that made them sparkle. In fact, Clara saw there was no light at all.

The air in the cottage seemed thick, and Clara was struggling to catch a breath. The sounds of the room came from far away, familiar objects confused and blurred. Clara's body swayed. She heard Bill in the distance. "Nae, nae, nae."

The howl of anguish from Bill faded to silence as Clara slid to the floor. When she came round, she was aware of something cold and wet on her forehead and Mrs Crow looking into her eyes. For a blissful moment Clara forgot where she was, but then the room came back into focus and she saw her mam lying on the bed, eyes closed, arms folded. Her face was pale. She looked like a doll.

Bile rose in her throat. She ran outside to the garden and threw up. With nothing left to expunge from her body, Clara stood, grabbing hold of the wall as her legs gave way beneath her. Once her strength returned, she walked over to a bucket of water and splashed her face. She smoothed down her hair, took a big gulp of fresh sea air and walked back into the cottage.

Bill was weeping beside Anna's bedside. In sixteen years, she had never seen him cry. He got up and lay beside Anna on the bed, his head next to hers. Clara noticed her mam was lying on fresh sheets and decided that must've been the work of Mrs Crow. The old lady was packing items into her leather bag. Clara walked over to thank her.

"Oh, pet, there's no need. I couldn't help yer mam or the bairn," she said, eyes watery with tears.

But Clara's eyes were dry, her body numb. After seeing Mrs Crow out, she walked across the small room to where Bill and Anna lay, looking as if they had just taken to bed for a catnap.

"Da, do you need anything?" He lay with his eyes closed and didn't respond. She tried again, whispering in case he had fallen asleep. "Da?"

"The one thing I need is the one thing I canna have." Bill's voice was hoarse. He placed his arm gently across his wife's still body.

Clara retreated to her side of the room, drawing the curtain across. Still, no tears would come. She climbed into bed, still wearing her boots. A wave of exhaustion swept through her and she lay on top of the bedsheets, a blanket wrapped around her, waiting for sleep to come. Her small toy rabbit sat on the cabinet beside her and she picked it up, hugging it to her.

Clara could hear the quiet rhythm of her da's sobbing. Sleep eluded her. When Bill's sobs turned to gentle snores, Clara got up, crept across the cottage, and clicked open the door. Outside, the birds began their dawn chorus, and the sky was no longer black but navy, growing lighter by the minute. She walked to the harbour, then on towards the castle. When she reached it, she began climbing across the rocks that led to the water's edge.

Looking out at the open sea, Clara wished it would whisk her away to wherever her mam had gone. Grief welled inside her until it became an uncontrollable force. Clara released a scream that filled the vast sky around her, scattering sea birds into the air and bouncing off the castle walls before heading out to sea. She screamed until her throat stung, and it was then that the tears came.

"I want my mammy," she sobbed as she crouched at the water's edge, hugging her arms around herself. "I want my mammy!" she screamed at the sea. "I want my mammy!" she screamed at the sky.

Sinking down against a rock, she cried until her head pounded and her eyes ran dry. She let a hollow sadness invade her body, one that she wondered if she could ever shake.

Chapter 23

April, 1913

Clara woke to the sound of gulls calling to one another as they glided above her head. Her body clicked and creaked as she straightened herself up from her rocky resting place. She raised her face to the sky, watching the birds floating on air without a care in the world. *Fly me away with you*, she wished, but the birds ignored her pleas, ducking and diving as currents moved them around the bright blue.

Clara shook her head free of grief and began marching towards the village. She couldn't fall apart. She was all Bill had, and must care for him as her mam would have wished.

As she passed the harbour, she saw the familiar figure of her da wading out towards his boat. Clara stopped and watched as he leant against its side, unable to pull himself aboard. Even from a distance, she could see the violent movement of his body as sobs heaved his shoulders up and down. She heard the roar as he cursed fate, cursed God, cursed life. Then, in one quick movement, he was on his boat. He unfurled the sail, sat back, and steered the vessel out to sea.

A sense of dread filled Clara as she opened the door to the cottage. Inside, she found Mrs Crow, sitting by her mam, now covered in a sheet. Tendrils of auburn hair spilled from its edges and Clara sat herself beside Anna's body, running the strands of hair between her fingers.

Mrs Crow looked at Clara. "Are ye alreet, pet?"

Clara didn't know how to answer her. "I will be, someday," she said. Mrs Crow nodded in understanding.

They sat for a while in silence until Mrs Crow shifted in her seat and asked Clara if she would mind her returning home.

"You go. I'll watch over her," said Clara, motioning to the still shape of her mam. Mrs Crow gathered up her coat and let herself out of the cottage.

Clara lay down on her side and looked at the form of Anna beneath the sheet. She sang to her, barely above a whisper and with her voice catching as it caught with tears.

"O my Love is like a red, red rose
That's newly sprung in June;
O my Love is like the melody
That's sweetly played in tune.
So fair art thou, my bonnie lass,
So deep in love am I;
And I will love thee still, my dear,
Till all the seas gang dry.
Till all the seas gang dry, my dear,
And the rocks melt with the sun;
I will love thee still, my dear,
While the sands o' life shall run.
And fare thee well, my only love!
And fare thee well awhile!
And I will come again, my love,
Though it were ten thousand mile."

Clara didn't notice the fat tear that slipped off her cheek and soaked into the sheets covering her mam. She didn't know how long she lay there, but she was becoming drowsy when a soft knocking on the door caused her to sit up.

"Hello?"

The door opened a crack, just wide enough to see the familiar face of Jimmy. "Is it all right if I come in?"

"Aye."

Jimmy came into the room, taking his cap off at the sight of the body laid out on the bed and holding it to his chest. He stood for a moment till Clara motioned him to come and sit beside her.

"I saw ye da down by the harbour. He asked me to check on ye."

"I'm fine," said Clara.

Jimmy put an arm around her, and she turned into him, burying her face in his shoulder and soaking his gansey with her tears. The sobbing eased, and she moved away, wiping snot and salty tears with her sleeve. He gently reached up and pushed away a strand of hair that had stuck to her forehead. He didn't speak, but lowered her down onto the bed beside Anna and sat with her until she fell asleep.

Clara woke to the sound of the kettle whistling on the stove and for a moment everything seemed normal, but rubbing sleep from her eyes there was her mam, still and cold beside her. Jimmy took the kettle off the fire and glanced across.

"Sorry, didn't mean to wake ye."

"You came back."

"Na, I never left. Promised yer da I'd stay with ye and I don't break my promises." He looked away, embarrassed, and set about making her tea. Clara raised a hand and rubbed at her throbbing forehead.

"How long have I been sleeping?"

"I don't know, but it's morning now, so a good while."

"My da?" Clara asked, looking anxiously around for any sign he had returned.

"He hasn't been back here yet. Give him some time, Clara. He'll be right."

Clara wanted to believe him, but she knew something had shifted and without Anna to hold them together, life wouldn't be the same again.

"What happens now?"

"Ye mean with yer mam?"

"Aye."

"I think she'll stay with yous longer, then I s'pose there'll be a funeral."

"What happens at a funeral?" Clara asked, ignorant of the ways of the world.

"Well, at my grandad's there were hymns. The vicar read from the bible, then we buried Grandad in the churchyard. A few people came back to the cottage, telling stories about him and such like."

"Oh," said Clara. The thought of Anna being buried beneath the island soil horrified her, but it would happen, and in some ways, she wished it would happen sooner rather than later. All the while Anna's body lay in the cottage, Clara felt she wouldn't be able to breathe.

Jimmy stayed a while longer until they heard Marnie out on the street calling his name. "Better get going," he said, reluctant to leave her until he was sure she'd be alright.

"Thank you, Jimmy. I'll be fine here."

Clara waited for Bill to return, but day turned to night and back to day and still he wasn't home. Jimmy called by in the evening to let her know that he'd seen Bill out on his boat and he wasn't showing any signs of returning to the harbour.

By the following afternoon, Clara was pacing the length of her cottage. She had lost her mam, she couldn't lose her da too. As dusk was settling in, Bill finally walked through the door.

"Where've you been?" Clara shouted, full of rage that he should leave her to deal with this alone.

"Oot," he said, keeping his head down and not looking at her.

"What about Mam?"

"What about her? She's gan. Nowt we can dee fer her now."

"Aye, there is. We need to sort a funeral."

"I've bin to the vicar. It's happening tomorrow."

In the event, the funeral passed by in a blur of grief. The entire island turned out, plenty crying, not just the women. Kindly arms patted Clara and Bill, people speaking words of condolences that merged into one long expression of sympathy. There was no wake afterwards. Instead, Bill went out on his boat and left Clara alone.

*

Clara lost both parents the day Anna died. In the weeks that followed, she searched desperately for signs her kind-hearted da had returned. Bill had barely uttered two words to her since the funeral, spending his time either at sea or at the Crown Inn, only returning to the cottage to sleep. He could no longer look at his daughter, and it hurt her almost as much as Anna's death. Clara gave him a grace period of three weeks before confronting him.

"I'm still here, Da. Why won't ye talk to me? Why won't ye look at me?" she asked one night after he had stumbled home from a drinking session. Bill ignored her, but she wasn't prepared to let him this time.

"Da? DA!" she screamed, pushing in front of him, standing inches from his face.

Clara didn't see his hand, but felt the hot sting of his palm against her cheek. She bent double, hand to her face, stumbling across the room and cowering in a corner. Bill moved towards her, but as she flinched, he backed away. Sitting beside the fire, he put his head in his hands. Clara wasn't sure how long they stayed like that. After a while, pins and needles crept up her legs, and she inched her way up to standing. She edged across the room but stopped short at the sound of his voice.

"Yer too much like her, Clara," he said through the muzzle of his hands.

"What do you mean?"

This time, his voice was louder. "Ye remind me of her, Clara."

"Isn't that a good thing?"

Clara jumped as Bill slammed his fist down onto the table. "Nae, it isn't."

Not wanting to anger him further, Clara crept through to the bedroom and buried herself under her blankets.

Chapter 24

June, 1913

A month had passed since their altercation, yet father and daughter were no closer to being reconciled. Clara cooked Bill's meals and took care of the household tasks Anna had attended to, hoping this might break the hard casing that now surrounded his heart. It was all to no avail. He ate in silence and spent most of his time away from home. It seemed the ghost of the cottage was Clara, for Bill looked right through her.

One evening he didn't return home, and Clara sought him out. She tried the Crown first, peering through its grimy windows until Old John came out and informed her Bill was not there. She called at all the island pubs, but Bill was in none.

Frustrated, Clara began roaming the island paths and was coming down from the Heugh when she caught sight of him. He was talking to Rachel Watson. Clara could think of no reason for Bill to talk to Jimmy's sister and moved to join them.

As she descended the rocky slope, Clara glanced up and noticed an intimacy to their movements. She hung back. Bill held Rachel's hand. Perhaps as a comfort? Instinct told her not to interrupt. They walked away, and Clara followed at a distance. As they neared her cottage, she expected them to part ways, but they continued. She watched as they entered the Watson cottage and closed the door behind them.

Clara was waiting at the kitchen table when Bill returned. He looked surprised to see her, but hung his jacket and made to go to his bed.

"Da, where have you been?" she asked, stopping him in his tracks.

"Doon the pub."

"No, you haven't. You were with Rachel Watson."

Bill spun round. "What business is it of yers who I've bin wi'?"

Clara slunk back into her chair. "Da," she said. Her broken voice caught him off guard. For a moment, she noticed kindness return to his eyes, and longed to wrap her arms around him.

He sat opposite her at the table. "Rachel and I are to marry."

"What? W... w... why?"

"I need a wife. I need a son." He pushed back his chair, signalling that the conversation was over.

Clara watched speechless as he retreated to the bedroom. Anger bubbled up inside her. She was no longer a child who would follow demands without question. She marched through to the bedroom and found him sitting on the edge of his bed, head in his hands.

"How could you?"

"I have to, Clara. I need a son. I told ye."

"She's only a little older than me!" Clara screamed, wanting to shake him from his madness.

Bill looked up and even in her emotional state Clara could see that the hardness had returned to his eyes.

"It's settled," he said, and turned his back on her.

Clara could not bear to be near him. She returned to the kitchen, grabbed an armful of blankets from the chest, and slammed the door. She ran to the harbour, anger spurring her on. The harbour was pitch black. The dark of the night and lapping of waves brought a calmness that quietened her soul. She picked her way over small rocks until she reached the fishermen's sheds.

"Jimmy?" she whispered.

"Clara?" His voice was full of sleep and she was sorry she had disturbed him.

"Can I sleep here tonight?" she asked, stepping into the shed.

"What's happened?"

"Don't you know?"

"Know what?"

"About Da and Rachel. They're getting married."

Jimmy laughed. "Yer having me on. Why are ye really here?" He sat up and tried to judge her expression, but it was impossible in the moonless night.

"I'm not messing around. I saw them together. He admitted it."

Jimmy was now wide awake. "Come here," he said. Clara fumbled her way through the darkness to where he lay. He reached for her hand and guided her down beside him.

"Tell me everything."

Clara told him everything she knew, which wasn't much.

"Poor Bill," said Jimmy.

"Poor Bill? There's nothing poor about our Bill. He's been a brute since mam died. He's barely spoken a word to me. Now, he's courting a lassie half his age, *marrying* a lassie half his age."

"Aye, I'll admit that's peculiar, but really, Clara, he's not in his right mind."

"I lost her too, and I'm not going round acting the fool."

Jimmy pulled Clara close, and she leant her head against his shoulder. "Try to get some sleep. Things will feel better in the morning."

Clara snuggled down beside him and curled up in his arms. "Goodnight," he said, kissing her hair.

Proximity to Jimmy was a comfort, but Clara's mind churned over Bill's announcement, and sleep eluded her. He had betrayed both her and Anna. She could never forgive him. Careful not to wake Jimmy, she sat up and made her way through the shed until she felt the cool night air on her face.

Up and down the harbourside she paced, tripping and stumbling on rocks, cursing when her arm grazed as she fell. Clara hurled stones into the water, the gentle plop as they landed doing nothing to salve her broken heart. She began feeling around the ground, gathering large rocks in haste, filling the makeshift basket of her skirt before marching over to her father's shed.

With a loud cry of despair, she hurled the rocks, hearing them bang against the wooden walls, which she hoped would dent. A satisfying splintering rang out as a rock hit the small glass window.

"What are ye doing?" cried Jimmy, woken by the sound of breaking glass. He pulled Clara's arm back as she went to throw another rock. "This won't solve anything."

"Maybe not, but it's made me feel better." She managed a small smile and sank down on the grass, some of her rage abating. Cold air pinched at her skin and she let Jimmy guide her back to his shed without protest.

*

The wedding was a muted affair. They honoured all the traditions; the petting stone, the guns, the gate toll. What was missing was joy.

Bill went through the motions, but didn't once look at his bride as he spoke his vows. He trained his eyes on the floor and there was an unmistakable crack in his voice. Clara closed her eyes, longing for the day to pass. There was no big island celebration. Clara was the only one sitting on Bill's side of the church and although Jimmy's large family filled the pews to her right, the church felt empty. There were fewer people than on any given Sunday, and the congregation that trooped out behind the newlyweds was quiet. Everyone had loved Anna. No one wanted to be in the church that day.

Clara waited as the congregation filed out. The sound of the footsteps on the hard stone grew distant, and she walked to the front of the church to light a candle. "I won't forget you, Mam," she said.

Chapter 25

June, 1913

Alex Watson benefited from the marriage, striking a deal with Bill that meant the *Mary Lou* was now seaworthy. He displayed a newfound swagger, hollow chest now puffed, holding conversations with Robert in quiet corners.

By now, the herring were on their migration from the Scottish islands, and it was almost time for Jimmy to leave. Only Clara knew of his plans. He would have slunk off unseen, but he was an honourable man and if he were to start a new life, he must end his old one well. With a deep breath, he knocked on the cottage door.

"Wat?" Rose looked up in surprise as Jimmy walked through the door, the first time he'd crossed the threshold in six months. Alex moved to get up from beside the fire, but Rose put a firm hand on his arm and, for once, he complied. Jimmy stayed close enough to the door to make a quick escape should he need to.

"I'm leaving to work the herring."

Alex didn't even look up. "Good riddance," he said, tossing a piece of wood into the fire.

Rose looked up from her knitting and frowned. "Ye canna go," she said, picking up her needles and resuming her work.

"Aye, I can," said Jimmy, unperturbed.

"Nae." When she looked up, she had tears in her eyes.

"It's not forever," Jimmy lied, hoping this might placate her.

"There're the bairns to think about and yer da's boat," she said, sounding more desperate.

"Mam, ye've not allowed me near the bairns for ages, and Da wants Robert to skipper the *Mary Lou*. Ye don't need me here."

Rose gave a quick cough to disguise the tears welling in her throat. Her reaction caught Jimmy off guard and he went across to squeeze her shoulder. She reached up and patted his hand.

"When dee ye leave?"

"Tomorrow," he said, and stepped out onto the quiet island streets.

Jimmy had seen Bill heading towards the Crown so knew Clara would be alone with Rachel and keen to escape awhile. He knocked on the cottage door, but it was Rachel who answered.

"Is Clara in?"

"Aye," she said. "Clara, Jimmy's here."

Clara appeared from the bedroom, and Jimmy asked if she fancied a walk.

"Aye, I'll fetch my shawl."

"How are ye?" he asked Rachel, keen to break the awkward silence that lay between them.

"Fine," she said, with none of the joy of a newlywed.

Jimmy coughed and shuffled his feet, hoping Clara would appear soon and save him from his awkwardness. "How's Bill?"

"Dinna kna. He's either on the boat or at the pub." Rachel held his eye, challenging him to press further. Clara appeared, and without acknowledgment walked past her stepmother into the evening light.

"Everything all right?"

"Not really. I'm a spare part in that cottage. Da ignores me and I ignore Rachel, despite her attempts to lord her position over me."

"What will ye do?"

Clara snapped her head round and gave a hollow laugh. "Not much I can do, is there? We can't all go swanning off when it pleases us."

Jimmy said nothing but thought to himself it was she who wouldn't leave the island. She was making her own bed, as his mam would say.

"I might get married," Clara said, looking to judge his reaction.

Jimmy felt stung, but kept his voice level. "Aye? And who do ye plan to wed?"

"I don't know, but there's plenty to choose from," said Clara, flouncing off ahead so that Jimmy had to jog to keep up. When he reached her, he grabbed her arm to stop her.

"Clara," he said, avoiding her eyes. "It's my last night on the island. Can we not argue? Please?"

Clara's breath caught at his words. She had long known this moment was coming, but hadn't expected it would come so soon.

"Let's go to the caves. I've left some things in there I need to fetch before I leave." Without waiting for her answer, he led the way through the village and towards the secret path.

Inside the cave, Jimmy moved to the small pile of driftwood he had gathered earlier that day and lit it with a match. Soon, flames were lapping at the wood, casting shadows against the rock walls that danced as Clara moved nearer to him. She sat close, but not so close that they were touching. The cave was quiet, its stillness only broken by the crackling of the fire and the pounding of waves onto the rocks below.

It was Clara who broke the silence. "I don't want you to go, Jimmy."

"I know."

She sighed in frustration, but didn't take her eyes from the dancing flames. Jimmy spoke again. "I don't want to leave ye."

"Aye, you do," she snapped, staring at him hard.

"I want to leave the island, not ye."

"It's the same thing," she whispered.

He reached across for her hand, but she pulled it away. Her body ached for him to hold her, but if she let him touch her, her resolve would break, and she would give him her all. She couldn't let that happen.

"I'll write," he promised.

Clara gave him a weak smile. "So will I."

Clara looked at him in the firelight, pressing his image into her mind.

"I should get going," he said, and Clara nodded. Jimmy reached to the back of the cave and picked up his bag of books from their hiding place. He placed a lingering kiss on Clara's cheek and handed her an envelope from his pocket. "Read it when I'm gone," he said, before turning his back on her and walking away.

Clara stayed in the cave long after he had gone, twirling the envelope round in her fingers and staring at the fire. She thought of the life and the man she could have had. "I love you, Jimmy," she said, but only the waves heard her.

Clara turned the envelope over in her hands, then tore open the seal and pulled a piece of paper from it.

Dearest Clara,

I hope one day we can find each other again.

All my love, Jimmy.

Below it, he had written the words of a poem:

Ae Fond Kiss

Ae fond kiss, and then we sever;

Ae farewell, and then forever!

Deep in heart-wrung tears I'll pledge thee,

Warring sighs and groans I'll wage thee.

Who shall say that Fortune grieves him,

While the star of hope she leaves him?
Me, nae cheerful' twinkle lights me;
Dark despair around benights me.
I'll ne'er blame my partial fancy,
Naething could resist my Nancy;
But to see her was to love her;
Love but her, and love forever.
Had we never lov'd sae kindly,
Had we never lov'd sae blindly,
Never met—or never parted—
We had ne'er been broken-hearted.
Fare thee weel, thou first and fairest!
Fare thee weel, thou best and dearest!
Thine be ilka joy and treasure,
Peace. enjoyment, love, and pleasure!
Ae fond kiss, and then we sever;
Ae fareweel, alas, forever!
Deep in heart-wrung tears I'll pledge thee,
Warring sighs and groans I'll wage thee
Robert Burns

*

Jimmy was up before dawn the next morning. He entered the cottage, taking care not to wake his sleeping family. Leaving was harder than he had expected, and as he stared down at his sleeping sisters, he found it difficult to tear himself away. Hair obscured Marnie's face, her small pink mouth just visible. Jimmy placed the lightest of kisses on it and his heart twisted. He gathered his bag and looked around the cottage for the last time.

"Wait," came a whisper, and Jimmy saw his mam slip from her bed. "Wait," she said again, beckoning him to follow as she headed to the yard.

When they were out of earshot of the cottage, Jimmy spoke; "Mam, I have to go now."

"I kna, I kna," she said, flapping her hand to shush him. She disappeared into the privy and came out holding the little tin of shillings.

Jimmy shook his head as she held it out towards him. "No, Mam. Ye keep that," he said, pushing her hands away.

Rose gave a frustrated sigh. "Jimmy, I've bin saving this in that stinking privy fer years. I've suffered beatings by yer da, hunger and temptation, but I've kept its secret. Ye're damn well taking it wi' ye, lad." She thrust it back towards him.

Jimmy did something that surprised them both. He flung his arms around his mam. She stood stiffly as he embraced her, but as he drew away, he saw tears swimming in her eyes.

"Now ye can gan," she said, handing him the tin before turning away.

Jimmy did as he was told and felt a small part of his heart breaking off as he closed the cottage door for the last time.

Chapter 26

June, 1913

Rag rugs still adorned the stone floor, and Clara still wrapped up in the patchwork quilt each night, but everything else in the cottage had changed. Days merged into one in a blur of chores and strained faces. The members of the household were engaged in a dance of sorts, avoiding each other's company, making excuses to be out of the house and sitting in different rooms when they were home.

Bill had got what he wanted, and Rachel's stomach grew larger with each passing day. She didn't complain about the pregnancy despite her terrible sickness, and Clara admired her for it. Rachel was meek, quiet, and seemed resigned to the unhappy life she led. There was a mutual apathy between the women. It was a surprise to both when Bill gathered them at the table one evening.

"Clara, we need te have a talk," he said, not meeting her eyes.

"Aye?"

"I think it would be best if ye made yer own way fer a while."

"What do you mean, Da?"

"It's plain as day we're nae gittin' along too well together in this house," he said with rare candour.

"I hope you're not blaming me for that?"

"Na," said Bill, looking down at his hands. "Na."

"Well then, what do you mean?"

"Things are changing here. There's a bairn on the way, a fresh start." He patted his wife's hand with little enthusiasm. "I've written yer grandparents. They'd be happy fer ye te stay with them a while."

"But I've never met them."

"Na, but they will treat ye well, give ye a better life than this one."

"What about the bairn? What about the work here? Ye'll need me here to help ye." Her voice was rising with panic.

Bill shifted in his seat. "I've arranged fer Marnie to stay here. She'll help with the bairn while Rachel attends te the chores."

"You're sending me away," Clara whispered, a ripple of fear running through her.

"Just fer a time. I think it's fer the best," said Bill.

"I won't go!" Clara shouted. "You can't send me away!"

Bill looked at her, his face twitching with emotion. "It's done. Ye leave next week." With that, he walked away.

Rachel sat, picking at grains in the table's wood with her fingernail.

"Did you know?"

Rachel shook her head, then stood up and followed her husband outside.

Over the following days, Clara threw herself into changing Bill's mind. But nothing could break the hard wall of resistance he had erected around him. After four days of trying, Clara admitted defeat.

Her remaining days on the island were slipping away like grains of sand through a timer, and her soul ached at the thought of leaving her home behind. She took to spending every waking hour walking the island shores, committing its sights and sounds to memory and filing them away within her heart. She felt her mam walking with her and, whether real or a trick of the mind, her presence gave Clara courage.

As dawn broke on her last day, she rose early and walked through the quiet village. In the hidden caves, she settled down to watch the sun rise over a calm sea. She barely noticed the display of colours floating on the water as her mind drifted over her life until this point. The tide was in, and while its waters hugged the island, they could not force her out. But the tide would not hear her pleas and receded as she knew it would.

Rachel had gone to see Rose, and Bill busied himself in the yard as Clara collected the last of her belongings. She wanted to take the patchwork quilt, each square stitched with Anna's love, but it was too heavy. Instead, she slipped the little patchwork rabbit into her bag, a memory of her mam and glorious spring days when she thought happiness would last forever. The rattle of Reverend Barn's trap approached beyond the window. It was time to leave.

"Goodbye, Da," she called, not expecting a reply. She was lifting the catch on the door when Bill appeared in the room. His large body still filled the space, but his essence had shrunk. Clara remembered the days when his laugh rattled through the room, shaking ornaments that now were still.

She glanced over her shoulder. "Goodbye."

In two strides, he had crossed the room and Clara found herself swamped within his arms. She breathed in his scent as her cheek pressed against his chest, her throat thick with tears. He ran a rough hand across her back, clinging to her, unwilling to let go.

"I'm sorry. I'm sorry," he said with a desperate urgency. Then, in one swift movement, he released her, turning his head so she would not see his tears.

"I love ye, Clara," he choked, before heading out to the yard.

Clara crossed the threshold of her home for the last time. Reverend Barns reached down with a hand to help her up. Beside him, Clara kept her eyes fixed ahead. She had said goodbye to the island she loved, now it hurt her to look at it. The vicar was doing a great kindness in driving her, but Clara could not bear to make conversation. Sensing this, he moved the horse along, leaving Clara alone with her thoughts.

Water glistened on the sands, and the horse ambled along, spraying torrents of water into the air as its muscular legs fought the currents. Mid way across, the island's pull overwhelmed Clara and she turned for one last view of her home. The island squatted against sea and sky, nature's hues of yellow, green and brown punctuated by the grey stone of dwellings. The sky wrapped around its edges, meeting the sea and slipping into it with reflections of wispy white.

Clara closed her eyes and kept them shut until splashes of water gave way to the clacking of hooves on firm ground. For the first time in her life, she reached the mainland.

SEAHOUSES

Chapter 27

June, 1913

Jimmy thought his bones might fall out of his body as the train rattled over the tracks. He had reached Beal on foot, then bought himself a third-class ticket for the princely sum of one shilling and sixpence. As miles swept by, his seat became harder and his backside ached. Wind whistled through the carriage and soon he was wearing most of the clothes from his bag. Relief flooded him as the train pulled into Chathill and he disembarked.

"You catching the branch line to North Sunderland, lad?" called the guard.

"Na. I fancy a walk," said Jimmy, waving as he turned away.

Ahead of him stretched open countryside. It was a relief to be on his feet, away from the incessant bangs, clanks and hoots of the train. He had thought little beyond his initial escape and now wished he had formed a plan. Uncertainty tugged at him as he wondered whether this was all a mistake. What if no crew took him on?

Seahouses was his first port of call. He hoped to find his way to the pub he remembered from the night of the rescue.

After walking for an hour, Jimmy found a grassy bank to rest on. He drank from his water flask, trying to push pessimistic thoughts from his head. All his life he had strived to be the antithesis of his da, sure and steady. Now, he risked it all on a gamble. One thing he knew with certainty; the silver darlings were out there, primed and ready for the chase. Given the chance, he would prove himself an asset to the hunt.

The miles slid by beneath his feet. Dusk was seeping in, and Jimmy wasn't keen to enter a new town after dark. He headed towards the empty dunes and found a comfortable place to settle.

His body welcomed a break from its ramblings, and his mind welcomed the stillness of the open sky. Head on his bag, Jimmy gazed at the darkening sky, stars breaking through the gloom. The night was cloudless and despite the cold it would bring, Jimmy would stay dry. He lay still, watching the stars intensify, forming a luminescent blanket. Tiredness swept through his body, and he closed his eyes. He fell sound asleep and though the cold woke him several times, on each occasion sleep won out.

The sun edged up from the horizon and loud squawking caused Jimmy to stir. Gulls circled high above, and the sky turned pastel blue. He propped himself up on an elbow and looked around. The imposing hulk of Bamburgh Castle towered over the coastline, offering protection and beauty in equal measure. The sand in front of him swept down to clear, calm waters. To his right, wide rocks snagged the air, shimmering pools emerging among them as the tide receded. The song of the dawn chorus signalled it was early, but Jimmy was restless to begin his adventure. He brushed sand from his bag, slung it over his shoulder, and made his way along the beach.

Worry plagued his mind as he reached the harbour. He had been expecting an expanse of boats. Though busy, there were no Skaffies, Fifies or Zulus that characterised the Scots herring fleet. Had he mistimed his island escape? He hoped not, for the coins in his tin wouldn't see him through for long.

His stomach growled. It had been hours since he had eaten. He perched himself on the harbour wall and pulled out his notebook and pencil before replacing them in his bag. Best to wait until he was more settled before writing to Clara. He wanted her to think him a success, not a man with no plan, no job and no food in his belly.

From the harbour, he noticed the island nestling on the horizon. He pictured Clara baiting lines and felt a sharp pang of regret that he had left her behind. His eyes settled on the Farne Islands, enjoying their impressive barrenness, before hitching his legs onto the wall and making himself comfortable against the hard stone.

Retrieving a book from his bag, he laid himself out on the harbour wall and read. By the time he emerged from the imaginary world of Dickens, the harbour had grown busy with locals, readying nets and lines for the season ahead.

Jimmy swung his legs down and jumped from the wall. He nodded to the fishermen he passed as he walked along the harbour. With the map of his memory, he found the King's Arms where the landlord was putting out his board.

"Ye open?"

"You're keen, aren't you, lad?" laughed the fat publican, signalling for Jimmy to follow him inside. "What can I get you?"

Alcohol was the last thing Jimmy wanted. He longed for a bowl of oats and a cup of fresh milk, but keen to fit in, he ordered an ale.

"Stan," the publican said, leaning across the bar to shake hands. Jimmy introduced himself. "Where've you come from? I've not seen you before."

"Sir, I have been here once, with the Holy Island lifeboat crew."

Stan squinted at him and scratched at his stubbled chin. "Aye, I remember that young lad with the ship's crew."

"He'd been fishing," said Jimmy, and as the memory flooded back, the publican slapped the bar and let out a loud guffaw.

"Aye, I remember now! You're a long way from home, aren't you?"

Jimmy was keen to avoid too many questions. "It's time I made my way in the world."

Stan hesitated, weighing up whether to question Jimmy further, then deciding against it he laid a pint down on the bar.

"You looking for work?"

"Aye, I'm hoping to join a herring crew."

Stan scratched his chin. "Hmm, you're early. Most of the Scots crews are due end of the week. Will you be alright till then?"

"Aye," said Jimmy. He smiled at Stan and cradled the glass in his hands, wondering how he would manage a full five days with no work or board. With a few large gulps, he finished his pint and thanked Stan.

"Come back Friday lunchtime. I'll introduce you to some fellows."

Jimmy was despondent as he left the pub and headed back to the harbour to make a few enquiries with local crews. None needed an extra pair of hands and he slunk away, embarrassed by his misfortune. He called in at a grocer and filled his bag with enough bread, milk, and fish to last a few days. After a quick glance around, he decided the best route would be to follow the coast and headed south.

Jimmy walked for several miles until fine sand turned to smooth round rocks the size of a man's head. Clear water rushed back and forth, and above the beach, the sky slipped from blue to pink. Wisps of cloud lay in arrows across the sky, pointing to grand ruins that stood stubbornly above the shore. He climbed the grassy bank behind the beach, standing among crumbling castle walls.

Heavy stone rose in towers to the sky, its curved walls evidence of man's tenacity and engineering. He contemplated setting a camp within them, but there was an eeriness to the place that made him reconsider. Instead, he found a section of the outer walls where two joined, making a pleasant shelter from prevailing winds. He pinned his sou'wester upon them with several large rocks and crawled inside his shelter. The mossy grass made a cosy bed. With no evidence of recent human activity, Jimmy was certain the only disturbance would be from the occasional rabbit.

Night was drawing in, his gansey keeping him warm against the chilly air. He ate a simple meal of bread and fish, then fell into the deepest of sleeps.

Determined to shake the moroseness of the previous day, Jimmy resolved to keep himself busy. He filled his days reading and exploring, glad to have packed several books, for absorbed in their worlds, time flew. On his final evening, he walked back along the beach, to be near the King's Arms when it opened its doors.

He arrived in Seahouses at dusk and found a comfortable position on the south beach. His eyes had just closed when he heard distant shouts. He sat up, and in the dim light saw two figures, wrapped together like lovers. Their movements abrupt and exaggerated, Jimmy realised this was no embrace but a fight.

Jimmy crept forward on his haunches, moving with stealth against the sand. Their aggression might have shocked other men, but for Jimmy it was familiar, and he remained calm. A stocky man knelt against the arms of another, pinning him to the sand. Against the dark sky, Jimmy saw blood spraying from the victim's mouth, in rhythmic spurts that matched the aggressor's punches. Thwack, thwack, thwack. The bloodied man lay on the sand like a rag doll, head whipping with every punch, unable to lift his arms in defence.

Something in Jimmy stirred. He was loath to intervene, but this was no fair match. The man on the sand could die if he didn't help. Now only an arm's length from them, Jimmy leaped up and onto the stocky man's back.

"Stop!" yelled Jimmy. "Stop!"

His arms wrapped round the man's neck, who struggled against Jimmy's weight, roaring and flinging himself back. Jimmy held tight.

"Get off me, ye bastard," shouted the man. Jimmy clung on. The man scrabbled around in the sand, then flung his right arm back towards Jimmy's head. Everything went black.

Chapter 28

June, 1913

When Jimmy woke, darkness surrounded him. He reached for his glass of water, but his hand sank into something soft. Fingers feeling around, he realised he was lying on sand, not the old chair in his cottage, or the floor of his shed. He tried to lift his head, but pain ripped through it and he winced. His hand reached for his forehead and touched the stickiness of blood running from his hairline to his cheek. Beside him was the man he'd tried to save. He was not moving, and Jimmy dragged himself closer. His face to the man's mouth, he sighed in relief as the faint tickle of breath reached his skin.

Jimmy slumped onto the sand and rested his hands on his chest. He lay still, considering the best course of action. The man was breathing, but needed help.

He turned himself onto his front and dragged his knees up under his stomach. Hands pushing down hard against the sand, he lifted himself upright. Dizziness made him stumble and a wave of nausea swept through him. He leant over, retching. Wiping saliva from his chin, Jimmy took big gulps of sea air until steadier on his feet. With the moon no longer swaying before his eyes, he crouched behind the unconscious man. He slipped his hands beneath him, levered him off the ground, then hooked an arm below the man's knees. The bruised body lay limp in his arms.

Soft sand caused him to stumble, and he almost dropped the invalid. With greater care, he walked on, feet shuffling under the man's weight. It was a relief to reach a solid path, and soon Jimmy found himself among the lights of the harbour.

"Help," he called. No one came. "Help!"

A curious party of men appeared beside a boat. They squinted in the darkness, then recognising the man in Jimmy's arms rushed towards him. Instead of the help he craved, they wrenched the man from his arms. A strong, tall Viking of a man gripped Jimmy's own arms behind his back.

"What did ye do to him? WHAT DID YE DO TO HIM?"

Jimmy's mind burned with pain and confusion. "I did nothing. I... I... tried to help!"

The tall man twisted Jimmy's arms tighter, causing him to yell out. Pain brought a moment of clarity.

"Check my hands," Jimmy begged.

His captor gave a final vicious twist of Jimmy's arms before yanking his hands out in front to examine them.

"I need a light," he called.

A man rushed over with a candle and held it to Jimmy's palms. The Viking turned Jimmy's hands over and studied his knuckles.

"Nowt there," he said. As he released his grip, Jimmy collapsed to the ground.

When he came to, Jimmy was staring at his feet, head between his knees. He sat up and the group of men surrounding him gave a collective sigh of relief.

"Glad you're alright, lad," said the tall brute who had pinned his arms back. Jimmy looked at him, confused. "You told us to check yer hands, remember? We can see that you did no damage to our friend here. Did you see the culprit?"

Jimmy recounted the man he had seen. On hearing the description, someone in the group muttered, "Martin," and the Viking declared, "I'll kill him."

"Calm down, Callum," said a slim man, stepping through the throng. "We need him, whether or not we like it. I'll deal with him my way."

"Aye, skipper," said Callum.

The skipper knelt beside Jimmy. "How can we thank you?"

Jimmy shook his head. "I would like to leave now."

The men moved aside to let him pass. Jimmy made his way along the harbour, finding his bag on the beach and sinking down beside it. He tried to stay awake, worried the other man might return, but tiredness won out and he was soon asleep. Next morning, Jimmy wondered if he had dreamed the night's events. He had slept longer than intended, and the sun was rising fast in the morning sky.

With no food in his bag, he drank the last of his water to stave off his hunger. At the water's edge, he splashed himself, revived as icy water trickled from his neck to his back. A week of salt water matted his curls, but at least he was clean. Pangs of hunger came in waves, but he grabbed his bag and headed for the town.

At the harbour, Jimmy let out a low whistle. In the light of day he saw hundreds of boats, all shapes and sizes, jostling for position in their haven. He wandered around, perusing the different boats, wondering if he would have the chance to work on any.

The King's Arms was open, and walking in, he saw Stan holding court behind the bar.

"What's happened to you?" Stan took in Jimmy's impressive gash.

"Wrong place, wrong time," said Jimmy. Stan laughed and handed him a pint.

"Ta," said Jimmy. He wanted to sit down, the ale making him light-headed on an empty stomach, but he was keen not to appear rude.

"Where did you stay last night?"

"It was late when I got back, so I slept on the beach."

"You hungry?"

Jimmy nodded, and the man shouted through to the back of the pub, "Mary, we got a lad here needs feeding up."

A plump lady waddled through to the bar and set a plate down in front of Jimmy. On it was a stottie, warm from the stove, filled with a slice of ham and a good dollop of pease pudding. Jimmy's eyes widened and his mouth watered.

"Ta," he said. "How much do I owe you?"

"On the house," said Stan, before moving off to sweep the floor.

It was the most delicious meal Jimmy had eaten since Anna's broth. With no one to check his manners, he took large bites, rubbing the pudding from his chin as it dribbled down in his haste. He ate fast, his stomach hurt, and he leaned back in his chair. He sipped his ale slowly, aware he must keep his wits about him if he were to impress the local men. The pub filled. Shyness crept in; he was an outsider amongst friends.

After attending to his customers, Stan appeared next to Jimmy. "Come with me, lad," he said, and Jimmy followed him across the room.

"This here is Graham," said Stan, motioning to a slim man in his mid-thirties with kind eyes and a cropped ginger beard.

"We've met."

Jimmy took a step back. With a steady gaze, the skipper from the previous night nodded a greeting. He moved forward and Jimmy flinched, eying the outstretched hand with suspicion. Graham offered his hand again. Sensing no aggression to Graham's movements, Jimmy took his hand in a gesture of friendship.

"Apologies again for last night. It was a most unfortunate way to cross paths."

Jimmy nodded but said nothing.

Used to smoothing out confrontation, Stan moved the conversation on. "Graham, this young lad is from Holy Island. He wants to make his own way in the world."

Graham caught Stan's eye, and his own creased in amusement.

"That right, lad? And how do you hope to do that?" he asked in his broad Scots accent.

"I'm looking to join a crew, sir. To work the herring." The inside of Jimmy's mouth had gone dry, but his palms were sweaty. Graham continued to stare at him.

"Got experience?"

"Aye, I've been working my da's boat since I was a bairn and I've done the herring season on the island the last few years."

"Can I ask why you're not helping your father anymore?"

Jimmy shuffled and stared at the floor. His hand reached to the gash on his forehead.

After a pause, Graham clapped his hands together. "Nae bother. You can work for me as a half share man and sleep on the boat. That sound alright to you?"

Jimmy shuffled and Graham, sensing the cause of his discontent, continued. "Look, lad, you need the work and after last night we're one man short."

"Is he... is he..."

"Oh no, lad, John's fine, at least he will be once he's back home under the care of his mammy. Not sure what state he'd be in if you'd not come to his rescue, though."

"And the other man... Martin?"

Graham's face darkened. "Well, he's staying... for now. He'll be on a tight leash, though, and I can promise you won't get any more trouble from him. How about it?"

Jimmy considered the offer. He needed the work and Graham seemed a sound enough fellow. He reckoned with the training his da had given him, he'd have no trouble avoiding any flying fists.

"Aye, alright then. Thank you, sir." Jimmy shook hands with more enthusiasm.

"One thing, lad," said Graham as he stood to leave. "My name's Graham, not Sir, so no more of that, alright?"

"Aye, sir. I mean Graham," said Jimmy, blushing.

As he headed for the door, Graham waved his cap in the air and called to Jimmy, "Start tonight, six o'clock sharp at the harbour. My boat's the *Star Gazer*." And with that, he left.

Jimmy continued to sit at the table, his head spinning with the turn of events. Stan placed a jug of ale down in front of him, the liquid spilling over its edges as it landed.

"Sounds like it's all settled then, lad?"

"Aye, it is. Ta."

Jimmy spent the rest of the day mooching around the village. He liked it, but didn't intend to get attached. He was following the silver darlings and would soon be on his way again.

Chapter 29

June, 1913

By half-past five, Jimmy reached the harbour. He searched among endless rows of vessels before spotting the neat curling letters of the *Star Gazer*. Graham was already on deck, and Jimmy strolled over. The boat was a beauty; a Zulu of eighty feet if she were an inch. Her pine mast stretched to the sky, and Jimmy thought she would graze the stars while gazing at them. Her bow stood vertical and proud while her raked stern hinted at speed and manoeuvrability. It impressed Jimmy to see she had a steam capstan, a technology which had not yet reached the island fleet. Her painted hull suggested someone loved her well. Next to her, the *Mary Lou* would look like a discarded child's toy.

"You're early," said Graham, glancing up from his nets.

"Aye, sorry."

Graham pulled himself up and looked hard at Jimmy. "Don't apologise, lad, it's a good start. Like her?" he asked, leaning against the mast.

"Aye, I love her."

Graham climbed up out of the boat and clapped Jimmy on the back. "Come on, I'll introduce you to the lads."

Jimmy followed Graham further along the harbour. A gaggle of men were leaning against the harbour wall and straightened on seeing their skipper approach.

"Lads, meet Jimmy. Jimmy, meet the lads."

A large man stepped forward, head hanging low. "Erm, I'm sorry for being so rough with you last night. Can we put it behind us and start afresh?" His eyes peered up from beneath his thickset brow, a warmth to them that made Jimmy smile.

"Aye, nae bother." Jimmy offered a hand to shake, but Callum pulled him into an embrace so tight it sucked the breath from him.

When freed from Callum's arms, Jimmy shook hands with the men, all different shapes and sizes but with the same rough hands; sandpaper skin calloused by thousands of yards of line, ropes, and salt water. He tried to match names to faces, but they threw introductions out with such speed he struggled to commit them to memory.

Martin lurked at the back. His head lifted and Jimmy recognised the black sunken eyes and thin lips. His face was purple and dried blood clung to a split on his bottom lip. He had not escaped the previous night's antics unscathed. Martin glared at Jimmy with dark beady eyes, lip curling despite the pain its movement caused.

"Shake Jimmy's hand," said Graham.

Martin didn't move. In two large strides, Graham reached Martin and hauled him up by a fistful of shirt. He didn't shout, but his calm voice held a great deal of power.

"Shake Jimmy's hand, or you'll be the one heading north in need of your mam."

Graham dropped Martin to the floor. He stumbled, then held out a hand. Graham seemed satisfied and turned towards his boat. The crew followed him.

"Right, lads, let's away," he said. The men all leapt into action.

Jimmy's first impressions of Graham proved sound, he was an excellent skipper. As his crew took up their oars and headed out of the harbour, he kept his eyes fixed on the sea ahead, small white crests forming as the summer breeze teased the water. As the moon ascended, its light fell in shards on the dancing waves and lit the sky in a supernatural glow.

"You know what to look for?"

The first test, thought Jimmy. Clues of silver darlings rolled off his tongue. Graham said nothing, but nodded, satisfied that Jimmy had some knowledge.

With the sails billowing and a fair wind behind them, the boat ploughed through choppy water, up and down as breath moves a man's chest. Graham straightened up, and Jimmy followed his line of sight. Gulls circled nearby, and below them the brooding sea had an oily shimmer to its surface.

Graham guided the boat to the required position and instructed the men to shoot the nets. The warp held the base of the net wall firm, corks and buffs bobbed above the choppy water. Taking his lead from the experienced crew, Jimmy helped lower the sails and mainmast, and the boat drifted with the tide.

"Get your rest while you can, lads, there'll be plenty of work soon, all being well."

They shared round oat cakes, salted beef and tea, and with bellies full, the men hunkered down in the hull to rest. Not long after midnight, with the wind whipping up and the troughs of the waves deepening, Graham woke them and instructed them to haul. Callum and Tom rushed to operate the capstan, and soon the warp wound in.

Shoulder to shoulder with the crew, Jimmy hauled in miles of nets. The catch wasn't the largest he'd seen, but enough to strain his muscles for a good five hours' hauling. Martin appeared with a large scoop net and Jimmy realised he was the scummer, reaching down to catch large herring which had escaped their mesh prison. Jimmy wondered if it was a demotion.

With the nets in, Jimmy grabbed a wooden shovel and helped sweep thousands of iridescent bodies into the hold. They hoisted the lugsails with the help of the steam capstan and the race back to the harbour began.

Dawn broke and the *Star Gazer* cut a fine sight as she sped through the rough seas, red-brown sails bloated with the strong north-easterly that battered the vessel and excited the waters below. Jimmy helped clean and store the nets and soon land appeared on the horizon.

Mooring up in the busy harbour was a task. Again, Graham's quiet skill and confidence proved an asset to the crew. Once tucked away in the busy harbour and fish unloaded in their swills, the men climbed back onto dry land.

"I'll see you at the pub," called Graham, heading off to the market to ensure they got a decent price for the catch.

The other men strolled along the harbour while Jimmy stayed aboard the *Star Gazer*. Callum looked behind him, and noticing Jimmy on board, jogged back to the boat.

"What you doing here by yourself?"

"Oh, I wasn't sure if ye'd want me tagging along," said Jimmy.

Callum let out a hearty laugh, "Come on, you daft idiot."

He offered Jimmy a hand and pulled him onto the dock. Jimmy fell in with Callum's loping strides and soon they had caught the rest of the crew.

Stan greeted them as they entered the gloomy interior of his pub, keen to hear the size of their catch. "So, they haven't thrown you overboard yet?" he asked, winking at Jimmy.

"Not yet," said Jimmy, taking the offered pint and sipping the froth from the top.

"He's alright, this one," said Callum, clapping Jimmy on the back and causing the amber liquid to rise, leaving Jimmy with a foamy moustache.

Jimmy wiped his sleeve across his lip and smiled at his crew members. Only Martin kept his mouth set in its hard line and didn't return his smile.

Graham returned from the market and treated his crew to another round. Setting Jimmy's pint before him, he leant in close and offered quiet praise for his work. Jimmy flushed with pride. The weather had taken a turn for the worse and there would be no fishing till it had passed. The crew settled in for a night's drinking, but with Alex never far from his thoughts, Jimmy made his excuses and left. Whatever path his life took, he would never become his father's son.

A few men were milling around the harbour when Jimmy returned, but with the wind howling and the sky turning black, it wasn't long before they retreated to the nearest pub. Jimmy settled himself down in the hull and pulled a canvas sheet across to protect him from the elements. The rain started, the splat of plump drops on the canvas turning to a constant barrage, the noise deafening. Trickles of water slipped through gaps in the canvas, and Jimmy adjusted the sheet. If he could stay dry, he would be cosy enough.

Chapter 30

July, 1913

Dearest Clara,

I hope this letter finds you well. I've made it to North Sunderland and have been working on a boat out of Seahouses. I'm only a half share man, but I hope it won't be long till I've saved enough for my own nets.

Graham, my skipper, is kind, though he's no soft touch. He reminds me of your da, though Graham's beard is ginger and his frame slight. He is from somewhere north of Aberdeen and the rest of the crew are from villages round about that area.

They're a friendly bunch. One is a tall Scot called Callum who has shown me the ropes. He looks like a Viking, with bright red hair and a flowing ginger beard. I'm a fair height but Callum dwarfs me, and you don't want to make him laugh, for he'll clap you on the back and knock the wind right out of you! Samuel is from the same village in the Highlands and seems suspicious of this 'southerner', but I shall win him round. Tom is a merry lad with a song to sing or a joke to tell. His good humour is most welcome after we've been hauling for many an hour. The only fellow I have trouble with is the boat's scummer, Martin.

Jimmy paused his writing. He wanted to tell Clara about the fight, but deciding it might worry her, he spared her the details.

I think he resents me being brought into the crew halfway through the season. I try my best to have a friendly word when I can, but he doesn't seem interested in anything I have to say. If I am being honest, he reminds me of my da, an unhappy soul.

The other men are right enough. All are experienced with the herring and have welcomed me as best I could hope for. I think I've proved myself hardworking and most have accepted me into their little gang.

Herring are plenty here, and my first few weeks on the boat have been busy ones. We returned on our third night with ten creels. You can imagine the fuss that caused among the Herring Girls on our return!

I've been sleeping in the boat, which is not that different from the old shed. It's comfortable since I found the smoothest place in the hull. On dry nights, I look up at a blanket of stars. I can see the island in the distance, and I often think of you.

How is everyone at home? Are things more comfortable between you, Rachel, and Bill? The bairn must be on its way soon. It's a strange thought. I will be their uncle and you, their sister. What a funny turn life can take. Send my love to all on the island and tell my mam I am safe and well.

I shall be in Seahouses for a few months yet, so you can write to me at the King's Arms. They are good folk there and will pass the letter on. All for now, Jimmy.

Jimmy crammed away his paper and pencil as the crew approached the Star Gazer. Rumours were circulating of a large shoal further down the coast, and they headed off early to try their luck. It was a fine evening, a half moon rising in the evening sky and clear calm waters. There was just enough wind to propel the *Star Gazer* along, and all signs were hopeful.

After shooting the nets, the men took their rest. Dawn was breaking before Graham called on them to haul. By now, they had the routine down to a fine art and all took their positions to begin their work. The net didn't feel too heavy, but the crew hoped that there might at least be a few crans' worth in the haul.

They began hauling, but it soon became clear something was wrong. As the nets rose, the muscles in Graham's face clenched. A few herring lay silver, blue and green within them, but these were the exception. With horror, the men hauled net after net of rags, large holes ripped through, frayed twists of hemp playing in the water like ghostly fingers. Repulsive severed fish heads, eyes staring out from bloodied faces, lay strewn within the broken nets.

"Dog fish," said Graham.

It was a grim job hauling the miles of nets. Some they could save, most were beyond repair. A few perpetrators remained caught, and the delight Martin took in destroying them sent an uncomfortable ripple through the crew.

Ruined nets lay in haphazard piles, for there was no point storing them properly. After raising the lugsail and turning to shore, the men sailed home in silence. Graham kept his eyes ahead, speaking to no one.

With arms full of broken nets, the crew walked along the harbour and made their way to Craster yard. Damaged nets carpeted the ground as they surveyed the extent of their losses.

"I bet you're happy to be a half share man," said Martin. He sucked hard on a pipe yet still managed a sneer, which Jimmy ignored.

"Shut your mouth unless you've something helpful to say," said Graham.

If Martin were chastened by his skipper's rebuke, he didn't show it, leaning back against the wall of the yard, his dark eyes disappearing beneath a plume of smoke. Jimmy was not happy. Lost nets would cost them dear, but it relieved him he hadn't yet made enough to buy his own.

They sorted the nets into piles, those that could mend and those that were goners. With the work finished, the men stood back, surveying the disparity between the piles. Only four nets were worth mending. One thing was certain, they would not be leaving Seahouses with much money in their pockets.

"Best go see about buying some nets," said Graham.

The crew followed him out of the yard, but Jimmy stayed behind, more an outsider than since he joined the crew. A red-faced woman in a grimy oilskin apron appeared, hands on her hips, taking stock of the scene before her.

"Terrible night for you, so I've heard."

"Aye, right it was."

"Need a hand with these nets?"

Jimmy managed a faint smile. She disappeared, returning moments later with two stools.

"Come on then, what you waiting for? These nets won't mend themselves."

Jimmy sat down and set to work. Grateful for her help, he would make sure he recompensed her from his own pocket. Her endless chatter soothed him, and his spirits lifted as they began rectifying the damage inflicted.

It was hours before the crew returned, tired and irritated by the dent in their purses. They laid their new nets down in a neat pile at one end of the yard. Jimmy and the woman had mended a quarter of one net when they appeared, and Graham gave Jimmy a nod to show his gratitude for the progress made.

"It'll be a few days before we can head out again. Get some rest and we can meet back here tomorrow to tar. Watch ye don't drink too much tonight. We're low on funds as it is." With that, Graham strode from the yard.

Jimmy stayed with the woman. His speed impressed her, and his mind turned to Rose, who had trained him up well over the years. They worked until the light was fading and Jimmy's stomach growled.

"Come to mine for some food?" the woman asked.

"Aye, ta," said Jimmy.

The woman introduced herself as Maisie and led Jimmy through the town to a small cottage not much bigger than his childhood home.

"Mam, Mam," grubby children cried as their mother returned. Her brood met Maisie with a list of demands. She gave them each a quick hug before stoking the fire and laying bowls on the table.

It was impossible to guess her age, but Jimmy placed her around the forty mark. He couldn't count the number of bairns, for they tore round the cottage, running in and out to the yard and mingling with friends on the street.

Her home contained only a few tired items of furniture, but the warmth of the woman towards her bairns made the space homely. Jimmy offered to help, and she set a large bowl of potatoes in front of him.

"Peel those."

Maisie was fascinated to learn Jimmy had grown up on the island she saw from the harbour. "It must be a right magical place," she said. "I often make up stories about it for the bairns when I'm trying to settle them."

He liked the woman, and reluctant to shatter her illusions, spoke of the caves, the ruined priory, walking along the shore. His tales thrilled

Maisie. When she questioned him about his family, he spoke of Marnie, skipping any details of his da. She was no fool, and knew there was more to tell, but not chose not to press further when she sensed her questions hit a nerve.

With the potatoes peeled and boiled, Maisie hollered through the cottage and with a scampering of footsteps, the place was filled with children. She looked round the room.

"Billy, Sid and Katie, head on back to your own house and eat your own food." Three impostors giggled and ran out of the cottage.

The meal was a simple one of potatoes and smoked fish, but it filled Jimmy as much by Maisie's kindness as the food. Her table was not big enough for all to sit at and five boys and four girls sprawled across the room, some on chairs, others on the floor. At a guess, the children seemed aged from five to eighteen and Jimmy blushed as he caught one of Maisie's teenage daughters staring. She was pretty enough, but Jimmy was saving his heart for Clara.

"Is yer husband out fishing?"

"No, my Dan's been gone four years now. Lost him to the sea in a winter storm. Now it's just me and the bairns."

There was sadness in Maisie's voice and Jimmy thought her Dan must have been a fine fellow for her to still grieve his loss. He admired Maisie for keeping the house while being the sole earner.

"The older bairns help me out. We're lucky to have the herring call on these parts, and there's plenty of work here if you want it enough."

When the meal had finished, Jimmy helped Maisie's pretty daughter clear away the plates. His hand brushed hers and she giggled. Jimmy blushed at the curious tingling the touch had brought.

"Well, I'd best be off. Ta very much for yer kindness. Will I see ye at the yard tomorrow?"

"Aye, I'm there every day," said Maisie, giving Jimmy a warm hug before sending him on his way.

*

Jimmy woke early and headed straight for the yard. Maisie was already at the nets and Jimmy resolved to pay her more than the going rate. He settled himself down beside her. They had been working for two hours when the crew arrived to bark and tar the new nets. Graham strolled over to check Jimmy's progress and clapped him on the back on seeing the net half mended.

"I reckon we'll be at sea by the end of the week," he said.

Callum, Martin, Samuel and Tom trudged round the yard and Graham confided, "King's Arms," before walking over to chivvy them along.

As the sun rose to its highest point, Maisie's daughter arrived with a basketful of oatcakes and bread.

"Thought you could do with some feeding," she called. The men dived into the basket.

They offered thanks through full mouths, and it was a merry group despite their misfortune. Jimmy caught the young girl's eye, and both blushed. Callum noticed and gave Jimmy both a wink and a sharp dig in the ribs.

"Something there takes your fancy?" he whispered, spraying Jimmy with crumbs.

"Shut up," said Jimmy. Callum laughed.

"Herring lassies are a perk of the job," he said, grinning. Jimmy ignored him. No girl could match Clara's wild island beauty, and he would not give up on her.

Chapter 31

September, 1913

The dawning of a Sunday signalled a welcome rest for Jimmy and the crew. He woke to the scatter of golden shards on cornflower blue water. Jimmy wished he could share the view with Clara.

He pulled out his writing paper but put it away again. The past weeks had been the same. He had little new to tell. The dog fish had spared them after the fateful night, and the fishing had been fair. Graham seemed pleased with his work, but no grand moments occurred that lent themselves to pen and paper.

It irked him that Clara had not written, but he decided she must have her reasons and he would not break his promise out of spite. He pulled out a book from his bag and leaned against the warm, smooth wood of the boat to read. Footsteps approached, and a shadow blocked the sun. Startled, Jimmy blocked the sun with his hand and saw Graham standing on the quayside.

"What you got there, lad?" said.

Jimmy held up his copy of Robert Burns for Graham to see.

"Any good?"

"Aye," said Jimmy. "That's why I didn't notice ye standing there."

Graham chuckled. "You're a clever lad, Jimmy. You'll make a fine skipper one day. Your big brain will waste away if not."

"I enjoy being part of the crew," said Jimmy. "Besides, anything away from my da is right by me." He grinned at Graham.

"Aye, well, you're a good worker, that's for sure. I just don't like to see a big brain like yours being wasted. Come on, I thought I'd take you to church."

With his book packed away, Jimmy jumped up onto the quayside to follow Graham. He led Jimmy up through the village to where the little Presbyterian church stood. Most of the pews were already full, and the hum of conversation was heavy with Scots' voices. Jimmy followed Graham to a pew where the rest of the crew sat, and they squeezed themselves into the small space. Quiet descended as the preacher took to his pulpit and heads bowed in prayer.

No man could underestimate faith when he threw himself on the mercy of the elements daily. At the first hymn they stood, and Jimmy saw men outnumbered women two to one. A few families stood at the front, all dressed in their Sunday best. Hearty male voices followed the organ's melodies, singing praise and thanks to their Creator. Jimmy found it hard to believe in God as his da's fists flew, but here he was drawn into the collective fervour.

As the service ended, the men filed out, shaking hands with the preacher as they stepped into the warm autumn sunshine. The village was quiet, people resting in their homes. Graham suggested they take a stroll, and the crew followed him towards the beach.

Change was in the air; the nights were drawing in and the herring were diminishing. Restlessness grew among the crew, who sensed the time was approaching when they would move on. Other vessels had already left, and the harbour had lost its characteristic bustle. For several days, the men debated whether Great Yarmouth or Lowestoft should be their destination and they settled on the latter. They knew Lowestoft well, and most were keen to return.

Callum regaled them with stories of herring lassies he met there. "An excellent reason to return to Lowestoft, lads!"

Graham turned to Jimmy. "You coming with us?"

"Aye, if ye'll have me?"

Graham laughed and clapped Jimmy on the back. The thought of putting more water between himself and the island pleased Jimmy. Perched on the horizon, he hadn't broken from its shackles. Seahouses was close enough for Alex to find, and they were near enough fishing the same waters.

"A change will be good," said Jimmy.

The crew sat themselves down on the sand and began making plans for their journey. Graham explained the route and the areas they would need to watch out for.

"All being well, we'll be in Lowestoft within the week."

"What's it like?" asked Jimmy.

"Full of pretty lassies!" said Callum, to cheers from the other men.

"I think we should leave first light," said Graham. The crew knew not to question Graham's judgment, for it always proved sound. Still, his announcement provoked anxiety among the men.

"Will that leave us time to prepare for the journey?"

"Aye. We have enough food stored now and thanks to the wretched dog fish, the nets are freshly tarred." Graham looked out across the sea. "I've heard talk of foul weather coming. If we don't leave soon, we could be stuck for another week, losing money by the day. Set off first thing and we'll make the start of the Lowestoft season. Say any goodbyes you need to. Let's meet back at the King's Arms at five."

With minds at rest, it was a merry crew who entered Seahouses for the last time. Jimmy went to say goodbye to Maisie. It being a Sunday, she was in her cottage and opened the door red-faced.

"These bairns will be the death of me!" Fanning herself with her hand, she stepped aside to let Jimmy in. "You off, lad?"

"Aye, we set sail fer Lowestoft at first light."

"Ah, what a time you'll have there! That's where I met my Dan. Fond memories I have of that place. It's cold, mind, and they talk funny." She grinned at Jimmy.

Jimmy thanked her for her kindness and promised to call the following year. She gave him a warm hug. "Farewell, young Jimmy. Take care of yourself."

He kissed her cheek and could have sworn she blushed. Maisie waved him off from her doorway as he strolled away toward the King's Arms.

As he stepped into the pub, Jimmy realised he had come full circle. He leant over the bar to shake Stan's hand.

"Ta for all yer help. I'd still be sleeping on the beach if it weren't for ye."

"No bother at all, Jim," said Stan. He poured a round of drinks for the crew. "On the house!" he said and found himself in receipt of back slaps and bear hugs.

Graham raised his pint. "To the *Star Gazer*!"

"To the *Star Gazer*," came shouts from around the pub. Glasses clinked, and the atmosphere was merry. One quick drink turned into several pints, and Jimmy almost fell into the water as he made his way back to the boat.

He'd asked Stan if any mail had arrived, but as usual, the answer was a shake of the head. The drink didn't fill Jimmy with cheer, instead it was a maudlin soul who settled down under canvas that night.

He turned over and over all the reasons Clara might not have written. It had been several months, and he had sent three letters, all receiving no reply. His emotions swung from anger to despair that some terrible fate had befallen her. He soon fell asleep, but woke throughout the night, dreams of Clara dragging him from his sleep.

*

Dearest Clara,

I'm not sure if ye have been receiving my letters, but I haven't yet had a response, so I hope you're alright. How are things on the island? I've not heard from my family either, not that I expected to, but I hope all is well.

We leave Seahouses first thing, bound for Lowestoft. If you would like to write to me, you can send a letter to the post office there. I'll check in often, so I don't miss it. The season here has been good, plenty of silver darlings ready for the catching. I enjoy working with the crew and Martin has left me to myself.

The thought of our journey south excites me, but I shall be sad to be further from you. I must go now, for it's only a few hours till we leave, and I should get some rest. I'll write again with news of Lowestoft. All for now, Jimmy.

Chapter 32

September, 1913

At dawn the crew arrived, bleary-eyed and suffering the effects of the previous evening. Their first two days of sailing passed without incident. The wind was behind them and the *Star Gazer* cut an impressive sight as she tore through open water. Jimmy and the men worked in shifts and rested when needed, but bursts of sleep were short, for excitement kept them alert.

On the third night at sea, a fat blob of rain landed on Jimmy's cheek, waking him from his brief slumber. Graham sat straight-backed, face strained, staring at the sky. Dark clouds rushed through the air, catching one another and turning black. Another dash of water to the skin. The wind was strengthening, its low whine becoming a cry, emitting a powerful scream across the vast sea.

"It's a north-easterly," shouted Graham.

All men were awake, their bodies tossed around with each mountainous wave. Jimmy grabbed hold of the gunwale as the boat heaved onto a crest and plunged back down. There was no haste to the crew's movements, for what they needed were careful, clear heads. Water lay like oil on the deck. One misstep and they would skid overboard.

The bow cut through banks of water, slicing through sharp as a knife. Foam clung to the men's beards and vision blurred with a barrage of spray. Graham guided the vessel near enough to the land to follow its curve, but far enough from the rocks that could scupper them.

Three months of sailing together proved a useful advantage, for no voice carried above the squall and the men read each other's movements by instinct. An almighty gust caught the lug sail and tore at its corner like tissue paper. Jimmy prayed the sail would hold long enough to get them to safety. The men fought on, and as the wind eased, they knew they had won.

"We're through it," yelled Graham, barely visible beneath the hood and cap of his sou'wester.

"Where are we?" asked Jimmy.

"Good question, lad. We'll wait for daylight before I answer that."

No one cared where they were. They were alive. That was all that mattered.

Daylight broke through thick raging clouds, and the men found their bearings. Impressive cliffs rose from angry waters, their white flanks a beacon against the grey sea and sky.

"We're at Flamborough Head," called Graham. "The lug needs urgent attention. We'll call into Bridlington Harbour to get it seen to."

The crew raised their hands to show they had heard the skipper. Fortunes changed, and on a rising tide, they entered the quay with ease. With the anchor down, a pilot boat came alongside, handing bread, beef and water to the grateful crew. The lugsail needed repairing, and the pilot assured Graham this would be no problem. He offered to take them to dry land, and they welcomed the suggestion.

Bridlington was a delight. Everyone was hospitable. It had everything a seaman could wish for and proved a welcome change from the *Star Gazer*. By the following evening, with the lugsail mended and fresh supplies on board, they headed back to the open sea.

The weather was kind, and it wasn't long before they passed the Humber with East Anglia in their sights. Off the coast of Great Yarmouth, drifters littered the sea on the trail of herring. The *Star Gazer* weaved a path through them, caught in veils of smoke that poured from their chimneys. Graham stood beside Jimmy, pointing at the steam drifters.

"If the herring are kind to us, we'll be sailing one of those next year."

As they neared Lowestoft, all men gazed at the land growing ever larger before their eyes. A creamy ribbon of sand wrapped the coastline, stippled with small boats and guarded by squat tin huts. Beyond it lay a jigsaw of buildings, squeezed together and shrouded by smoke that poured from roofs.

Graham climbed to the bow and spread his arms wide. "Welcome to Lowestoft, lads. The most easterly point of England."

Cheers of relief filled the air. "To the herring!" said Samuel.

"To the herring lassies!" said Callum, and Graham rolled his eyes.

A tugboat helped them into the harbour, and they moored up beside vessels of every shape and size. Grand buildings fringed the outskirts of the harbour, presiding over the frenetic activity below. The crew threw their bags and kists onto the harbourside and grinned as their feet settled on dry land. They pushed their way through crowds of fishermen, buyers and herring girls, swerving to avoid the crans being winched from boats.

"Off to The Grit, lads," called Graham, and the crew followed him as he disappeared through the crowd.

NORTH SHIELDS

Chapter 33

June, 1913

Reverend Barns pulled the trap to a halt beside Beal station. "Whoa," he called, the horse whinnying as her hooves scuffed the dirt track. He jumped to the ground and helped Clara climb down. After fetching her bag, he looked her square in the eye.

"Do you want me to wait with you?"

"No thank you, sir. I'm fine," she lied.

"Very well," he said, unconvinced by her bravado.

Before driving off, Reverend Barns pointed out the platform Clara must wait on and explained what she might expect from the train. He turned the trap around before reaching down and squeezing her hand.

"Go well, Clara, you will be in my prayers." With a look of sadness, he let her hand go and jerked the horse's reins, and the trap disappeared back down the track.

Clara took a deep breath and squared her shoulders. A porter appeared to assist with her bag and soon she was on the platform. She had taken care with her appearance. Her long auburn hair sat pinned beneath a bonnet, and she had worn her smartest dress. Her boots were well polished, and she had replaced the missing buttons on her jacket, one of the few items of her mother's that Bill had allowed her to keep. Only her eyes betrayed her as a novice traveller.

She clasped her gloved hands together to stop them shaking and took deep, careful breaths to stem threatening tears. Her legs twitched, and she fought the urge to pace the length of the platform. Instead, she stood stock still, allowing only her head to move as she scanned the horizon for signs of the train.

Far in the distance, a small puff of white cloud appeared above the treetops. Clara watched it grow larger, turning from grey to black and billowing out over the countryside.

A roaring, clattering sound grew louder until it became almost deafening. Clara's eyes grew wide as the train approached. Struck by awe and terror in equal measure, she watched as the vast machine thundered towards her. It filled the air with screeching and scraping of metal on metal and a plume of thick grey smoke. The train shuddered to a halt, emitting a violent blast of steam with a piercing squeal that sent Clara's hands to her ears. Men with blackened faces appeared through the smoke, fanning themselves with sea air, a welcome relief from the heat of the cab. A porter appeared, picking up her bag and guiding her towards a carriage. He opened a door and signaled that she should climb aboard.

"You need to get in, miss," he explained. "The driver will want to be on his way." He took her gloved hand and helped her climb the steps.

Clara found her way to a seat and settled herself down. The carriage was near empty, bar an elderly gentleman reading a broadsheet. She let out a sigh of relief. At least she would not need to engage in conversation. Sitting on a comfortable chair, she rested her head against its tall back.

With the shrill scream of a whistle and an enormous blast of smoke, the train jerked forward. Gripping the edges of her seat, Clara steadied her body against the sporadic movements of the train. Only when it settled into a steady motion did she let herself relax. A greasy film covered the window, and Clara pulled on a leather strap to lower it. Cool air flooded the compartment and soothed her tense features.

Countryside rushed past in a blur, the train skirting the line of the coast. As the island appeared on the horizon, she turned her face away, staring at the blank wall ahead. She could not confront her emotions in this public space. Her bravery had its limits, and Clara was determined to hold on to her composure for as long as she could. When she felt it was safe, she turned her gaze back beyond the window.

Shrouded in smoke from the train's funnel, Clara pressed her face nearer the opening to get a better view. The stench of coal stuck heavy in her nostrils and flecks of soot caught her eyes. She whipped her head back and pulled the window so only a sliver of breeze slipped through. The last thing she wanted was to turn up on her grandparents' doorstep as sooty as a chimney sweep.

The herring girls' tales of freedom and independence played on her mind. They told of the sights they had seen and adventures they had had. The difference, thought Clara, was they had chosen their path, whereas she had little choice. But it was up to her to make the best of it.

The rocking of the carriage calmed her. Clara's head nodded against her seat and she drifted into a semi-conscious slumber. Her head snapped up each time the train slowed.

Clara stirred as the train arrived at an enormous station. The platforms were teeming with bodies and she spun around, trying to get her bearings. The elderly gentleman behind her was folding his paper, and Clara turned to him.

"Excuse me, sir. Could you tell me where we are?"

"Miss, this is Newcastle. Where are you heading?"

"North Shields."

"You need to change here, miss, and catch another train. Best be quick about it."

A guard walked past the carriage, checking doors were closed before the train moved on. Clara grabbed her bag and rushed to the door. She fumbled with the handle. Noticing her distress, the guard came and assisted.

"Could you tell me where I can find the train to North Shields?"

"Aye, miss, you want that platform there," he said, pointing in the direction Clara must go.

"How long till the next train leaves?"

"You've got fifteen minutes, pet. No need to panic."

Clara wove her way through the station. People thrust themselves past her and in her confusion, she collided with a suited man who shouted for her to get out of his way.

Screeches of whistles assaulted her ears, along with shouts of unkempt young men and cries of children dragged along the platform behind harassed mothers. Clara moved on, eager to be past the chaos. She reached the platform and didn't have long to wait before the train arrived. She was growing accustomed to the noise and smells of these metal monsters and found herself a seat with ease.

Soon the train was speeding on, turning pitch black as they went through a tunnel. Clara relaxed as daylight flooded in once more, but her relief was short-lived, for beyond the window she saw they were high above the land, racing across a large iron viaduct. Her knuckles whitened as she gripped the seat tightly, grateful when the train pulled into the station. It was less crowded than Newcastle, and finding her way out onto the street was straightforward enough. Unsure of the direction she should take, she followed a path down towards the river.

Throughout the town sprawled towering buildings of red, brown, and grey. She recognised the salty tang of her island, but here it mingled with smoke that left an unpleasant taste on her tongue. It tinged the air dull grey and an acrid smell caused her to cover her nose.

A sign announced she had reached Fish Quay, which equalled Newcastle station in its bustle. She pushed her way through crowds of men and herring girls, all engaged in the business of finding gold in silver darlings. Ahead of her lay a river, its gaped mouth meeting a vast expanse of grey sea. Loath to linger in the intimidating crowd, she pushed on.

Clara climbed a mountain of steps, edged by tightly packed buildings that oozed a stench of squalor. A toothless man, clothes stained and face grimy, lurched from a doorway. Clara let out a small yelp, sidestepping him and pushing on higher. She turned several times, but the man remained leaning against a crumbling wall, sucking on a pipe and showing no desire to follow her.

Children clothed in rags ran in and out of windowless buildings, and several times Clara felt the slime of human excrement beneath her boots. At the top of the stairway, she leaned against a low wall to catch her breath, rubbing her boots against the stone to remove any filth. Clara walked on. Streets widened and houses took on a more genteel appearance. She stopped to ask a passing woman for directions. The lady looked Clara up and down, surprised by her destination.

"They won't welcome ye selling up there," she said.

Not understanding the woman or knowing how to reply, Clara nodded and continued on her way.

She walked higher through the town and along a cobbled lane, past towering houses that would have dwarfed her island cottage. A folded piece of paper lay in the pocket of her skirt. She pulled it out and reviewed the map Bill had given her.

Clara studied the numbers on the houses until she found a polished brass plaque with 20 displayed on it. She looked up at the house. This must be it. It seemed to stretch to the sky, four floors displaying large windows whose glass glinted in the sunlight. There was no salty residue clinging to them the way it covered windows of her cottage. The frames were crisp, bright white.

Clara took a deep breath, placed her hand on smart black railings and walked up the stone steps. The red front door housed a large brass knocker that sat in the jaws of a lion's head. Clara put her bag down and rapped the knocker three times. She heard scurrying footsteps approach. The door opened and a uniformed lady stood, wiping her hands on a pressed white apron.

"Yes?" she demanded.

Clara opened her mouth to speak, but no sound came out.

"We're not buying anything," said the lady, before moving to shut the door.

Clara stepped forward and pushed the door open again. "I'm not selling anything. I'm here to see my grandparents. I think they live here?"

The lady stared hard at Clara. Clara stared back. The pinched features and grey hair pulled back from her face gave her an unwelcoming appearance.

"Wait here," she said.

Clara stood on the doorstep, wondering what she should do. Minutes crawled, still no one came. Clara turned and heard the door open behind her. An old man in a smart suit stood in the doorway, a shiny pocket watch poking out of his breast pocket. On seeing her, he lurched back as if punched in the chest. Grabbing hold of a polished table, he recovered himself, placed an eyeglass to his eye, and leaned forward. "Anna?"

"N… n… no. Anna was my mam. My name is Clara."

Clara thought she was going to have the door slammed on her again, but the man staggered inside, calling over his shoulder, "Well, don't stand there like some street urchin, come inside."

Chapter 34

June, 1913

A large tiled hallway led into a grand imposing room. As Clara walked through, she clutched the doorframe and gasped as she took in her surroundings. Images of exotic birds stroked the towering walls. Unlike the practical worn wood of her island cottage, here were sumptuous cushioned chairs and settees in many shades. She had to restrain herself from rushing over and caressing the silk fabrics. Every surface housed ornaments, and lush plants crowded all corners of the room.

"Sit down, sit down," the old man muttered, and motioned to a wooden-framed armchair of soft crimson velvet.

Clara edged through the room, wary of knocking into a decorative table and sending its contents tumbling. On her chair, she perched at its edge, feeling drab against this technicolour backdrop.

The woman in the starched apron reappeared, and Clara's grandfather leaned in close to mutter something in her ear. The woman scuttled off and her grandfather sat himself on a settee. Clara opened her mouth to break the silence, but he held up his hand to stop her.

"Best wait, my dear. Your grandmother will be along any minute to hear all you have to tell us."

Uncomfortable in the silence, Clara shifted and looked at the floor. Her grandfather's fingers rapped on a polished table and the loud tick-tock of a clock rang out. The maid returned with a silver tray, laying its contents out on a low-lying table.

"Thank you, Sibyl," her grandfather said as the maid retreated once more.

His crossed legs twitched and his left hand rested on his face, stroking a grey moustache. Clara searched for signs of her mother in his features, but found none. The clock ticked on. An elderly woman appeared in the doorway. Her back was stooped, and her white hair was thinning. As she moved through the room, her black skirts rustled like the marram grass of the island's dunes. A lump came to Clara's throat at the memory of her island and she pushed it away.

The lady sat herself down opposite Clara and looked up. Clara held her gaze. The woman studied her.

"Andrew, what is all this about? Who is this young woman?" Her voice was clear and cool, displaying no emotion and triggering a fit of nervousness in Clara.

"This young lady claims to be our granddaughter."

"A... a... aye, I am," said Clara, her usual forthrightness deserting her.

"Speak up, girl."

"I am Clara, your granddaughter," she said, this time with more confidence. Why should she be nervous or ashamed? It wasn't her fault they had never met.

"We weren't expecting you."

Clara met this news with surprise. Hadn't her da said he had written?

"Oh... I... I'm sorry. My da said he had written to you."

Her grandfather snorted, "I wouldn't trust anything *that man* says." He wrinkled his nose as if he had caught the whiff of a foul smell in the air.

Clara bristled. Bill had hurt her, but she knew at heart he was a good man and didn't like the tone her grandfather was taking. In the room's silence, she wondered if she had ever seen her da write. Could he write? Surely, he wouldn't have lied to her about it? But he wasn't himself anymore, so anything was possible.

Her grandmother reached down and rang a little silver bell. Its tinkling rang out through the room and Sibyl appeared.

"Pour the tea, please, Sibyl," said the old lady. Clara's eyes widened at the sight of the maid pouring tea from a china pot into china cups. Why couldn't her grandparents pour their own damn tea?

Sibyl handed Clara a cup and saucer covered with pictures of pink and blue butterflies. 'My little butterfly'. She pictured Anna sitting at the table, chiding as Clara's mind drifted everywhere but the task in hand. Clara smiled at the memory.

"Is there something amusing, child?"

"No, grandmother. I'm sorry, I was just thinking of home."

"By the looks of it, this is your home now, girl, and it doesn't appear we have a lot of say in the matter." She glared at Clara. "We want no talk of that wretched island in our home," she added in a venomous whisper.

"There, there, Phyllis," soothed her grandfather, patting his wife's hand.

"I shan't be staying long," said Clara, though she had nowhere else to go. "It will be nice to get to know you." She squeezed a small smile.

"We'll see about that," muttered her grandmother.

After they'd sipped their tea in silence, Phyllis rang the silver bell.

"Sibyl, show Clara to the guest room."

"Yes, ma'am."

Clara replaced her cup and saucer on the tray, gave her grandparents a polite smile, then followed the maid from the room. Sibyl was smaller than Clara, but insisted on carrying Clara's bag. When Clara offered to help, the maid seemed offended, despite her panting. She led Clara up a wide oak staircase, its treads covered in deep, thick carpet.

The room Clara entered was the size of her cottage. Thick curtains held back the darkness outside, soft lamplight giving its features a warm glow. Once Sibyl had departed, Clara sat herself down on the bed, sinking into its heather-like softness. Dark wood and rich hues filled the room. Printed flowers poked their paper petals out from beneath an endless array of framed pictures and photographs on the walls. A small girl peered out with serious eyes, hand resting on the knee of a woman swathed in long skirts, buttoned up tight in a stiff blouse. Clara stroked the photograph, for the child must be her mam.

Running her fingers over the papered walls, Clara journeyed through an array of exotic lands, painted in delicate water colours and vivid oils. She searched through the solemn faces, gazing out of frames, scrutinising them for traces of Anna's likeness.

At a polished dresser, Clara picked up an ornate silver frame, its metal twisted in intertwining curls. Inside was a young woman Clara recognised as her mam. It must be the last photograph before she left for the island. She hugged the frame to her chest, its black and white presence bringing more comfort than any luxurious furnishings. Her bag sat waiting for her to unpack, but Clara climbed onto the bed and, lying on her side, placed the frame opposite her. It was the first time she had seen Anna's face in months, and a mix of love and agony twisted in her stomach. She began speaking, telling Anna of all that had come to pass. What would her mam think, she wondered, to see Clara lying on a bed in her childhood home?

Clara whispered at the photograph. "Can you see me, Mam?" As she spoke, a light flutter of breeze tickled her face and she hugged the frame close. A knock on the door startled her. She rushed across to the dresser and replaced the photograph before settling herself in an armchair. "Come in."

Phyllis stood in the doorway. "Dinner will be served in the dining room in fifteen minutes. Please be prompt." Without waiting for a response, she closed the door and Clara heard her footsteps receding.

Sadness slowed her movements, but Clara forced herself out of the chair and unpacked her small collection of belongings into the dresser. Its decorative ornaments rattled as she pulled open heavy drawers, and Clara wondered at the usefulness of such trifles.

She splashed her face with water from the washstand and dried it with the soft towel hanging from the rail beside it. Her reflection stared out from the opaque glass and Clara paused. She placed the towel back on its rail and once again reached for her mam's photograph. From mirror to photograph, she saw herself reflected in both. A deep yearning welled inside her for the life she had left behind. She dabbed away tears with the corner of the towel, then stood, pinching her cheeks and taking a deep breath.

Keen not to be late, Clara checked her reflection and made her way down the imposing staircase. Unsure which was the dining room, she had tried several doors, to no avail, when Sibyl appeared beside her.

"Can I help you, miss?"

Clara wondered if Sibyl suspected her of stealing the family silver. "Aye, I'm looking for the dining room?"

Sibyl pointed to a door further down the hallway, and Clara nodded her thanks. There was a sadness to the sight of her grandparents siting at a table of a dozen chairs, all but two unfilled. They looked up as Clara entered and both frowned. Clara was unsure what she had done wrong. She walked across the fine Turkish carpet, took her seat, and smiled at them.

Phyllis cleared her throat. "It is polite to change for dinner, young lady."

"Phyllis..." her grandfather warned.

"No, Andrew, it is best she understands correct etiquette from the start."

A deep blush rushed from Clara's neck until it prickled her scalp. "I'm... I'm sorry, grandmother, I didn't know." She studied the silverware on the table in dismay.

"Do you have other dresses in that small bag of yours?"

Clara paused as she thought of the clothes she had packed. She had dresses, worn from years of working, unlikely to meet her grandmother's high standards. Before she could answer, Phyllis jumped in.

"We shall buy you some outfits tomorrow. You are a pretty girl and we cannot have you being made plain by such dull clothes."

Clara wondered how within a few brief hours she had slipped from one world to the next.

Sibyl arrived with platters of meat and vegetables and served the food onto plates of fine china. Clara ate with care, allowing frequent furtive glances across the table in order to emulate her grandmother's table manners. She sipped her glass of claret, welcoming the warm sting as it slipped down her throat. The trio ate in silence, the sound of clinking and scraping of silver on china filling the room. Clara noticed her grandmother picked at her food like a small bird, and despite her restraint, Clara was the first to finish the meal.

Unsure how to start a conversation, Clara distracted herself by examining the room. Geometric hues of oak and gold covered the walls, contrasting with the leafy green of the curtains and brightly patterned carpet. As in her bedroom, framed photographs and paintings littered the walls. The mantel housed bronze objects, candlesticks, a clock and two vases. More muted than the drawing room, the dining room still held an air of opulence.

Andrew leant against his high-backed chair and crumpled his napkin onto the table. Sibyl came in to remove the plates and he thanked her, but seemed unable to find anything else to say. Clara tried to fill the silence.

"Thank you. That was a delicious meal. On the island we usually had..." but before she finished, her grandfather interrupted.

"Well, it will be an early night for me," he said, standing up and nodding to the two women before leaving the room.

They had conducted the entire meal in an awkward silence, and Clara wondered what her grandparents spoke of when alone. Sometimes a gulf is too wide and deep to cross, and Clara sensed mealtimes were to be hard. It was clear her grandparents wanted no mention of the island, but it was all Clara had ever known and she had nothing else to talk about. Andrew and Phyllis were no different from her da. She was too much like Anna, and her presence hurt them.

Chapter 35

June, 1913

Clara woke on her first morning in her grandparents' house with a sense of foreboding. The dress she had travelled in lay on a chair beside the bed and Clara stood to pull it on. She moved to the window and drew apart the heavy curtains.

Across rooftops she glimpsed the familiar blue of the sea. With a hand held against the cold glass, she watched as gulls leaned into the air, gliding their way out and up along the coastline. Clara tore herself from the view and rubbed at the imprint she had left on the glass. She slipped on her boots and tiptoed downstairs.

The house lay shrouded in sleep. With no one awake, she explored her new home a little more. All the doors were closed, and she turned the handle to the drawing room, doing her best to avoid any creaking that might wake the household.

The ringing of the grandfather clock startled her. Its loud chimes caused the house to stir. She heard movement upstairs, and Sibyl scuttled past the drawing room to the stairs, taking them two at a time. Clara thought of the effort it had taken Sibyl to carry her bag and wondered if the maid had been trying to make a point. Floorboards creaked above her, feet crossing back and forth. A door clicked shut and soft footsteps came down the stairs. Her grandfather appeared at the drawing-room door. He looked surprised to see Clara, as if he had forgotten she had arrived the day before.

"Good morning, Clara," he said, reaching for his coat and hat.

"Good morning. Are you off for a walk?"

"No, I'm heading to the shipyard. We are working on an important contract and if I'm not there, my men will be idle."

"Oh," said Clara. "Will you not be having breakfast?"

"No time, dear girl," he said, and rushed out of the door.

Clara stepped back into the drawing room and, after examining some ornaments, made her way to a piano that filled one corner of the room. It was made of the same polished dark wood as the furniture, and the ivory keys were a rich cream. Clara sat on the piano stool and pressed a key with her forefinger. No sound came, and she tried again. A note rang out and filled the vast room, crisp and clear. She continued to move a finger up and down the keyboard, intrigued by the ability of ivory on metal to create such a pure sound.

Clara heard her grandmother, the fine satin of her dress rustling like autumn leaves as she descended the stairs.

"I heard the piano," she called, entering the room.

"Oh, I'm sorry, grandmother. I hope I didn't wake you?"

"No, no," said Phyllis as she crossed the vast carpeted floor. She settled herself down on the stool, causing Clara's muscles to tense at the proximity of the sombre woman.

"The last person to play this piano was your mother," she said, her eyes fixed on the keys.

"Oh," said Clara, taken aback. "I'm sorry if my playing has upset you."

Her grandmother didn't answer, but spread her fingers over the keys. "She was a fine musician," she murmured. Her fingers pressed down and a few notes rang out.

"Do you play?" asked Clara.

"I used to." She stared at the keys beneath her fingers.

Clara whipped her hands back just in time as Phyllis slammed down the lid, enclosing the keys in darkness.

"Sibyl is waiting to serve breakfast."

Clara followed her grandmother to the dining room. They sat at the dining table, each as uncomfortable as the other.

"Are you educated?" Phyllis asked.

"Aye."

"Yes."

"Pardon?"

"We say 'yes' in this house. We do not speak like commoners."

"Yes," said Clara, struggling to keep the annoyance from her voice. "I attended the island school until the age of twelve."

"Humph, well, I suppose that is something. Can you read and write?"

"Aye, I can."

Phyllis winced at Clara's turn of phrase. "Did you have a proper teacher at the school?"

Clara suppressed a smile. "Yes, grandmother. I had a very stern schoolmistress called Mrs McKinnon."

Phyllis seemed satisfied and made no more attempt at conversation. She set her plate aside and rang a small bell to summon Sibyl. "Sibyl, please make sure the carriage is ready to take us into town in half an hour. I am taking my granddaughter shopping."

Clara met Phyllis in the hallway half an hour later. After issuing instructions to Sibyl for lunch on their return, she led Clara outside and into a waiting carriage. The decadence of using a carriage to travel the half mile into town shocked Clara, but she kept her opinions to herself. It was a bumpy ride across uneven streets, and Clara thought how much more comfortable the journey would have been on foot. Outside a grand-looking shop, the driver jumped down and helped Clara and Phyllis down the steps. Clara thanked the driver, but Phyllis said nothing.

She followed Phyllis into a bright room where different fabrics hung from rails on every wall. An eager young woman dressed in fine silk rushed across to them. She gave Clara a quick glance before turning to Phyllis, certain where the money lay.

"How can I help you, madam?"

"As you can see, my granddaughter needs some new clothes." She waved her hand to show Clara's current dress was most unsuitable.

"Certainly, madam. Did you have any colours in mind?"

"Yes, green would suit her complexion. Avoid crimson or pink. They will leave her looking washed out."

Clara stood mute beside Phyllis. The shop girl scurried round, picking out fabrics and bringing them to Phyllis for approval. With a tape measure in hand, the young girl manhandled Clara, checking the measurement of her hips, waist, and bust. She had never experienced such a level of scrutiny. Sweat prickled beneath her arms as the shopkeeper held the tape measure to her breasts. The young girl jotted measurements onto a pad of paper, and Phyllis held out her hand to inspect them.

"Good, good, the same as her mother's." She handed the paper back to the girl.

"We can have the dresses delivered to you a week today."

"Very well."

Phyllis turned and Clara followed her from the shop, relieved the ordeal was over. Back at the house, Phyllis disappeared upstairs and Clara retreated to her bedroom. A knock came on the door.

"Come in," Clara called, but no one entered. "Come in," she called again. She moved across and opened the door. Sibyl stood, the top of her head just visible beneath a pile of dresses in her arms. She pushed past Clara and threw them down onto the bed.

"Your grandmother says you are to wear these until your new outfits arrive. They were your mother's," she added before retreating from the room.

Clara sat on the bed and looked through the garments. They were island shades of green and blue. Silks and linens were plentiful, and the long full skirts fell across the bedsheets like paint on a canvas. Her hand stroke against jade green silk. Clara tried to imagine her mam wearing the clothes. She looked beautiful in her island work clothes, and Clara could well imagine how many heads she would have turned in these fine skirts and bodices. She lifted a bodice to her face, hoping to catch Anna's scent, but the fabric smelt musty, and she let it drop. Another knock came on her door and Phyllis entered the room.

"I see Sibyl found the clothes. They are no longer in fashion, but will do until your new garments are ready."

"Thank you, grandmother. Were these really my mam's?"

"Of course," said Phyllis, sounding surprised. "I don't expect she ever wore fine clothes after she chose a life of drudgery."

Clara tried to speak, but her grandmother held up a bony hand in protest.

"Just be grateful you are the same size she was. Now, take off that disgusting outfit you travelled in and I shall have Sibyl dispose of it."

Clara clutched her arms tight around herself. "I'll bring it to Sibyl when I've changed," she said, with no intention of doing so.

"Very well. Please be ready for lunch in half an hour."

Once alone, Clara picked out a simple teal skirt and bodice and hung them across the back of the armchair. Removing her old dress, she folded it into her bag and stuffed it at the back of a drawer, hoping Sibyl wouldn't find it. With difficulty, she squeezed herself into the flowing skirt and tight bodice. Once it was fastened, Clara found it was hard to move or breathe. She tried to lift her arms, but the stiff fabric held them back. Meters of thick silk slowed her and her strides became shuffles. Clara thought about the walks she had taken around the island. No wonder her mam had swapped silk for cotton on her arrival.

*

Clara made it through lunch unscathed. Once more, conversation was stilted and scant. Phyllis kept glancing at her across the table, and Clara wondered if she had left a trace of food on her face.

"I need to lie down," said Phyllis once Sibyl had cleared the plates. "Make yourself at home in the drawing room. There are books you can read if they are not too difficult for you."

Alone in the dining room, Clara sighed and tucked her chair under the table. She pulled a book from the shelf in the drawing room and sat down and read. Before long, she became restless, eager for activity. Grateful for the forethought to pack her needles and yarn, Clara went to retrieve her knitting from the bedroom.

As she climbed the stairs, she noticed a strange squealing coming from her grandparents' bedroom. She crept along the corridor. Phyllis's door stood ajar, and Clara held her breath as she peered through the crack. Her grandmother sat on a stool by the dresser with her back to the door. She was rocking back and forth and Clara realised with alarm, her hands were tearing at the thin white hair on her head.

The squeals continued, turning to grunts. Phyllis's hands moved from her hair and balled into fists, hitting at the legs beneath her skirt. Clara was an intruder but couldn't tear herself away. She moved her head as close to the door as she dared. Picture frames covered the dresser, the same beautiful face staring out of each.

"Anna, Anna, Anna," Phyllis groaned, hitting herself harder and rocking with such urgency Clara worried she might fall.

Noise from downstairs made Clara jump, and she whipped her head from the door. Phyllis heard it too, pushing back her stool, which tumbled to the floor. Clara ran to her room. Phyllis's door squeaked open for a moment, before being slammed shut.

Clara's entire body was shaking. The woman she had seen was so far removed from the dour elderly lady with whom she'd spent the morning. She looked down at her skirt and wondered if it was her likeness to Anna that had caused such an upset. Not wanting to disturb Phyllis further, she pulled her knitting from her bag and stayed in her bedroom until her grandfather returned. When Phyllis came downstairs to greet him, she was her usual composed self, and Clara wondered if she had imagined what she had seen.

Chapter 36

August, 1913

Life in her grandparents' home was proving a peculiar mix of tedium and unease. Despite the bright colours of its rooms, sadness filled the space like an unwelcome houseguest. As the weeks wore on, Clara realised her grandparents spent little time together.

When at home, Andrew would be in his study while Phyllis kept to her bedroom. Clara knew her grandfather no better than the day she arrived. He offered pleasantries if their paths crossed and maintained a jovial veneer, but gave nothing of himself away. Most days Phyllis did not appear until mid-day, complaining that a headache kept her in her bed. She was often silent, but prone to sudden bouts of irritation that left Clara on edge. Weight had dropped off her since Clara's arrival, and no amount of styling hid the ever-growing bald patches on her scalp. Grey skin hung from sharp cheekbones, and her hunched back seemed more pronounced as she shuffled through the house like a ghost.

Several times, Clara heard mournful whimpers, grunts, and cries filtering through the thick bedroom door. If Andrew was aware of his wife's condition, he didn't show it. Only Sibyl appeared concerned. Clara found her loitering outside Phyllis's door, worry etched across her face. She spent an inordinate amount of time dusting the hall ornaments, and Clara suspected she positioned herself there to hear the little bell and respond with haste. It was clear Sibyl thought Clara was to blame for Phyllis's distress.

A source of discontent for Clara was how to fill her time. She had almost knitted an entire blanket since her arrival, but had run out of wool. All the books that caught her interest had been read, those remaining too dry to hold her attention. Clara began walking each morning. With Phyllis bound to disapprove, she timed her outings to ensure she was back before her grandmother appeared. Sibyl knew what she was up to, but Clara was certain she wouldn't burden her grandmother with the information.

One morning, Clara was thumbing through a book when her grandfather appeared.

"Goodbye," he said, grabbing his coat and striding across the hall.

She stayed in her position for several minutes on the off chance that he might return. When enough time had elapsed, she threw her book down on the settee and rushed through to the hall to put on her coat. She had one arm through when Sibyl appeared. The maid stared at her, and Clara stared back. Sibyl folded her arms, but ignoring her, Clara turned and let herself out of the front door.

Memories of her first encounter with the town still firm in her memory, Clara opted to stay closer to home. Not five minutes from the house, she had discovered the most glorious park. On reaching it, Clara passed under its wrought iron entrance and began strolling its well-laid paths. Women dressed in fine clothes passed her, parasols out, anticipating the sun breaking through. Clara felt self-conscious and out of place, before remembering that with her new clothes she fitted in with this upmarket set, in appearance at least.

She strode across the well-manicured lawn and made her way to the wooded area. Her first visit to the woodland left her awestruck, for no such environment existed on her barren island. The rustle of leaves and uplifting birdsong filled her with peace and provided a welcome respite from the oppressive atmosphere of the house.

Clara ran her hands across the rough bark of an old oak and gazed up at its canopy of leaves, beautiful with the luminosity of late summer. She walked for a while before deciding to return home. The risk of being caught alone was not worth the momentary peace the park delivered.

At the house, she let herself in and listened. All was quiet, no sign of movement other than the distant clanging of plates from the kitchen. Clara had just hung up her coat when Sibyl appeared, carrying a silver tray.

"Your grandmother is not well and shall remain in bed."

"Thank you for letting me know, Sibyl. Is there anything I can get for her?"

"I need no help, thank you."

Clara lingered in the drawing room, but finding nothing to fill her time, she headed upstairs. She had no wool to knit, and leaving the unfinished blanket on the bed, walked downstairs to find Sibyl. The maid was busying herself by reorganising the well-stocked pantry.

"Excuse me, Sibyl."

Shocked to find someone in her domain, the maid jumped. "You shouldn't be in here."

"Sorry, I just wanted some advice."

"Huh, very well." Sibyl looked intrigued and paused her work for a moment.

"I was wondering if you know somewhere to buy yarn?"

"That I do, but you have another think coming if you think I'm going to be your skivvy."

"No, I'm not asking you to get me some. I will buy it. Just tell me where to go."

"They do not allow you out on your own."

"Aye, but that hasn't stopped me so far."

Sibyl huffed.

"It would give you an afternoon to yourself..."

The thought of Clara being out of the way seemed to work. "If I tell you and you get caught, I will deny all knowledge of your escapades."

"Fine," agreed Clara.

Sibyl gave Clara directions to a little haberdasher. "You didn't hear that from me. Understand?"

"Aye. Thank you."

Sibyl ignored the thanks and went back to the task in hand. Clara was nervous about venturing into the town, but any excitement was welcome and if it meant negotiating the slums, so be it.

She had a small allowance from her grandfather stashed in a silk purse. She retrieved it and slipped it into the pocket of her skirt. On her way out, Clara paused beside Phyllis's door. All was quiet. If she was quick, the chance of being caught was slim.

Sibyl's directions were efficient, and Clara found the small shop with ease. She browsed the yarns, selecting a variety of colours. At the counter, she paid with the money in her purse and experienced a rush of independence. She thanked the shopkeeper and tucked the brown paper bag under her arm.

Buoyed up by her success in the shop, she walked the long way home through the town. It had been a lonely few months and Clara had spoken to no one outside the household since she arrived.

She headed to Fish Quay, its bustle now comforting rather than frightening. The sight of fishing boats moored up made her heart twist.

Was her da out at sea today? She tried her best not to think of home, but she missed Bill. She saw a young man unloading swills onto the quayside and her thoughts turned to Jimmy. The shots of anticipation with each visit from the postman became twinges of disappointment, as day after day no letter arrived.

Clara walked across to a small boy selling winkles wrapped in paper. She handed him a coin from her purse, and stabbed a pin into the makeshift cup, enjoying the taste of home as she wandered through the busy streets.

Time was getting on, and she would need to brave the warren of squalid steps. This time she kept her wits about her, side-stepping suspicious objects and liquids that flowed down the stone.

She crumpled the paper in her hand and looked up. A man was walking in front of her, dressed in a smart suit and top hat. He turned, and Clara flung herself backwards into a doorway. The moustached face of Andrew was unmistakable, and she did not dare get caught walking alone against her grandmother's wishes. She expected her grandfather to continue, but he paused and knocked on a door. A woman, not much older than Clara, appeared. Tangled fair hair hung loose around her shoulders and her bodice gaped at the top, exposing large round breasts. Clara clapped her hand to her mouth as the woman draped a dirty arm around her grandfather's neck. She waited for him to push the woman away, but he gripped her backside and pressed his mouth to hers. Andrew glanced up and down the street, and Clara held her breath. The woman grabbed Andrew's shirt and pulled him through the door of her home.

Clara saw him kick the door, and it slammed shut. She waited a moment, then rushed up the steps, no longer caring what stuck to her boots provided she got away unnoticed.

Chapter 37

August, 1913

By the time she reached the house, Clara was sweating. In her haste to get inside, the door slammed and Sibyl rushed through to the hallway, shushing her. She looked Clara up and down.

"Whatever happened to you? Your grandmother is stirring. Hurry upstairs and change before she sees you. And make sure you have a wash, you stink of fish."

Clara grabbed her skirt in her hand and took the stairs two at a time. Closing the bedroom door behind her, she leaned against it, trying to slow her heartbeat. With her breathing more regular, she threw the bag of yarn onto the bed. She took off her hat and unpinned her hair. The image of her grandfather filled her mind, and she retched into the basin in disgust.

A quiet knock came on the door.

"Who is it?" she called, wiping traces of bile from her mouth. Quiet knocking came again and Clara moved to the door, opening it just an inch. Sibyl stood holding a large basin of warm water. Clara let her in and the maid set the heavy container down.

"Thank you," she whispered.

"This isn't for you, it's for her. I don't want her upset by your behaviour. The less she knows, the better," Sibyl said, pointing toward Phyllis's room.

"Well, thank you anyway."

With Sibyl gone, Clara grabbed a cloth and began sponging herself with the water. Its warmth was comforting and the tension in her muscles eased as she wiped sweat from her brow and neck.

Once changed, she made her way downstairs, reaching the hallway just as Andrew walked through the door. Clara blushed and kept her head down, refusing to catch his eye.

"Evening, Clara," he said to her back, as she scurried through to the dining room. Phyllis sat at the table, playing with the napkin in her lap.

"Are you feeling better, grandmother?"

"A little."

"Can I help?"

Phyllis shook her head and stared at the table. Andrew entered, but neither woman looked up.

Sibyl brought in their meal and they ate in deafening silence. Clara was the first to crack.

"How was your day?" she asked, holding her grandfather in a steady gaze.

Unfazed, he dabbed his lips with a napkin and smiled. "Oh, so, so. Run off my feet as usual. I didn't get to see daylight till closing time."

Phyllis dropped her cutlery with a clatter against her plate. "Excuse me," she said, as she stood and hurried from the room.

"Well, I think that is my cue to head to my study. Have a good evening."

Once again, Clara found herself alone.

*

In her bedroom, Clara waited till she heard her grandfather leave before heading out onto the landing, keen to avoid their polite charade.

She had crept as far as the stairway when Phyllis appeared. It surprised Clara to see her dressed and wearing her coat.

"Are you alright, grandmother?"

"Yes, dear, I thought you could take me with you on your morning jaunt."

Clara looked at Phyllis, her face reddening. "I... I... I'm not sure what you mean."

"Oh, don't play the fool, girl. My window faces the street. I know you've been sneaking out each day. You're not as clever as you think."

Clara looked at her, open-mouthed.

"Well, come on then. Is it far?"

"N... n... no, just to the park."

"I think I can manage that."

Phyllis had taken to walking with a stick and leaned on it as she crossed the landing. Shock crossed Sibyl's face as she appeared on the stairs and saw the two women together, each dressed in their outdoor attire.

"Do you need me to call the carriage, madam?"

"No, Sibyl, I do not. My granddaughter is taking me to the park."

"But... but..."

"That's enough, thank you. I don't need you fussing, I shall be alright." Phyllis crept her way down the long staircase. Clara opened the door for her and offered her arm, but Phyllis brushed past her, insisting her stick was enough support.

Once over the shock of having a companion, Clara found herself frustrated by her grandmother's presence. The usual five-minute walk took thirty, and she brought with her the stale, close atmosphere that Clara longed to escape. Inside the park's gates, Phyllis pointed her stick at a bench and suggested they sit down. They sat a good meter apart, Clara playing with her fingers as a distraction from the awkward stillness.

"I know everything that goes on inside our house... and out of it," said Phyllis, turning and staring hard at Clara.

"Sibyl?"

Phyllis laughed, "Oh no. Sibyl is a good keeper of secrets. My body might fail me, but my mind is as sharp as a pin, I can assure you."

An unspoken truth sat between them.

"I know our home is no place for a young woman. I am sorry for that." Her candour left Clara dumbstruck. "I cannot change the way we are, but I can consult some friends on how to go about finding you a husband. That might solve things."

The thought horrified Clara. "Grandmother, I don't want a husband. I want to go back to the island. But I can't, and will learn to make the best of things."

"Very well."

They sat on the bench watching people walking past.

"I would like to go home now."

Clara stood and helped her grandmother to her feet. "We were happy once, you know. Losing a child... it does strange things to people."

Before Clara could think of a reply, her grandmother had moved off and Clara knew the conversation had ended as quickly as it had begun.

Chapter 38

September, 1913

Since their trip to the park, Phyllis had been warmer towards Clara, and her daily walks continued without secrecy. Among the town's lanes she thought of Anna, walking the same streets all those years before. In her mind's eye she saw her da, reaching down to help the young woman refill her spilled basket, and her heart hurt.

She had heard nothing from Bill since she arrived with her grandparents. She told herself the lack of correspondence made it easier to move on, but she didn't want to move on. The island filled her dreams and in the small hours she would be back mending lines with Anna, or reading in the caves with Jimmy. Sometimes she even found herself back in the schoolroom with Mrs McKinnon.

Thoughts of home clustered in her mind and she walked on blindly. Her face to the floor, eyes bathed in tears, she stumbled along Fish Quay. With a fright, she walked straight into something large and solid. Stumbling back, Clara lifted her eyes and realised with horror the solid shape was a woman.

The woman spun round and glared at her. She had a creel on her back and its fishy contents lay splayed out on the yard floor, eyes bulging in lifeless regret. A slap of insults and screams hit her hard. She could not understand the words but recognised them to be Gaelic and there was no doubting their sentiment. Clara rambled words of apology and tried to move away, but the woman was strong and grabbed hold of her arm. She squirmed beneath the woman's tight grasp, the skin on her forearm twisting in a burn.

A small crowd gathered, and a female voice joined the kerfuffle, scolding the older woman for her aggression. With reluctance, the woman released Clara from her grip. Clara stumbled back, rubbing a sore arm against her skirt. She kept her head down, ashamed at the scene she had caused. A voice was speaking to her, English words filtered through a soft lyrical Scots accent.

"Apologies for my friend there. She's a little highly strung."

Clara lifted her eyes to respond but stopped short at the familiarity of the stranger's face, untamed flame red hair escaping its headscarf. The other woman was staring hard, as if pulling a memory from the deep recesses of her mind.

"Clara?"

"Kitty?"

They stared at each other for a moment, before leaping forwards into a firm embrace. Exclaiming declarations of surprise, Kitty linked her arm into Clara's and led her to a quiet patch of harbour wall.

"You've gone up in the world since we last met," said Kitty, taking in Clara's fine clothes and bonnet.

Clara groaned. "I wish I hadn't."

Kitty took hold of her fingers, searching for a ring. "Well, I can see it's not a man, so tell me, Clara love, how did you come by this turn in fortunes?"

"How long do you have?" asked Clara, giving her friend a sad smile.

"Don't you worry, I'm finished for the day. You can talk all night if you need to."

Clara began her tale, wiping away tears, her friend reaching a comforting arm around her or squeezing a hand when she needed encouragement to go on. When Clara had finished, Kitty took her hands in her own.

"What are you going to do?"

"What do you mean? I can't do anything. I'm wanted nowhere and there is nowhere I can go."

Kitty stared at the boats bobbing in the harbour. "Clara, how attached are you to your finery?"

Clara shook her head. "Weren't you listening to me? I don't want it. I don't want it," she whispered.

"Alright, lassie. Can you meet me tomorrow evening?"

Clara nodded.

"Good. I'm not promising anything, but I might have a way out for you."

Clara looked at Kitty with curiosity, but her friend jumped off the wall and walked away, calling over her shoulder as she went, "Tomorrow."

Clara jangled with nerves as she walked back to her grandparents' house. She wished Kitty had just told her the idea. She suspected she might try to set her up with some young man or other.

It displeased Phyllis that Clara had stayed out so late, and Clara's attempts at conversation were met with a stony silence. Andrew was at the office and the two of them sat awkwardly at dinner, Sibyl glancing from one to the other, and she cleared away plates, wondering at the cause of this latest disagreement.

The following evening, Clara made her excuses and headed down to the herring yard. She lingered by the outer wall, not wanting to risk bumping into the angry woman from the previous day. Kitty appeared, removing her oilskins and cloth headscarf as she walked. Clara smiled as a frizz of ginger broke free, sticking out in all directions except those Kitty would like.

"You came," Kitty said, the hint of surprise in her voice.

"Of course I came," said Clara, and they walked arm in arm to the harbour wall.

Away from flapping ears, Kitty turned and looked at Clara. "How would you feel about coming to Lowestoft with us next week?"

Clara almost fell off the wall. The name Lowestoft sounded familiar, and she was sure she had heard stories of it when they were on the island.

"How could I do that?"

"Well, you know we work in threes?" Clara nodded and Kitty continued, "Well, we've got a little spot of bother. Your remember Alice?"

Clara nodded again, remembering the plump girl with broad shoulders and a broad grin.

"Well, Alice got herself mixed up with a local boy a couple of months back and her monthlies haven't come since."

Clara looked confused.

"She's expecting..."

"Expecting what?"

"She's expecting a bairn, Clara. Pregnant. With child. In the family way."

Clara flushed, not only with embarrassment at the subject but also that it needed spelling out. "Oh."

"Aye, well anyway, she's been sick as a dog the past two months and doesn't show any sign of improving. She's spoken to the lad and thankfully he has agreed to wed. But it means she can't come to Lowestoft and we'll be short one lass."

"You want me to take her place?" asked Clara, wanting to be sure she understood.

"Aye, well, that's if you can still remember how to gut fish?"

Clara laughed. "I think so. It might take me a while to get as quick as you though, and I don't want to hold you back."

Kitty smiled. "We'll be much worse off one person short." She nudged Clara. "What do you think?"

"Aye, I'll do it. When do we leave?"

Chapter 39

October, 1913

Guilt plagued Clara as she contemplated leaving her grandparents, but she hoped her absence would be a relief. She couldn't tell them her plans. They wouldn't allow it, of that she was certain. Instead, she would write to them.

Twice more she met with Kitty, and Alice agreed to swap her kist for Clara's carpet bag. Each time they met, Clara smuggled a few items out with her, not that she had much to take. Her fine clothes would remain in North Shields, creating a sad bundle as they joined with those Anna had left behind. She still had the clothes she had arrived in and in these she would leave.

With the small allowance given her by her grandfather, Clara bought the apron, boots and warm clothes she would need for an East Anglian winter. Sibyl had been keeping a close eye on her and knew something was amiss.

Finally, the morning of her departure arrived, and Clara took one last look around her bedroom. She planned to leave a note on her bed, but had second thoughts. She didn't trust Sibyl to pass it on. Slipping quietly from her room, Clara crept down the stairs, made easier by the plush carpet, and, finding her grandmother's book, slipped the note inside.

She gathered her bag and coat and made for the front door. As she turned the handle, her grandmother appeared at the top of the stairs.

"Is that you, Clara?" she said, in a voice that sounded timid and frail.

"Aye," said Clara, forgetting herself. "Sorry, I mean yes."

"Are you going?" Something in the way she said it made Clara stop short. She looked up at her grandmother. There was no need to pretend. They couldn't stop her now.

"Yes, grandmother, I'm going. I'll be away for a while, but I promise I'll write. Thank you for everything you have done for me."

"Will you be safe?"

Clara dropped her bag and took the stairs two at a time. She lifted Phyllis's thin, papery hands in her own. "I'll be safe. I'm going away with some good female friends. One day I hope to return home to the island. It isn't what you want to hear, but your daughter loved it there as much as I did. She was happy, oh so happy, and above all she was the most wonderful mam I could have wished for."

Phyllis gave a small choke. "I loved her," she said, tears weaving their way down the crevices of her aging skin.

"I know," said Clara. She bent and kissed Phyllis's cheek. "I'll write," she promised, and with that she ran down the stairs and let herself out of the door.

Grief eclipsed the excitement of leaving. She would keep her promise and write, but would she ever see her grandparents again? It seemed unlikely.

Kitty was waiting for Clara at the end of the road. "Are you sure about this?" she asked, holding her palms to Clara's cheeks and staring hard into her eyes.

"Aye, I'm sure," said Clara. Hand in hand, they walked towards the harbour.

Kists lay in ramshackle piles beside a cart, ready to take to the station. The atmosphere was bittersweet. Excitement brimmed at their new adventure, but leaving friends and loves behind tinged it with regret. Alice waved them off and wished Clara well.

They squeezed themselves into the cart. A hard-edged kist prodded Clara's back and only a sliver of Kitty's flaming hair poked above the luggage. At the station they uncurled their stiff limbs, and the driver helped them load their kists onto the train. The platform was brimming with herring girls. They might have been in the Highlands, for it was Scots and Gaelic chatter that bounced off the station walls.

A whistle shrieked, and they jumped aboard the train. In their third-class carriage, they didn't notice the hardness of the seats, or the freezing air whistling through gaps in the walls. With a sly smile, Kitty reached into her bag and pulled out a bottle of gin. She passed it round, each girl taking a slug from the bottle.

Hours flew past, girls singing merrily as the train rattled their bones like shells in a bag. They taught Clara the songs of their homeland and by the end of the journey she knew them by heart.

The train crept into Lowestoft station with a squealing of metal and a hissing of smoke. After the long journey, the girls were black with soot, but their spirits remained high. They unloaded their kists onto a cart and jumped on the back. Kitty yelled directions to the driver, and they made their way to their lodgings.

"We're headed for The Grit, girls," she cried.

Lowestoft buzzed with life and its drifters were packed in so tight you could walk from one side of the harbour to the other without touching a drop of sea. Men in ganseys and sou'westers streamed around the dock. The air was alive with cries and laughter of both men and girls.

Their lodgings were in a house on Rant Score East, belonging to a Mrs Creek, a most unwelcoming host. She held her nose, complaining of the bad smells the girls brought with them. They unloaded their kists from the cart and heaved them up the bare wooden staircase.

Kitty kicked open the door of their room and held it open with her foot as her roommates stumbled in under the weight of their kists. The room was bare other than three sets of rickety bunks, one chair and a small dresser. Hooks were nailed into the walls to hang their oilskin aprons, and their clothes remained stored in the kists that doubled as seating.

The girls scrambled to choose their bunks, taking Clara by surprise. She ended up with the only bunk left. A rosy-cheeked, middle-aged woman called Heather lay on the bunk above. Clara noticed the other girls giggling, descending into snorts of laughter.

"Bad luck, Clara," said Cassie, patting Clara on the arm before bursting into another fit of giggles.

"What?"

Kitty tried to speak, but with each attempt she began spluttering.

"You drew the short straw," explained a thin young girl, and she pointed up to Heather, her features twisting with mirth.

"It's all lies, Clara. Don't believe a word they tell you about me," said Heather with a wink.

When they had calmed down, Kitty explained that not only was Heather a terrible snorer, but the herring did strange things to her bowels. "Your bunk will tremble through the night, that's for sure."

The giggling resumed. Clara couldn't imagine any amount of snoring would keep her awake after a day's work. At least she hoped it wouldn't.

She threw herself down on her bed, the effects of the lengthy journey clear in her tired limbs. But Kitty was having none of it.

"No time for sleeping, lassie, we need to look around... see the sights." She winked at Cassie, who giggled at the prospect of eying up a few fishing lads.

Clara wanted to protest, but excitement got the better of her. She picked up a shawl and moved to the door, noticing the other girls stuffing balls of yarn into their pockets.

"I thought we're going for a walk?"

"Aye, we are, but you'll soon see we are never idle," said Kitty, handing Clara a spare ball of yarn and a pair of needles.

The girls headed out of the house in a raucous cloud of chatter. Mrs Creek huffed as they passed. Out on the street, the girls picked up their needles, knitting as they walked. Unused to such multitasking, several times Clara bumped into lamp posts and carts as she stole glances to check her stitches. Watery daylight slipped into solid darkness. The streets were full of life despite the gloom and biting October air.

Had she come to Lowestoft directly from the island, the stench of rotting guts, shouts, cries and songs of the fisherman would have been overwhelming. With so many bodies around, it was hard to walk in a straight line, never mind while knitting at the same time.

"You alright?" asked Kitty.

"Aye, I am."

"Good," said Kitty. "You're about to have the best three months of your life."

THE GRIT

Chapter 40

September, 1913

The Grit was the place to be, and 1913 was the year to be there.

"What's The Grit?" asked Jimmy, as Graham led his crew away from the harbour.

"It's where we'll be living for the next while," said Graham.

"Paradise," said Callum, and the crew laughed.

They walked some more before Graham turned to Jimmy and, spreading his arms wide, announced, "The Grit."

In front of them stood a grand church. "Christchurch, the fishermen's church," said Graham.

Despite the cold, a group of children were gathered in the church square. Huddled together on their haunches, some played marbles, while others were whipping round a skipping rope, jumping at the speed of lightning.

"That'll keep them warm," said Jimmy.

"Reckon they'd let us join in?" asked Callum, running towards the children. He jumped into the middle of the rope. It caught around his ankles, pulling children down with him as he tumbled to the floor.

"Away with you," called Graham. "The rest of us are freezing to death here."

"Just having a little fun, skipper," said Callum as he rubbed a grazed elbow.

Beyond the church lay rows and rows of terraces, cut with steep staircases, that Jimmy was told were the Scores. A pub graced every street.

"More pubs per head than anywhere in the world," said Callum.

This place would be heaven for Alex, thought Jimmy.

The Grit was a town within a town. Jimmy had seen nothing of Lowestoft, but wondered why anyone would venture beyond the cliff when everything you could need was here. A mile long and half a mile wide, The Grit had shops of every kind; butchers, chemists, sweet shops, bakers, toy shops. There were laundries, factories, net stores, fish-houses and pickling yards.

Girls in oilskin aprons wandered around knitting as they walked. Grubby children tore in and out of unlocked front doors. Women were out in their yards hanging washing on lines, and men were heading to the pubs.

"We're up here," said Graham, leading his crew along the dubiously named Anguish Street. Jimmy hoped the name wasn't an omen. Before they reached it, the door was flung open and a ruddy middle-aged woman rushed out to embrace Graham.

"Good to see you, Josie," he said, kissing the woman's cheek.

"Likewise, looks like you've got a young'un with you this year," she said.

"Aye, this is Jimmy."

"Welcome to my humble abode," she laughed, shaking Jimmy's hand. "Now, let me look at the rest of you. Callum, I think you've grown even taller, and Martin's cheery as ever I see." She greeted the rest of the crew, even Martin, with warmth and humour. "Settle yourselves in and I'll bring you up a cuppa shortly."

"Come on, lads, let's do as we're told," said Graham, winking at Josie. The cottage was tiny, a two up, two down, with a staircase in the middle.

"Privy's out in the yard," said Graham as he took the stairs two at a time.

Their room was bare other than a small chest of drawers and a pile of blankets in one corner.

"There are your beds," said Graham, picking up a blanket and laying it out by the window. "Not exactly luxury, but the herring will have us away on the chase most of the time."

Josie appeared with a tray of steaming mugs. "How do you like The Beach?" she asked Jimmy.

"Oh, I've only seen it from the water."

Josie looked confused, and Graham jumped in to explain. "This is The Beach, Jimmy, or The Beach Village, or The Grit. They're all the same thing."

"Oh, I see. I'm used to a place with more than one name."

"Where you from, lad?" asked Josie.

"Holy Island, but its old name is Lindisfarne, and some people still call it that."

"An island, hey, bet that's a nice place to live. Do they have pubs, though?"

"Aye," laughed Jimmy. "Plenty of pubs."

"Good," said Josie, setting down the tray in the middle of the room. "You out on the boat tomorrow?"

"Aye," said Graham. "I'd like to be out tonight, but thought the lads deserved an evening off."

"Ah, you're a kind skipper, Graham. I hope these lads appreciate you. There's talk around the village this will be a bumper year. Enjoy your night off, lads, cause it might be the last you get in a while."

The men thanked their host and sipped the hot tea.

"You hear that, lads? A bumper year, let's hope the silver darlings are ready for us." Graham clinked his mug against the others.

"I reckon it's time for something stronger," said Callum.

"Alright, lads, but not too much. I want you at your best when we head out tomorrow."

"Aye, skipper," they all agreed.

Despite the number of men at sea, the Rising Sun had a quiet busyness to it. Old boys sat playing dominoes, men propped up the bar, and only two tables were free.

"I'll get these. What are ye having?" The crew gave Jimmy their orders, and he headed to the bar.

"Not sin you in here before, you after the herrin'?" asked the publican.

"Aye, arrived today."

"Crabbin', Mike," said the man, holding out a hand.

"Jimmy."

"Looks like it'll be a good season. Plenty of crans comin' into the harbour already."

"That's grand," said Jimmy. Back at the table, he passed on the news to his crew.

"Like Josie said."

"Aye, do ye think they're right?" asked Jimmy

"I do," said Graham. "These are true fishing folk. They know the signs. If they say there are plenty of silver darlings, there are plenty of silver darlings."

"I'll drink to that," said Samuel.

Three pints in, Callum turned to Martin. "You going to play us a tune, lad?"

Martin scowled.

"Oh, come on, lad. Don't hide your light under a bushel." The men laughed.

"Can ye play?" asked Jimmy.

"Aye, but I try not to," said Martin.

"There'll be a pint waiting if you do," coaxed Graham. This did the trick, and Martin slunk across the room to the piano.

"When did he learn to play?"

"His mam sent him for lessons. Wanted him to be a cut above the other lads. Explains the enormous chip on his shoulder," said Graham. Everyone laughed.

"Every pub here has a piano," said Callum. "Saved from a wreck years back. Martin hates it, can't escape the damn things he says."

The piano struck up, drowning out their laughter. Jimmy looked on, amazed. His dour crewmate sat by the piano, eyes closed, face animated.

"For someone who hates playing, he sure seems to enjoy himself."

"Aye," said Graham. "He loves it really."

With a pianist in their midst, the crew were a hit with the locals and it was a merry evening. They would look back on the night fondly, for the locals' predictions were right. They would barely see The Grit over the next few weeks, for the silver darlings had arrived. Sea and silvery scales would fill every waking hour.

Chapter 41

October, 1913

The twelfth of October 1913 was a day Jimmy would never forget. On the evening of the eleventh, they set off from the harbour along with hundreds of other boats. Frustration creased Graham's face as they trailed behind the new steam drifters, but there was a good wind and they were not far behind. Like many vessels, their destination was Smith's Knoll, around thirty miles out. As they approached, they saw a mass of gulls circling, and in the fading light, the water below turned silvery green.

"Looks like a good night," said Graham.

They shot over two miles of nets and settled down for scran and sleep. Boats were bobbing on the water as far as the eye could see, the red-brown sails acting as flags to show they were all after herring.

"I hope there's enough to go round," complained Martin.

"Well, there's enough for the gulls, so I'd say there's a good chance there's enough for us," said Graham.

Graham was right. Far from too little, the nets were full to bursting.

"Hurry, lads, we have to beat the steamers. I need you to work harder than you've done in your life," said Graham.

They hauled and hauled, muscles straining, sweat pouring until herring spilled from the hold and across the deck.

"Any more fish and the boat will sink. Throw the rest back, lads," said Graham.

They didn't like to see money slipping down beneath the waves, but speed was of the essence. If they didn't leave soon, the other boats would be in first and the price would drop. They hoisted the sails and headed for land. Some steam drifters were ahead of them, but they had worked hard and were in the middle of the pack.

"Next year I'm saving myself the worry and getting a boat with steam," said Graham as Ness Point came into view.

By the time they arrived, the harbour was already a hive of activity. Quarter crans covered the ground with more swung onto the quayside every minute. Merchants and salesmen eyed the catches, checking for quality and price. With such a large catch, the unloading was a long job. It was several hours before the fish were aboard the cart and headed for the yards.

"I'll meet you at the Rising Sun," said Graham, heading off to the fish market.

*

The crew were through their second pint by the time Graham joined them. He walked into the middle of the room and shouted, "ten million fish! Ten million fish they reckon was brought in today."

Cheers erupted through the room.

"Get a good price, skipper?" asked Samuel.

"Not bad. A good thing we weren't the last in though, for the price had dropped right down by the time I left."

"To the *Star Gazer*," said Callum, clinking glasses with his crewmates.

"I'll get a round in," said Graham. He appeared back with a tray of whiskies. "To Lowestoft," he said, and glasses clinked once more.

*

Dearest Clara,

I've been checking at the Post Office when I can, but still no news from you or the island. I can't pretend I'm not disappointed. Then again, perhaps you've been busy, or found yourself a new fellow?

Well, I'll share my news. We reached Lowestoft some weeks back, and it's quite the place I can tell you. I reckon ye could fit twenty of Holy Island in the town. I'm living on The Grit, a village beneath the cliff where the main town sits. It's hard to tell where The Grit ends and the fishing begins, for it stretches right to the water and everyone here is in with the fishing. There's a place called the Denes where the beatsters work on the nets, but nets are everywhere, strung up on every pole and hook that's spare.

The Gritsters seem to welcome us fishing folk from the north and though they have little in the way of coins, they're a colourful bunch, full of warmth and mirth. Many a local man has married a Scots lass, and the Gritsters are a peculiar mix of north and south. They're a tough breed, that's for sure. Never have I met such hardworking folk.

We've had our work cut out since we arrived. The silver darlings must have a fondness for the place, for the sea all around turns silver by night, and you've never seen so many crans of herring come onto shore by morning. There's talk ten million herring were landed in just one day. How they counted them I can't say, but I've seen with my own eyes the mountains of fish and can well believe it true. We've barely set foot on land, and when we do, it's to sleep and nothing more.

There was one night when we went to see a show at the Palladium. That was quite something. And there's always time for a pint in the Rising Sun, but mostly it's just sleeping. Where Callum gets his rest from I can't say, for while we are dozing he's often out chasing the herring lasses. The chase of the herring is enough for me!

Graham is talking of getting himself a steam drifter next season. I wouldn't mind being on the crew when he does, for they fly through the water faster than the darlings themselves.

You might grow tired of all this talk of fish, so that's all for now. If you have time to respond, it would be welcome. I miss you Clara and would love to hear how Marnie and the bairns are doing. All for now, Jimmy.

Chapter 42

November, 1913

Jimmy refused the coaxing of his crewmates to go to the dance. It had been a long week and he could barely lift his arms, never mind hold a lassie. He would put up with the lads' ribbing for the chance of a few hours by himself.

"Think of the lasses that will be there, Jim," said Callum. "Tonight might be the night you meet the girls of your dreams."

"Go on with ye, keep talking to me and ye'll miss yer chance with the herring girls."

Callum looked alarmed and headed for the door. "Alright, just don't blame me if you end up a lonely old man with just a book for company."

Graham shooed the men from the room. Once in a comfortable position, Jimmy pulled a copy of *Middlemarch* from his bag. He had read every book he owned several times and wished he had brought more with him. He could recite the poems of Robert Burns by heart and longed for new reading material. But Callum's jibes had left him unsettled. That there would ever be anyone but Clara had never crossed his mind. But she had refused him.

Frustrated and growing weary of the book, he packed it away and crossed the room. At the mirror, he checked his appearance and tried to smooth down wayward curls. If he ran fast enough, he could catch the lads. Sure enough, they were in striking distance, and as he reached them, panting, they turned in surprise.

"Look who's here," cried Callum. "Couldn't resist the lassies, huh?"

"Hmm. Actually, the prospect of reading *Middlemarch* for a fifth time was worse than an evening with ye."

"Well, I have no clue what you're going on about, but I'm pleased you're here," said Callum, slinging an arm across Jimmy's shoulder.

Rather than go straight to the dance, they called in a pub filled with fishing crews. Several groups must have been there a while, for the noise inside was deafening and men swayed unsteadily, covering the floor with splashes of amber liquid. With all seats taken, Jimmy and the crew huddled in the centre of the room.

He regretted his decision to come, for the inebriated men reminded him of Alex and were all too familiar. A bear of a man stumbled back from the bar, knocking into their group and sending beer raining through the air.

"Watch it," snarled Martin.

"What did you say?" said the man-bear, spinning round to face them.

"I said, watch it."

Graham laid a steadying hand on Martin's arm. With a vile gurgling sound, the man sucked phlegm up from the depths of his lungs. He paused a moment before depositing it on Martin's boot. Nervous laughter rippled through the room, and the man turned back to his pint. Martin lurched forward, but Callum held him back.

"It's not worth the trouble, Martin. Leave it."

All the crew felt uneasy, but Martin seemed ready to comply and stood scowling as Callum tried to keep the conversation going. Then, without warning, Martin turned and tapped the man-bear on the shoulder. As they faced each other, Martin flung his head back, whipping it forward with an almighty crack. He caught the man on the nose. Blood poured from it, and as it soaked his shirt, a murderous look entered his eyes. Within seconds, a full-blown fight had broken out, fists flying indiscriminately. They knocked over tables and glasses splintered, the frantic landlady screaming at the men to get out.

Jimmy found himself dragged across the room by Callum's forceful grip. They emerged onto the street, followed by a glass that missed their heads by an inch. Both had escaped unharmed and moved to the safety of a shop doorway to wait.

"Should we go back in and help?" asked Jimmy.

"No, best wait it out here. They'll be alright, should be out soon."

"*Middlemarch* seems suddenly appealing," said Jimmy. Callum laughed, unfazed by the situation.

The doors of the bar opened and Martin emerged, held up by Graham and Samuel on either side. He pushed them away, but when they let go, his legs buckled and he fell to the floor.

"There won't be any dancing for this one tonight," said Graham, and Martin scowled. "I'm taking him home."

"Want us to come?" asked Callum.

"No, we'll be right. I don't want you to miss out on seeing your admirers."

"Ta, skipper."

Callum helped Jimmy to his feet, and the crew made their way to the hall. Jimmy wasn't sure he had ever seen so many people in one place. The hall was a mass of bodies, some gyrating to the music, others talking in groups, couples finding a moment of passion in not so quiet corners.

"Drink?" shouted Callum above the din. Jimmy nodded. The rest of the crew dispersed among the crowd, but Jimmy stood still, waiting for Callum to return. Uncomfortable among so many strangers, he wished he had persevered with his book. Callum didn't return, and Jimmy looked for him at the bar. It was lucky Callum was tall, or Jimmy would never have noticed him among the group of women.

"Excuse me," he said, but no one let him through. "Excuse me!"

Callum was regaling the enthralled women with a tale of the sea. A young girl pressed herself close to the giant Scot. Jimmy stood on tiptoes and reached above the women's heads, tapping Callum on the shoulder.

"Ah, Jimmy, sorry, I got distracted. Here's your drink."

"Thanks," said Jimmy, pushing through the throng.

"Girls, meet my friend Jimmy. He's been lonely since we arrived."

Jimmy met Callum's wink with a scowl. Callum grinned and slipped his arm round a girl's waist. She giggled and perched herself on his lap. Jimmy shuffled as hungry eyes looked him up and down.

"I'd love to have his hair," remarked a thin girl, who couldn't be much older than sixteen.

"I'd love to have his eyes," said another.

"I'd love to have him!" shouted a plump middle-aged woman, and laughter erupted. Someone's fingers pinched his bottom hard, and Jimmy jumped, turning puce and looking round for the culprit. This prompted more laughter, and once again he wished he had stayed at home.

On balance, Jimmy was the more attractive of the two, but his awkwardness left him overshadowed by the manly confidence oozing from Callum. He was an easy target for the girls. They loved a joke at a man's expense, and Jimmy's blushes gave them a suitable reward.

The herring girls were an altogether different breed. Independent and sure of themselves, they would take no nonsense from any man.

Here it was a woman's world. Jimmy would need to draw on his experience of eight sisters to help him better understand the fairer sex.

"Let's dance," someone called, and the gaggle of herring girls pulled Callum into the throng. Jimmy remained at the bar, grateful for a moment of solitude. He surveyed the scene before him, young men strutting about thinking they were the bee's knees, when anyone with half a brain could see it was the lasses in control.

His eyes scanned the room, settling on two girls deep in conversation. One had her back turned, but there was a familiarity to her movements. Jimmy's glass slipped from his hand and shattered on the floor. *Clara*.

*

Fragments of glass scattered in all directions, but no one noticed above the hum of music and voices. Jimmy couldn't catch his breath. His heart pounded in his ears and he steadied his weak body against the bar. What was she doing here?

Before Jimmy could decide what to do, a man with a child's face approached Clara. He led her to the dance floor and Jimmy watched as she spun round in his arms. Her hair glistened under the hall lights, her face beamed. She was happy. Jimmy hated the man with his arms around Clara's narrow waist, face pressed close, whispering sweet nothings in her ear. At that moment, he hated Clara, too. Hadn't she told him she would never leave the island? Yet here she was, dancing without a care in the world. Jimmy ordered a dram of whisky and downed it in one gulp. He turned back to the dance floor, but Clara had gone.

Without saying goodbye to Callum, Jimmy slipped out of the back door. The whisky had gone to his head, and he stumbled his way round the side of the building. Rounding the corner, he saw Clara sitting on a bench. He stayed in the shadows unobserved. They were too far away for him to hear their conversation, but Clara was smiling. Jimmy felt sick. The pair stood, and he watched as they slipped away into the dark night. Sucking in deep lungfuls of sea air, Jimmy waited for his head to clear. He slunk down against the wall and tried to process what he had seen.

Clara. In Lowestoft. His Clara, only she seemed older somehow, and she wasn't his anymore. She hadn't even told him where she was. Did she care so little for him? Anger bubbled inside him, and instead of returning home, he went back inside the hall. At the bar he ordered a whisky, then another, then another. By the time Callum appeared with two girls in tow, Jimmy was swaying, slurring about some girl called Clara to whoever would listen.

"Looks like your friend has had a bit too much," laughed one of Callum's companions. Callum looked worried. He had never seen Jimmy drunk or out of control.

"You alright there?"

Jimmy slung unintelligible words at Callum and lurched towards the dance floor. Bodies parted as he lunged back and forth, girls screeching as he stepped on their toes. A woman approached and took him in a firm grip. Jimmy couldn't see her out-of-focus form, but knew she was plump and older than most in the room.

"Come on, lad, let's get some air."

The woman guided Jimmy outside towards the beach. He staggered a few steps forward, but the cold air hit him hard. He bent over, retching up mouthfuls of bile-flavoured whisky.

"Here, wash your mouth out with this."

Jimmy took a sip from her hip flask and forced the bitter liquid down his throat. He stumbled down the beach and splashed his face with freezing seawater. Feeling better, he thanked the woman for her kindness.

"Where you heading, lad?"

"The Grit."

"Me too, let's walk together."

The woman linked her arm in his and they trod across the beach, scuffing up fine sand as they went.

"Right, I'm off this way," she said, pointing towards Lighthouse Score. She held him in a tight embrace and Jimmy sank into the warmth of human contact. She moved to let go, but Jimmy clung on. The woman's manner shifted, and she began running her hands through his hair. Jimmy's own hands ran up and down her back. He felt a stirring inside him, at odds with the aging unattractiveness of the woman he held. Her breathing grew heavy as she tugged at his hair.

"You want it, do you?" she whispered, menace in her voice.

No, thought Jimmy. *I don't want it. I don't want her.* But his body disobeyed his mind, and he pressed hard against her in reply. All his anger at Clara was pouring out, sending him down a path of self-destruction from which he couldn't free himself.

She kissed him hard. Her mouth was slippery and left his face sticky. She pulled him behind the fishermen's sheds.

"You done this before?"

"No."

"I'll show you the ropes."

Jimmy wanted to stop but didn't know how. She reached down, unfastening his trousers and taking him in her hand. Skirt pulled up, she guided him to where he should be. Tears ran down his cheeks as he gave himself to her. He finished with a shudder. She straightened her skirt.

"Not bad," she said, before heading off across the beach.

Jimmy stood in a daze. He walked down to the water's edge. The cold didn't touch him as he removed his clothes, folding them in a pile on the sand. It was only when he stepped into the water that the temperature had an effect, tearing through him till it reached his bones. He sat cross-legged in the waves, enduring the pain of the water as a fitting punishment for his actions. Perhaps, he thought, he was his father's son after all.

Chapter 43

November, 1913

Callum looked across at Jimmy. Two weeks had passed since the night of the dance, and still his friend was no less tetchy or withdrawn. Any spare moment they had, Jimmy's nose was in a book, and Callum hadn't even got him across the threshold of the Rising Sun. He could count on one hand the words Jimmy had spoken since that evening.

Rumours swirled among the herring girls, but they were so out of character for his friend, Callum struggled to believe them. When asked, Jimmy would neither confirm nor deny their authenticity, so Callum gave up trying. All that could raise a smile from Jimmy were the pages of a novel. Callum left him to it.

Jimmy's demeanour hadn't gone unnoticed by his skipper, but Graham had little time to worry, for the silver darlings kept coming. Besides, Jimmy hauled as hard as ever and seemed to salve his frustrations at sea, working twice as hard as other men. Graham was satisfied that out among the crashing waves, Jimmy would work out whatever was troubling him.

*

"Where are you spending Christmas, Jim?"

Jimmy shrugged and continued to read. If his actions at the dance had taught him anything, it was to keep as much distance between him and Alex as possible. Stay too close, and his da's poison could swirl around him like the island mists, settling on his skin before making its way to his heart.

"Jimmy?"

Head in his book, Jimmy ignored his friend. Callum reached down and yanked the book from his hands.

"Whatever happened that night, whatever you did, it was down to you. Stop taking it out on the rest of us. Bloody hell, Jim, we've been tiptoeing round you for weeks. Get your head out of your own arse and stop being such a pain in ours."

The crew held their breath. Jimmy stared at Callum. Then, for the first time in weeks, he smiled. "Sorry," he said.

"Apology accepted."

"Have I really been that bad?"

"Worse. Your eyes are more doleful than the bloody herring."

Jimmy laughed, and Callum pulled him to his feet and gripped him in a bear hug. "Why don't you spend Christmas with me?" he said.

"Ye sure? What about yer mam?"

Callum laughed. "If I bring you home, Mam will think I'm on the straight and narrow at last. You're a middle-aged woman's dream, Jim."

Jimmy winced at his choice of words, and Callum wondered if the rumours were true. "So, what do you think?"

"If yer sure yer mam won't mind, then I'd love to."

*

On their last night in Lowestoft, they headed out in search of a party, even Jimmy agreeing to one final celebration. The price of the herring had dropped, but what a sight it was to see the crans mounting up on the quay.

It was hard to find space in a pub, with every crew out in force. Singing filled the air, and it wasn't long before Jimmy had a pint pressed into his hand. Despite his promise to himself that he would never be drunk again, the celebrations continued long into the night and Jimmy soon lost count of how many pints he had sunk.

The party spilled onto the High Street, groups of lads mingling with groups of lasses in the hope of one last hurrah.

"Jimmy! Jimmy, come here," Callum waved from across the street. He was standing with women Jimmy had not met before.

"Come on," said Callum, pulling him over to the group. "Meet Kitty. She's tipsy and not making much sense, but she knows someone from your island."

Jimmy turned cold, but it wasn't from the November chill.

"Kitty, this is my friend I was telling ye about, Jimmy."

A girl with wild red hair was holding out a hand, and Jimmy shook it. The girl eyed Jimmy. "I've seen you before."

"Oh?"

"Aye, back on the island. I saw you in the yard. You were Clara's fella."

All colour drained from Jimmy's face. "How is Clara?"

Kitty was shrewd enough to realise she had put her foot in it. "Oh, aye, she's grand. Won't stop talking about the island, though." She looked nervous.

"Is she going back soon?"

"Um, no." Now Kitty looked very uncomfortable, but Jimmy probed further.

"She told me she'd never leave. Why's she not going back? Has she met a fellow?"

Like a caged animal, Kitty looked for an escape, but finding none, she faced his question head on. “Aye.”

Jimmy turned on his heel and strode down the street. He heard both Callum and Kitty calling after him, but didn’t turn back. A safe distance away, a wave of nausea rushed through him, and he darted down an alley to vomit behind a pile of boxes. He emerged, wiping his mouth to raucous laughter and jibes from a passing group of fishermen.

The streets were heaving and finding his way through with a mind addled by drink proved tricky. A large group of men were walking towards him, and Jimmy stepped into the road to avoid them. The whinnying of a horse pierced the air and Jimmy turned to see a barrel-laden cart hurtling towards him. The last thing he remembered was a disgusting cracking sound. Then the world went black.

Chapter 44

December, 1913

A bright light pierced his eyes as Jimmy peeled his lids apart. His room was noisy, but not with the gruff Scots voices he was used to. He could hear squeaking wheels in need of oiling, and a jangling of metal and glass. Footsteps clacked against a smooth floor, and voices mingled together in a hum of East Anglian drawl.

He tried to sit up and get his bearings, but pain ripped through his limbs and he laid his pounding head back down. His lips were dry with a terrible thirst. He reached for the chipped cup he kept beside his bed, but his fingers clutched at thin air.

"Graham," he said, but only a croak came out. He tried again, "Graham?" This time, a whisper escaped his lips.

He felt a small hand gripping his, then an urgent call. "Nurse! Nurse!"

Jimmy smiled, certain the voice was Marnie's. He closed his eyes to slip back into his dream. The next time he woke, it was dark other than a small light in the corner of his eye. Again he tried to sit, again he slumped back down. Panic rose in him. Something heavy was pressing on his stomach and he reached to push it away. The object lifted with a sudden movement that startled him.

As his eyes adjusted to the gloom, he saw a figure leaning in towards him. His breath was fast and his heart raced. A whimpering came from his mouth, that he seemed unable to stop. As a light dazzled him, the monster at his bedside became an angel, bright blonde curls glowing in the lamplight. Jimmy rubbed his eyes and stared hard at the angel above him.

"Jimmy?" said the angel.

"Marnie?"

"Aye," said Marnie, and squeezed his hand.

"Am I dreaming? Am I dead?"

"No, my love, you're not dreamin'. Nor dead." She ran her hand across his forehead, marred by congealed blood around a still weeping wound. Her hand ran up to his curls and swept over a stubbly patch of skin held together by tiny stitches.

"Where am I?"

"You had an accident. You're in the hospital. It's late now. Try to sleep and we can talk in the morning."

Questions rushed through Jimmy's mind, but the effort of thinking tired him more. However hard he fought, sleep proved a potent adversary, overwhelming him.

*

A fresh breeze scuffed Jimmy's closed eyes, causing them to flicker towards the morning light. He remembered dreaming of an angel. Disorientated, he lifted his head a few inches. In a chair beside him lay his sister, curled in a ball, golden hair spilling across her face in a messy halo.

Eight neat beds lay side by side, some empty, some with curtains drawn. An austere nurse emerged from behind a curtain, surprised to find Jimmy's wary eyes upon her.

"You're awake, I see. About time." She glared at Jimmy as if she had caught him sleeping on a job. "Get some more rest," she contradicted. "I'll be back on my rounds shortly."

The voice of the nurse intruded on Marnie's sleep and she stirred, uncurling herself from her cat-like pose and brushing curls from her eyes.

"Mornin', sleeping head," she said.

"Where am I?"

"In hospital, don't you remember? I told you last night."

"No, I mean, where am I? What place is this?"

Marnie looked confused. "You're in a hospital, in Lowestoft. You had an accident, Jimmy, and they brought you here."

"But... but... why are you here? How did ye get here so quick?"

Marnie threw back her head and let out a hearty laugh. "How long do you think you've been here, Jimmy?" she asked, laughter dancing in her eyes.

"Since last night," he said, irked that she found his predicament amusing.

Marnie moved over to the bed and sat beside Jimmy. "Jim, you've been here two weeks," she said, the laughter disappearing as quickly as it had come. "We thought you may never wake."

She reached across and clasped his hand in her own. Jimmy lay staring at the peeling paint of the ceiling, confusion addling his mind. He tried to lift his head again to look at his sister, but the effort was too great.

"I don't know why I'm here," he whispered.

As Marnie explained about the accident with the horse and cart, fragments of memory flickered across Jimmy's mind.

Fear and confusion crossed his face. "Where's the crew? I'm supposed to be with Callum for Christmas."

Marnie squeezed his hand. "The crew waited long enough for me to arrive, then they had to go back up north. Callum wanted to stay longer but couldn't risk delaying their voyage. They were here with you day and night, Jimmy. It was them that told the hospital where you came from. They sent word to the island, and I caught the first train I could."

Jimmy turned his head away so that Marnie couldn't see the tears in his eyes.

"When you're well enough, I'll take you home and care for you till you're back on your feet."

Jimmy felt the whitewashed walls of the hospital room closing in on him, breath being sucked from his lungs. Would his escape amount to only eight short months? Not even a year? Oh, how Alex would enjoy the sight of his crippled son returning with his tail between his legs. His hands balled into fists, and he kept his head turned from Marnie.

"What's wrong with me?" he asked through clenched teeth.

"Jimmy, you've broken near enough every bone in your body. The doctor says most are healing nicely, but your left leg isn't looking too great just now. At any rate, it will be months before you're fully back on your feet, so to speak."

"I need to sleep," he said with a coldness he regretted, for none of this was Marnie's fault.

Hatred boiled in his veins, not for Marnie, but himself. He had escaped the island to get away from his da, but by drinking himself stupid, hadn't he behaved just like him? Again. Maybe distance was no rescue from destiny.

Chapter 45

December, 1913

In the week since he woke, Jimmy had barely uttered a word, even to the sister he adored. He could cope with the physical pain of his broken body, but his heart was heavy and there seemed no way out.

From beyond his window, he saw a small wedding party making their way down the street. They were too far off for him to see well, but the bride reminded him of Clara. He remembered Kitty's words and hated himself for the fool he had been. He had sacrificed his love for freedom, and now he had lost both.

The nurses gave him short shrift, considering his glum attitude at odds with everything they knew men to be. Marnie's frequent visits just tied his noose tighter, and he met her kindness with a sullen demeanour.

Only an elderly, plump nurse named Marjory lifted him from his desperation. She threw open the curtains, letting the view and light flood in, propped winter greenery in a vase beside his bed, and offered home-made cakes that even in his self-pity he was polite enough to accept.

One morning after completing her rounds, she approached his bedside, a thick brown paper package in her hands. Jimmy kept his eyes lowered, but she continued to stand, holding out the package in front of her.

"Well? Aren't you going to ask what I have here?"

"No, Marjory, I'm not."

Marjory humphed and sat her plump backside down on the bed. She undid the string that held the paper tight.

"Hmm, what do we have here?" she teased, unfolding the brown paper.

Jimmy looked away, but curiosity got the better of him as he heard the familiar *thwap* of pages being thumbed. His movement was returning, and he propped himself up against his pillows.

"Oh, so you are interested, are you?" asked Marjory, holding the paper package behind her back.

"Come on, Marjory, ye've got me sitting up. What more do ye want?"

Marjory handed him the package, and Jimmy began pulling out book after book after book.

"Where did ye get these?"

"Your friends left them for you."

"What friends?"

"The friends that stunk of fish. George, I think they called the ringleader."

"Graham."

Jimmy stroked each cover and flicked through the books. He lifted his head. "When did they leave them?"

"A couple of days after you arrived, said they had to go and you might need some company." Marjory smiled, "Matron said you weren't to have them yet, thought they'd tire you out, but I reckon they're just what the doctor ordered." She winked at Jimmy and moved off to attend to her duties.

*

Jimmy was lying on his side when Marnie walked in. Tiptoeing to his bed, she realised he wasn't asleep but reading. She coughed to make him aware of her presence, but he didn't look up. She coughed again, and this time he looked at her, surprised.

"Sorry, Marnie, I was miles away."

Her heart filled as he smiled at her for the first time in a week. "What you reading?" Jimmy held up his book. "What is it?"

He looked at her. "Marnie, can ye read yet?"

Marnie flushed. "We didn't all get the chance of school," she said, plonking herself down in a chair.

"Would ye like me to teach ye?"

Her face lit up, eyes full of hope. "Would you?"

"There's not much else for me to do in here, is there?" he smiled. "Next time ye come, bring paper and a pencil."

Jimmy shifted himself so he was sitting. Moving was still painful. He had broken his right arm, and doing everything with the left was troublesome, but he was learning to cope. He stung with humiliation every time the nurses came to help with toileting and was determined to be back on his feet as soon as possible.

"Marnie, I'm sorry for how I've been, it's just the thought of going back to the island...."

"I know," she said. "But you're here for a while yet, so we can cross that bridge when we come to it."

"Marnie? Where are ye staying?" he asked, ashamed that he had not asked before.

"In one of the boarding houses. They were grateful for the business with all the herring lassies away for Christmas."

"Do ye need money?"

Marnie shuffled in her seat. "No," she said, her face pink.

"Where'd ye get the money for the room, Marnie?"

The pause that followed caused Jimmy to consider a raft of horrendous ways she might come by the money, and he looked at her, willing her to put his mind at rest.

"Bill," she said.

"What about Bill?"

"Bill gave me the money."

Marnie explained Bill's grief at sending Clara away, how he had descended into self-loathing that only eased with the birth of his son Benjamin. "Benjamin's a darling bairn," she added, smiling.

"He sent Clara away?"

"Aye, I dinna think he was right in the head after Anna's passing. He rushed to marry Rachel, as you know. In his own way, he was trying to do the best for all of them. He regretted it as soon as she left. Things are calmer there since Benjamin came along. It's not a conventional marriage and I can't see them having more bairns, but they rub along together fine."

Jimmy's mind raced with questions he needed answers to but knew where he must start.

"What happened to Clara? How did she end up here?"

Marnie noticed the longing in Jimmy's eyes, and sadness crossed her beautiful face. "I don't know, Jimmy. Bill sent her to her grandparents in North Shields. They sent word that she had left, but no one knew where she went. Hang on, did you say she's here? In Lowestoft?"

"Aye," said Jimmy, and lay back on the bed. Why had she not written to him? Couldn't she trust him with her plans? How could she be happy, away from her beloved island?

He would have to wait for more answers, for at that moment the nurses wheeled an elderly gentleman into the ward and began transferring him to the bed beside Jimmy's. The man was grey and Marnie took this as her cue to leave.

"I'll come back tomorrow. We can talk more then," she said, leaning down to kiss his head.

"Aye." As she walked away, he added, "Don't forget the paper and pencil."

Marnie nodded and waved.

Jimmy turned back to his book but found it didn't grip him as it had before. His mind was full of worry for Clara. If only he had waited longer, they could have left together. He could have protected her. If only he had spoken to her at the dance. "Damn it," he said to himself.

The grey man beside him groaned. Jimmy looked across. He had a neat moustache, cropped grey hair and his hands were clean and smooth, not the hands of a man that worked the boats. Beneath the grey tinge, his skin was pale and not the burnt brown of most of the town. Jimmy sighed, turned away and tried to lose himself once more in his book.

Chapter 46

December, 1913

Over the next week Marnie visited Jimmy daily, bringing a note-book with her and sitting on the edge of the hospital bed as Jimmy taught her the alphabet. She was a quick learner and within a few days they had moved on to simple words.

"I can see ye've been practising," he said, impressed.

Marnie brushed off the praise with, "Aye well, I've not much else to do," but still she flushed with pride.

They sat and talked some more, Marnie painting a picture of life with Bill and Rachel, the light that baby Benjamin had brought into the home.

"He's not the Bill you knew, but his old self is returning. His eyes are still sad, mind, and he rushes to the window each time he hears horses' hooves, hopeful that Clara has returned."

"Can they manage without ye there to help?"

"Oh, aye. I always considered Rachel a bit of a mouse, but she's fair bonny as a mam. Now Bill is more himself, she acts more comfortable and they've grown fond of one another. It's no great love story, but she pours all her love into little Ben and he shares it round to the rest of us."

"How's Mam and Da?"

"Same," said Marnie, not meeting Jimmy's eye and twisting her hands together. "Sally and Robert are becoming more like them each day."

Jimmy stared out of the window. Not enough had changed for him to return.

*

Jimmy stole a glance across at his neighbour. The old man seemed to be improving. His colour was returning, and he had extended periods where he was awake. Jimmy tried to catch his eye, but the man stared at the ceiling. He had no visitors, and Jimmy felt lucky to have Marnie with him. There were moments when he couldn't believe she was there. He'd always planned to send for her, but not like this.

Visiting hours ended, and they packed up the notebook for the day. Jimmy glanced across and saw the old man staring.

"Hello," Jimmy said, but the man turned his head and resumed studying the ceiling.

Marnie gave Jimmy a smirk and said goodbye. Jimmy picked up another book.

"What's that you're reading, boy?" said a husky voice. Jimmy snapped his head round. The old man stared at the ceiling, but Jimmy was sure the words had come from him.

"Pardon?"

"Are you deaf, boy? I asked what you are reading."

"Sorry, sir. It is a copy of *Great Expectations* written by Charles Dickens."

"I know who wrote it, boy," said the man. "What is your opinion of Magwitch?"

Startled, Jimmy hesitated, then grew in confidence, relishing the chance to discuss Dickens with a fellow enthusiast. They only stopped talking when a stern nurse hushed them. She left the room, and the old man turned back to Jimmy. The literary discussion had enlivened him. His cheeks had grown pink.

"Raymond Edwards. Pleased to meet you." Unable to reach far enough for a handshake, Raymond raised a hand in a salute. Jimmy introduced himself and returned the gesture.

"What is your profession, boy?"

"I'm a fisherman, sir."

"Huh! Is that so? Then tell me, where did a fisherman learn to read and converse like that?"

"I had an excellent teacher," smiled Jimmy, thinking of Mrs McKinnon and wondering if she was still at the island school.

Another silence followed before Jimmy summoned the courage to find the answer to a question that had been teasing him. "I hope ye don't mind me asking, sir, but what is yer profession?"

The old man's chest puffed out a little, and he answered with pride. "I'm a headmaster. I have given thirty-five years' service to my profession and I don't intend to stop now, even if my old ticker has other ideas. Do you enjoy fishing?"

Jimmy laughed. "Aye, I do, which is just as well as where I come from, there's not much choice about it."

"And do you intend to fish all your life?"

Jimmy lay mulling over Raymond's question. He wasn't sure his broken body would ever mend, never mind getting him back on the water.

"Hmm?" demanded the man, unimpressed that Jimmy had ignored him.

"Sorry, sir. I suppose the answer to yer question is that I don't know. I'd assumed there was little choice in the matter, but it seems fate has intervened. The doc tells me my leg may never heal, and I'm not much use to any crew without two working legs."

The old man gave a small 'humph' and resumed his inspection of the ceiling.

Sensing the conversation was over, Jimmy lay back and retreated into his thoughts. What would he do? Even if his leg healed, it would not be in time for the next season. His arm was healing well and his chest no longer felt crushed each time he breathed. The bruises on his face were barely visible other than a faint yellow tinge, yet his leg proved stubborn to mend. The nurses gave him crutches and he could shuffle along a few paces, using his good leg to bear his weight, dragging his other behind. It was a long way from working, though.

He thought of his time with Graham and the lads and his dreams of joining them on a brand new steam drifter. They had become a surrogate family, and he would miss them. If Marnie took him back to the island, he would be beholden to others for his survival. The harsh working life of the north was no place for a cripple.

That night, Jimmy dreamed of the island. He was running along the north shore, racing Clara through the shallow waters that licked the sand below. He was strong and fast, sprinting ahead of her, turning breathless and kicking jewels of salt water up in the air as she tried to catch him. As she reached him, he spread his arms, and she tumbled into them, clasping onto him to catch her breath. He lifted her high and spun her round and round, the toes of her boots catching the water, sending a rainbow of spray towards the sky.

When he woke he was still laughing, and the pain in his leg made him wonder if he had run across the firm sand rather than just dreamed it. Marnie walked into the ward and saw Jimmy smiling.

"What's tickled your fancy this morning, then?" she asked.

"I dreamed I had two working legs," he said.

She seemed both satisfied and saddened by his answer. Setting down her cloth bag, she looked at him.

"Jimmy, I don't want you worrying. I'll take good care of you once you're back home."

Jimmy looked down and studied his hands. "The problem is, Marnie, the island isn't my home."

Marnie sat on the bed and sighed. "I know, but I canna think what else we can do."

He took her hands in his and reassured her he would be fine whatever happened and that she mustn't worry. He reached over to her bag and pulled out the notebook in a successful attempt at changing the conversation.

After Marnie had left, Raymond eased himself out of bed and shuffled over to Jimmy, a piece of paper in his hand. He motioned to the chair beside Jimmy's bed. "May I?" Jimmy nodded and Raymond sat down.

"I know you can read, my boy, but can you also write?"

Jimmy laughed. "I can, sir."

"Good, then I wonder if you can help me? I need to write to my sister, but my hands are shaky these days. Would you mind?"

"Not at all." Jimmy took the pen and paper from Raymond and leant them against a book. "Fire away."

Raymond dictated a letter that was so dull Jimmy thought Raymond must hate his poor sister. On finishing, Jimmy handed back the paper and Raymond signed it with a flourish.

"That all right?"

"Yes," said Raymond, looking up. "Very good. Thank you, Jimmy," and with that, he stood up and shuffled his way back to bed.

Two days later, when Jimmy woke, Raymond's cubicle had its curtains drawn. Jimmy worried the old man's heart had given up the ghost. It was with surprise and relief that Jimmy saw the curtain open and Raymond step out dressed in a fine suit.

Jimmy whistled. "Very smart!"

Raymond walked the few paces to Jimmy's bed and sat down beside it.

"I am being allowed home today," he said with a smile. Jimmy smiled back but felt a stab of sadness that he was losing his companion. There was no word yet when he would be ready to leave.

"Jimmy, I have a proposition for you," said Raymond. "First, I must admit that I have lied. I don't have a sister. I have a brother, Alfred."

"Oh?"

"The letter was a test."

"A test?"

"Yes, it was back-handed of me, I know, but I needed to check your writing to be sure."

The conversation was becoming stranger and stranger.

"Sure of what?"

"Your ability. I've been watching you, Jimmy, teaching your young lady to write..."

"My sister," Jimmy interrupted, but Raymond waved his hand to show the woman's identity was of no consequence.

"I've been watching you teach your young... your sister to read and write. I know you have excellent taste in reading matter and can discuss a text as well as any university graduate. I had to check if you could write. Now I know you can."

"Thank you, sir, but why do ye need to know those things?"

"Because I want you to teach," Raymond said, as if it were the most obvious thing in the world. This revelation stunned Jimmy into silence.

"Ta, sir, that's very kind of ye to say, but I don't have the means to attend a training college. Besides, I'm not sure they would even let me in given my dodgy leg."

Raymond laughed. It was a strange sound, high pitched, like a young girl's giggle.

"It's your mind we need, boy. You could have one eye and three arms for all I care and I'm not talking about going to some fancy college. I'm talking about coming to work for me."

Jimmy's mouth fell open. "Is that allowed? I mean, can anyone become a teacher, just like that?"

"Of course not," said Raymond. He stroked his moustache. "I will have to present your case to the board, and I will offer to tutor you. You would not be on a full salary until you complete your training. It is an unconventional route, yes, but not unheard of."

"I don't know what to say," said Jimmy.

"You must mull over my suggestion. How about I come and visit you next week and we can talk it over some more? I could provide you with room and board in my school accommodation. Think it over, boy." Jimmy nodded and Raymond stood up. "One thing, Jimmy, you will need to work on that accent of yours. We teach my pupils in the King's English." He said the last words with a flourish to emphasise his point, shook Jimmy's hand and left.

When Marnie came to visit, she found Jimmy staring out of the window, face frozen by some hidden emotion. "What's the matter, Jimmy?"

Jimmy turned, and it shocked her to see tears rolling down his cheeks, spilling into his smiling mouth.

"Marnie," he said, eyes shining. "How would ye like to stay in Lowestoft?"

Chapter 47

December, 1913

Raymond was true to his word. A week later he appeared on the ward, waving across at Jimmy. His usual shuffle had quickened, and he looked jolly as he crossed the room to Jimmy's bedside. As soon as he sat down, he opened his mouth to speak, then paused.

"How are you? I apologise, I was going to launch right in there but realised I haven't asked for your verdict on my proposition."

Jimmy smiled. "Sir, if you are prepared to train up a crippled island boy like me, then I would be quite the fool to refuse."

Raymond smiled, and it surprised Jimmy to notice a line of strong white teeth.

"Good, good. I can see you have already been working on that dreadful accent of yours."

"I have been listening to the doc when he comes on his rounds. Unfortunately, my King's English is mostly medical terms, but at least it's a start."

Raymond giggled. "I am pleased you said yes, Jimmy, for I spoke to the board and the local authority and both will accept you into the school under my tutelage."

"Thank you, sir." Jimmy paused. "Sir... I dinna, I mean, I do not wish to push me, my, luck, but is there any chance my sister could stay with me, for a while at least? The doc says it won't be long till I'm out of here, but I'm going to need a bit of help till I'm back on my feet... or foot, as it may well be."

"Humph," Raymond said, pulling at the ends of his moustache. "The problem is, I only have one room, and I wouldn't expect the two of you to share."

Jimmy let out a loud guffaw that startled Raymond. "Sir, we grew up sharing one room between the twelve of us. I think we can manage."

"Oh, I see. Well, in that case, it won't be a problem. Would your sister help with the household chores? My regular lady June is getting rather elderly. I'm sure she would be glad of the help."

Marnie arrived, and Jimmy beckoned her over. "Let's ask her," said Jimmy.

It was an unlikely trio that sat in Jimmy's hospital bay discussing the future. Marnie was delighted with the arrangement. She had kept details scant when talking to Jimmy of the island. The situation between Bill and Rachel was improving, but Alex was growing worse by the day. With Robert taking up the drink too, she had wondered how Jimmy would survive their cottage, unable to defend himself against the aggression that swirled through the home.

"Sir, I would be most grateful to stay in Lowestoft and help both you and Jimmy."

"That is good to hear, young lady, but you won't be staying in Lowestoft. The school is in Somerleyton. Don't fret, it is only a few miles away, and I am sure you will like it."

They sat talking until Matron came to inform them visiting hours were over.

"It is only two days until Christmas," said Marnie as they stood to leave.

"That means it's six weeks that I've been in this bed," groaned Jimmy.

Marnie and Raymond agreed to visit Jimmy on Christmas morning, and it was a merry party that dispersed that evening.

On Christmas morning, the little group reassembled by Jimmy's bedside. Marjory had provided Jimmy with some paper for wrapping, and he presented both Marnie and Raymond with a book each from his collection. They handed their gifts to him. After opening two more books, Raymond handed them small wrapped packages.

"Open them," he said, twirling his moustache.

Inside each package was a key. "Is this...?"

"Yes," said Raymond. "As soon as you can leave, these are the keys to my home. I think it would be inappropriate for Marnie to arrive before you, so it's best you both wait until you are well enough, Jimmy."

"Yes," said Jimmy, remembering his King's English.

"Thank you," said Marnie, touched by his thoughtfulness.

The nurses brought a gramophone into the ward, and everyone was in good spirits. Matron swayed in time to the music, and Jimmy smiled in amusement. The three chatted for some time before visiting hours ended, and Marnie and Raymond stood up to leave.

"Thank you both for coming. I'm sure you had better things to do today than sitting in a hospital ward you've just escaped from," Jimmy said.

"Oh no, boy. If I wasn't here, I would be alone. My parents died long ago and my brother is overseas. This has been the happiest Christmas I have had in quite some time."

Chapter 48

March, 1914

It was two more months before Jimmy was well enough to leave the hospital. Marnie and Raymond visited regularly, but he was itching to escape the hospital's confines and begin his new life.

Seeing no sense in waiting, Raymond started Jimmy's training in the hospital ward. He talked through the curriculum and left documents for Jimmy to peruse during the hours devoid of visitors. The nurses complained about the growing pile of papers beside Jimmy's bed, but even Matron seemed impressed by his new career.

Marnie had worked through the money Bill gave her and found a job at a department store in town. It relieved Jimmy that she was taking to her new life well and relishing her financial independence. The only drawback to her job was how much it dominated their conversation. He had no interest in women's clothing or household goods and had to feign enthusiasm as she droned on about the disastrous love lives of her colleagues. Marnie ignored Jimmy's disinterest, for her new life thrilled her, and Jimmy was a good sounding board.

Jimmy's body grew stronger and he could walk beyond the ward with the aid of a stick. On the eve of his departure, the nurses gathered with Marnie and Raymond for an impromptu leaving party. They turned a blind eye as Raymond slipped a dram of whisky into Jimmy's glass.

"To Jimmy," toasted Marjory. "Here's hoping we never meet again."

"To Jimmy."

Jimmy wouldn't miss the hospital, but would miss the nurses who had kept him sane these past months.

On his last night in the ward, Jimmy couldn't sleep. If he were honest, the thought of his new career terrified him. Raymond had been so kind. Jimmy wanted to honour that kindness with competence and skill, but felt he possessed neither.

Jimmy was tucking in his shirt when Marnie arrived the following morning.

"Come on," she said, linking arms. "Raymond's waiting outside."

Jimmy followed her out of the ward to the applause of the nurses. Raymond sat waiting in a carriage and jumped down to take Jimmy's bag.

"Lowestoft station," he said to the driver. Tilting his head up to the sun, Jimmy swallowed big gulps of salty air. Despite the season ending, the smell of herring lingered and filled him with nostalgia for his time on the *Star Gazer*. His friends would all be in the warmth of their homes and families by now. He wondered if he would see them again.

Lowestoft station was quiet, and the train to Somerleyton quieter still. It was an effort to climb the train's steps, but Jimmy insisted on conquering them alone. The train passed by flat fields and marshy wetlands, but was soon pulling into the station.

"We'll get a cart to the schoolhouse," said Raymond.

"If it's alright with you, I'd like to walk."

Marnie and Raymond exchanged worried glances.

"It's a good mile's walk, dear boy. Might be best to rest that leg of yours."

"It'll be fine," said Jimmy.

Knowing there was no point in arguing, the trio began the slow walk to the village. They passed by farms and fields and, reaching a large common, Jimmy paused and leant against a gate.

"Everything all right, dear boy?"

"Yes, I just need to rest my leg for a moment."

Marnie and Raymond remained quiet. It was plain to both that Jimmy was struggling, his face twisting in pain with every step.

"Right, let's carry on," Jimmy said, and they followed, ready to catch him if his leg gave way. They passed the brickworks and a line of workers' cottages. By the time they reached the centre of the village, Jimmy was sweating.

"What's behind there?" he asked, pointing to a high red-brick wall with his stick. The wall snaked along for miles.

"Oh, that's the hall," said Raymond. "You'll get to visit it soon enough."

Turning a corner, they came upon a large green, picture postcard houses snuggled around its borders.

"Blimey, this is posh."

Raymond giggled. "I suppose it is."

The Sparrow's Nest above The Grit had a thatched roof, but this was the first time either of the siblings had seen thatch on the homes of ordinary folk.

"You see that building over there?" asked Raymond, pointing across the green. "That's the school."

A fine white building with a thatched roof dominated the green.

"The best view is from the other side," he said, leading them on.

Jimmy and Marnie gasped as they rounded the corner to the school. Two low buildings flanked a beautiful octagonal structure, topped with the same thatch. Raymond smiled at their reaction.

"I wish I had a photographer to capture your faces," he said. "Come on, let's get you settled in."

He led them through a red painted gate, into a small entrance lobby where coats, boots, hats and walking sticks adorned the walls. The first thing they noticed, stepping into the main room, was the light. It flooded in from windows on all sides, forming diamonds as it skirted the window's lead.

"Come upstairs and I'll show you your room."

The treads of the staircase, though well polished, bore the scuffs of years of footsteps. Above them, the building split into two rooms.

"That's my room there," pointed Raymond, "and this," he said, pushing open a door, "is yours."

There was nothing grand about the room. It contained only two thin beds, an armchair and a chest of drawers, but Jimmy thought it was perfect. Against one wall stood a simple fireplace, and Jimmy was sure they would be cosy on winter nights. Marnie rushed to the window and marvelled at the view outside.

"Look, Jimmy, from this side you can see the green, and from the other you can see miles of fields. I love it!"

Jimmy walked over to his sister and placed an arm across her shoulder. "I do too," he said.

That evening, as they sat by the fire in Raymond's sitting room, he gave Jimmy some advice. "The key is not to show any weakness. The pupils will assume you have been teaching for years. Don't give them reason to doubt it. Pretend you're an actor on a stage, fool them into thinking you're in control, and, whatever you do, don't forget your King's English!"

Jimmy nodded, but the advice filled him with nerves. Facing a room of young children felt far more intimidating than facing a storm at sea. He slept badly, tossing and turning as he played potential scenarios through his mind.

"You'll be fine," murmured Marnie, woken again by Jimmy's restlessness.

Jimmy sighed and waited for the morning to come. He woke with the dawn, finding Marnie already up and preparing for her own day's work.

"What time is your train?"

"Eight. I'm pleased you found a job near a station," she said, smiling.

Too nervous for breakfast, Jimmy was in the schoolroom an hour early, reading over and over his notes, checking his chalk was to hand, and when he could prepare no more, pacing the room.

At last, the bell went, and children filed in. They gazed at him in curiosity, and Jimmy took a deep breath. He took the register in the sternest voice he could muster, and the children remained compliant. He was harsher than he would have liked, sending two children to the corner with the dunce's hat, and rapping his cane loudly on the tables of those not listening. The newfound fierceness didn't sit well with him, but he couldn't risk losing control.

Time flew by and before he knew it, the dinner bell rang. The children came from families of either estate workers or brick makers and all ran from the school to their nearby homes. The afternoon went by in much the same way as the morning. As the first afternoon lesson was drawing to a close, he noticed two boys nudging each other.

"Stand up, boy," said Jimmy, rapping his cane against his palm. "What is all the commotion about?"

"It's his fault," cried the boy, pointing to his friend at the desk beside him. "He wanted me to ask about your leg."

Jimmy knew he should scold their insolence, but curiosity got the better of him. "What about my leg?"

"Well... well... we was wondering what happened to it..."

Jimmy crossed the room. He leant over the boy and saw that the young lad was shaking. His voice only audible to the child in front of him, he lied; "A crocodile attack." The boy gasped, and Jimmy winked to show he was joking, but the boy's eyes almost popped out of his skull. At break, boys huddled together and Jimmy could guess their conversation by the furtive glances they kept stealing his way.

Raymond appeared in the final half hour of lessons to check Jimmy was alright. Jimmy was grateful that Raymond had left him alone without scrutiny to settle in. Raymond was both surprised and impressed by the respect the children showed Jimmy, but couldn't understand why they kept eying his leg.

Jimmy didn't admit his tall tale to Raymond, but told Marnie when they were in bed that night. She was delighted his first day had gone well and impressed by his use of a white lie to win his charges round. She looked across at her brother. *He's found his way home*, she thought.

LOWESTOFT

Chapter 49

October, 1913

There was a fair nip in the air as the girls strode through Lowestoft. They hurried to the harbour and searched among boats for men they knew. It struck Clara that Kitty knew everyone.

"Kitty!" men yelled, waving from boats and blowing kisses her way. Some she answered with a kiss in return, others with a hand gesture that made Clara splutter with mirth. Cassie was no less popular, attracting wolf whistles from young hopefuls as she leant against the harbour wall. Heather had left them to it, searching out her husband to warn him against getting up to no good.

Financial independence brought confidence, and the girls held their own among men. But Clara, knowing no one, hung back. Many of the conversations were in Gaelic or Scots and she would've thought them arguments but for the smiles on faces. Were it not for her training on the island, her friends' crudeness might've shocked. Their grasp of English swear words was second to none. Conversations chattered on, comparing notes on voyages and sharing news from back home.

It was growing dark by the time they left. Clara had lost all sensation in her hands and could not stop shivering. She was used to the cold, but the easterly winds blew right through her and she made a mental note to put on more layers the next time she went out. Her bed was calling. The company, however delightful, proved exhausting after so many months on her own.

Back in the dorm, Clara struggled to sleep. Every time her body edged towards slumber, her mind chased sleep away. Too much had happened for her mind to still, and she gave in to its wanderings, listening to the gentle snores, and worse, from the bunk above as she thought back over the day's events.

She must have got just two hours' sleep, for before dawn had broken, the small dormitory came to life. The girls trudged out to the privy for their morning ablutions before readying themselves for a day's work. They pulled on thick sweaters, rolled up at the sleeves, twisted their hair into scarves and bound their fingers in cotton cloots. Arms linked, they headed down to the pickling yard, where they put on oilskin aprons and boots.

Kitty made Clara give them a twirl. "Look, girls, she's one of us."

Dawn was breaking, and with no sign of any fish, they settled themselves down on empty swills and pulled out their knitting. Despite the early hour and threatening easterly sky, spirits were high, and anticipation rippled through their group as they waited for silver darlings to arrive.

Carts carrying containers loaded with herring pulled into the yard. The women took up their positions at the farlin. Clara, Kitty, and Cassie stood together as a crew. Kitty, the packer, was their leader by default. Shoulder to shoulder with other crews, the line of women filled the length of the yard.

Soon silvery fish came tumbling from their containers into the trough, piling high in a mass of silver scales and bleak eyes. Clara gripped her small knife. Fish in hand, she cut a neat incision into its throat before pulling its gills and intestines through with a light slurp and throwing it into a tub. She was soon in her stride, flying through the fish almost as fast as they flew through water.

"Alice taught you well," Kitty called. Clara smiled but didn't take her eyes off her knife.

After three months of being idle, it took only a few hours to feel the effects of work on her body. Her back ached from bending over the farlin, and despite the cloots on her fingers, she gained several grazes as her knife slipped. She refused to lose pace, pushing through the pain and gritting her teeth. The surrounding atmosphere helped. Songs rang out across the yard, and thanks to the long train journey, she knew the words. The long line of girls joined in song, time passing with each note sung.

As I were a walking down by the seaside I saw a red herring washed up by the tide, And that little herring I took home and dried Don't you think I done well with my jolly Herring. Toorali ladi rye toorali laye Toorali ladi rye toorali laye Toorali ladi rye Koorali laye Don't you think I done well with my jolly herring?

Now what would you think that I made with his eyes: The finest of lamps now that ever did shine. There were big lamps and little lamps and lamps for to shine, Don't you think I done well with my jolly herring?

Now what would you think that I made of his head: the finest of ovens that ever baked bread. There was big ovens and little ovens and ovens to bake, Don't you think I done well with my jolly herring?

Now what would you think that I made of his gills: The finest of boats now that ever did sail. There was big boats and little boats and boats for to sail, Don't you think I done well with my jolly herring?

Now what would you think that I made of his back: Just as much money I could pack in a sack. There was sixpences shillings and crowns by the score, Don't you think I done well with my jolly herring...

It was a grey morning, but amidst the frenzied work, the spits of drizzle were negligible. Not once did they see the bottom of the wooden farlin, for each time they got close, someone would arrive with more fish, a waterfall of bodies piling up in the trough once again. Slice, thud, slice, thud, the work became hypnotic.

The call came for lunch, and the girls downed tools. Heather helped Clara rinse her wounds free of salt and bandaged fresh cloots around them. With several girls needing the first aid station, Clara was fortunate she had only minor grazes.

Kitty came round with herring and bread, and quiet descended as the girls devoured their meal. With plates cleared, some girls wandered off to chat to the lads at the dock. Clara suspected Kitty and Cassie might have joined them, but sensing their friend's exhaustion, they remained in the yard, taking up their knitting in solidarity. The crew looked up at the sky. Dark clouds were rushing through the grey and it didn't bode well for their afternoon.

The rain came at two and lasted till five. Despite the short-sleeved oilskins, rain was soon dripping from the hoods, rushing down the smooth surface and finding its way into layers of sweaters below. Standing in a muddle of fish guts and rainwater several inches deep, Clara wondered what Phyllis would think if she could see her now. Water streamed in rivers down her oilskin apron, collecting in puddles on her boots. Still the girls remained cheerful, Heather proving quite the storyteller as she led her workmates through the exploits of her youth.

It was a good day for the boats and boded well for the remaining season. As dusk fell, there was no sign of the work letting up. By now, Clara was dead on her feet, fish melting before her as her eyes lost focus. Their cooper, Richard, came out to seal the barrels. He took the girls' teasing in good spirits, responding to their jibes with a quick wit. He laid down some Naphtha flares for the girls to work by. In the light of the flares, fish glowed silver, like mystical creatures from the depths. Clara's black apron glistened with scales, and she looked like a most strange breed of fairy.

"Thirty barrels!" cried Kitty as the day drew to a close.

"Is that good?"

"Aye," said Kitty, drawing Clara into a tight embrace. "It's grand, Clara, grand."

Clara smiled. The walk home was arduous, every muscle in her body screaming in rebellion. She dragged herself into bed, falling asleep in seconds.

Chapter 50

November, 1913

Clara was dog tired. She sat on the floor of the dorm, back against the wall, head nodding as sleep came in waves. Kitty jumped from her bed.

"Come on, we're going out."

"*Noooo*," begged Clara, weariness pinning her to the floor. Kitty grabbed her hand and hauled her up to standing. She placed her hands on Clara's shoulders and shook her.

"You're a young lass. Stop acting like an old woman."

Clara smiled and yawned.

"No excuses," said Kitty, and flung a clean dress at Clara.

As she dressed, Clara hated Kitty for keeping her from her bed. Her body had grown used to the work as weeks passed, but tiredness remained a stubborn companion. But there was no point arguing with Kitty when an idea came into her head.

Clara ran a brush through her long auburn hair but made no more effort to be presentable. She intended to slip out from the dance and head home the first chance she got. The cool night air refreshed her, the mist of sleep receding from her mind.

They entered a hall filled with music and chatter. Couples were dancing, and groups of men and women huddled together, sharing jokes and sizing up their counterparts. Kitty ordered two gins, and they moved through the hall, searching for familiar faces among the crowd. The music revived Clara's soul, and she joined in the fun, laughing as lads came over to try their luck with her friends.

A young man had been loitering beside them for a while before they noticed him.

"Can we help you?" asked Kitty, turning from Clara and staring hard at the young man.

"Um, I was wondering if your friend would like to dance?"

Clara looked at the man. His face was childlike and his features nondescript. What struck Clara was his eyes. In colour, they were a watery blue, the blue of a winter sea rather than a summer sky, but they were kind.

"Aye, I'll dance with you," she said, handing her drink to Kitty. Kitty seemed taken aback by Clara's impulsiveness. Her eyes twinkled as she watched Clara melt into the pulsating sea of bodies.

It must have been the gin, thought Clara, surprised at her readiness to enter this man's arms. The band was playing a lively tune, and the man held her close, spinning around until dizzy. Her dance partner tried to say something, but Clara couldn't hear above the noise coming from the musicians.

"Pardon?" she shouted, moving her head nearer his ear.

"I'm Michael," he shouted back.

"Oh, I'm Clara. Pleased to meet you."

They danced a while longer before Michael moved his mouth close to her ear. "Can we get some fresh air? It's hot in here."

Clara would not normally have allowed herself to be alone at night with a young man, but something about Michael left her reassured. She followed him out into the darkness. Her instincts proved trustworthy as he showed her to a nearby bench and sat a respectable distance away.

"Thank you," he said with a wide smile. "I thought I might melt into a puddle if I stayed in there much longer."

Clara smiled. "Thank you for the dance. You're light on your feet and my toes are still intact."

"Where are you from?"

"Holy Island, up in the north."

"Oh, I've met a few lads from there before and seen it on a map. You're a long way from home. What brought you down south?"

Reluctant to spill her heart to a stranger, "The silver darlings," was all she said, and he seemed satisfied with her answer.

They talked a while longer, before tiredness returned, and Clara stifled a yawn.

"You're tired. Let me walk you back to your lodgings."

"Aye, thank you."

At her front door, Michael seemed nervous. "I...I... I'd like to see you again if that would be agreeable?" He looked at her like a child at an ice cream stand.

Clara smiled. "Aye," she said, "I would like that too."

"How about Sunday? Eleven-ish?"

Clara nodded and let herself into the house, waving at Michael as she closed the door. She had enjoyed his company, but as she fell asleep, it was Jimmy who occupied her dreams.

*

At a quarter to eleven on Sunday morning, Clara looked out of her small window and saw Michael pacing the street below. She tapped on the glass and he looked up, startled. She waved, smiled and raised her hand to show she would be down in five minutes. Her room mates were lounging on their beds and ribbed her as she smoothed down her hair and straightened her jacket.

"Someone's getting lucky tonight."

Clara glared.

"What's he like?"

"He's kind."

"Is he a good kisser?" asked Heather, and the other girls laughed.

"We haven't kissed yet. He's a gentleman," said Clara, with a haughty flick of her head.

"Yet," squealed Kitty, wrapping her arms around herself and making kissing noises at her friend.

"Stop it. I'm off for a walk, not a wedding." As Clara left the room, the echoes of giggles faded behind her.

"Hello," said Michael as she appeared from the house.

"Hello."

It took a while for conversation to move beyond pleasantries. Walking calmed them both, and they spent a pleasant morning strolling along the fine pale sand of Lowestoft beach. Michael spoke of his life growing up in the town and how much it had changed with the herring industry. He spoke with warmth about his family, and Clara hoped one day she might meet them.

For the first time in months, she spoke of her mam and the island with happiness, the lump of grief that sat within her dislodging from its resting place.

They walked along the promenade, enjoying the brief respite of a Sunday, all work paused, and the drifters tucked in harbour for the day. Michael showed her to his boat, the *Elizabeth*.

"My brother Joe named her after Ma," he explained.

Impressed by the steam trawler, Clara admired its funnel, the height of technology. Michael seemed pleased.

"It's Joe's boat. I'm only third mate, but he's a good skipper and great to work for. One day, I hope to have a boat of my own."

As they neared Clara's lodgings, Michael paused and looked at her, frowning. "Please tell me if I'm being presumptuous, but would you like to meet my family? We gather on a Sunday for afternoon tea and they are always welcoming of my friends." His feet shuffled as he spoke.

"Oh, so you bring female friends home to tea every weekend, do you?"

Michael flushed and looked crestfallen. "No... no... I..."

Clara reached out and placed a hand on his arm. "Michael, I'm teasing. I would love to meet your family." She linked her arm in his, motioning for him to lead the way.

Michael showed her to a small terraced house. It was narrower than any house Clara had seen, but hanging beside the front door were two baskets, ivy spilling from them. The front door was a cheerful red, and net curtains drooped like smiles in the windows.

"I'm back," Michael called to the waiting family.

The front door opened straight into a small room, stuffed with old armchairs, their pink flowers worn on the arms and headrests. A table sat in the middle of the room, well-polished and housing a jug of flowers. Clara smiled. The room reminded her of her mam. There was a gentle homeliness to it she hadn't felt for some time.

In the kitchen beyond, a small wooden dining table was the scene of lively conversation. Its occupants looked up, surprised, as Clara followed Michael into the room.

"Ma, this is my friend Clara. I've asked her to join us for tea, if that's alright?"

An elderly woman with a wide smile moved from her chair and rushed to Clara. "It is," she said, pulling Clara into a warm embrace that left her startled.

"Lovely to meet you, dear. Here, have a seat." She offered her own chair, which Clara took out of politeness.

Michael introduced Clara to the smiling faces around the table. "This is my dad, Ted, brother Joe, his wife Susan, and of course my mum Betty." He put an arm around his mother, kissing her cheek.

The family said their hellos. Betty leapt into a flurry of activity, bringing out plate after plate of scones and jam, tea cakes, sandwiches, and a large Victoria sponge. The chatter continued as the family ate. They asked Clara many questions and listened open-mouthed to her tales of childhood on an island. At one point, Betty placed a round, warm hand on Clara's, tears in her eyes.

"Your ma sounds wonderful, dear."

"Aye, she was."

Ted was so like Michael, the only difference being his face housed a thin beard and his hair was greying. Susan was a slip of a woman, not over five feet tall, with golden hair and deep brown eyes. She had a ready smile and seemed pleased to have another female at the table.

"How did you two meet?"

"At a dance," said Clara with a smile.

"You're the first girl he's brought home," whispered Susan. She winked, and Clara blushed.

"We only met last week."

"Looks like a whirlwind romance to me."

Clara smiled, but the comment worried her. She liked Michael, but wondered if it was his welcoming family that attracted her more than the man himself.

"Would you like to come over for a cuppa next week?" Susan asked. "I've not been out much since I fell pregnant."

"Oh, I didn't realise," said Clara, eying Susan's washboard stomach and wondering how any life could fit in there. "I'd love to, but I might struggle to get away from the yard. Work's been frantic these past weeks."

"What are you two whispering about?" asked Joe.

"Mind your own business," said Susan, folding her arms and grinning.

"Where are you stayin', love?" asked Ted.

"The Grit."

"Hmm, there's some wrong 'uns round there. You be careful walking them streets."

"Oh, I like it," said Clara.

"Humph."

"The townsfolk are snobby about us Gritsters," said Susan. "You're alright, just passing through, but me and Joe kept my address secret till we were sure Ted and Betty liked me."

"You grew up on The Grit?"

"Yep, loved every second. It was a hard life in lots of ways, no money, little food and suchlike, but as a child, it was paradise. All summer long we'd be down the beach, swimming, building sandcastles and making pictures from the pebbles. Ma would pack us lard sandwiches and tell us not to be home till teatime." Susan laughed. "If we weren't on the beach, we were playing at the Denes, or messing around the boat sheds or pickling plots. We had no money, no shoes or socks, but plenty of freedom."

Clara smiled, thinking of her own childhood. The Grit reminded her of the island, a close-knit community cut off from those around them.

The harshness of their existence resulted in both steeliness of its people, and a strength of belonging that meant anyone would do anything for their neighbour.

"I'd love you to meet my family some time. They live on Nelson Road, next to the church. You know it?"

"Aye, I think so. I know the church anyway."

"Maybe I could meet you there one evening after work?"

"I'd love that," said Clara.

It was disappointing when tea was over, and Clara knew she must leave or outstay her welcome. She thanked the family, and Betty again embraced her. Michael said he'd walk her home, and she noticed Ted patting him on the back as they left the room.

Clara was quiet as they walked, and a look of concern crossed Michael's face.

"I'm sorry, was that too forward? I shouldn't have introduced you to them so soon."

She stopped walking and smiled at him, looking into his kind eyes that were both hopeful and concerned. "Michael, I had the most wonderful time. It felt like home." And she blushed at her unintended candour.

Michael grinned and as they reached Clara's dorm, gave her a chaste kiss on the cheek. "Would you like to come again next Sunday?"

"Aye. Aye, I would."

Chapter 51

November, 1913

The next three Sundays Michael picked Clara up on the dot of eleven and they repeated their walk and Sunday tea. Clara found no time to visit Susan or her family, but talking with Michael's sister-in-law was a highlight of her weekends.

A slight bump showed on Susan's stomach, and Clara shared her excitement at the growing life within it.

"Have you thought of names for the bairn?"

Susan smiled, enjoying the sing-song nature of Clara's accent. "Lizzie, if it's a girl, Edward, if it's a boy. Joe wants to name them after his parents and, thankfully, they both have pretty names. I can't wait for him or her to arrive and meet you."

Clara didn't voice her thoughts to Susan that she would be long gone by the time the bairn arrived.

"Fancy meeting my family this week?"

"Susan, I'd love to, but I can never seem to get away from work in time."

"Well, do you think Michael would mind if I walked you home tonight? We could call in on my ma on the way to yours."

"I'm sure he can cope for one week. Are you alright walking round there after dark?"

"Oh, not you as well," said Susan. "I'm a Gritster. They look after their own. I'll be perfectly safe."

"It sounds like a wonderful idea then," said Clara.

After tea, the women said their goodbyes. Michael looked disappointed not to be walking her home, but Clara felt no guilt as she linked arms with Susan and waved goodbye.

Susan led Clara through a maze of streets and alleyways.

"This is Herring Fishery Score," said Susan, "and that's my old school." She pointed to a single-storey building near the bottom of the alley. "I remember little teaching from my schooldays, but I remember the toilets clear as day. Cor, they didn't half stink. Three troughs flushed just three times a day. The boys were even worse. Theirs didn't flush at all, and in summer stale pee perfumed the entire building."

Clara giggled, enjoying the impromptu tour. "How many people live in The Grit?"

"Hard to say, a lot more this time of year. A couple of thousand would be my guess."

"Phew, that makes my island seem tiddly."

"How many's there?"

"Couple of hundred. There's more when the herring come, but nothing like this."

"Did your school stink of pee?"

Clara laughed. "Not that I remember."

"Here we are," said Susan, standing outside a red-bricked cottage. "Got to do the special knock or Ma will think it's the landlord after his rent."

Susan tapped out a rhythmic pattern of knocking on the rough wooden door.

"That you, Sue?" came a voice from behind the door.

"Yes, Ma, let me in. It's freezing out here."

Several locks turned, and a small, impish woman poked her head round the door.

"Who's this?"

"Clara, Michael's girl," said Susan.

"Nice to meet you, Clara. Come on in, don't mind the mess."

Clara walked into a small sitting room, children filling every space on the floor. Susan went and kissed each in turn.

"My siblings," she said. "Six girls, seven boys. I'm the eldest."

Susan met Clara's gasp with a grin.

"Where do you all sleep?"

"I'll show you. Follow me."

Susan led Clara up a bare stairway. Above it lay two rooms.

"That's for the boys, this is the girls'," said Susan, pointing an arm at each.

A musty smell hit Clara as Susan opened the door to the girls' room. It reminded her of walking past the barns of the island farm. Clara's feet sank into a soft layer of straw. She looked at Susan, open-mouthed. Susan laughed.

"They treat us like animals here," she said with a grin. "Come on, lie down."

Clara followed her friend's lead and lay down on the straw. Susan threw her a blanket.

"Close your eyes," she said.

Clara did as she was told, pulling the blanket around her and closing her eyes tight.

"Makes sense now, don't it?" asked Susan.

"Aye, it does."

The straw made for a soft bed, and after a long week working in the yard Clara would've happily stayed the night, assured of a good night's sleep. She sneezed.

"Oh yes, that is one downside, I'll grant you. You get used to it though, and the smell. It's a very efficient system, really. We chuck the straw out of the window on a Friday ready for burning, then replace it with a fresh load. Saves on laundry. Took me a while to get used to a proper bed after I married Joe. Oh, don't you tell Betty about this, she'd be horrified."

Clara giggled at the thought of Betty and Ted seeing their daughter-in-law's childhood bedroom.

"What are you girls doing up there? Come down for some tea," called Susan's ma.

The girls headed back downstairs. Clara was a hit with the children, who asked her endless questions about the island. They reminded her of Jimmy's sisters, but despite the obvious hardship, the home contained none of the nastiness that came with Alex Watson.

"Lovely to meet you," said Clara, as the time came to leave.

"Call round anytime, dear. You know where we are now."

"Aye, I will, thank you."

Clara hugged Susan and watched as her friend made her way back through the dark streets of The Grit.

*

On their fourth week of meetings, as Michael dropped her home, he blushed and asked, "Clara, would you mind if I kissed you?"

Clara met his blush with her own. "I suppose not," she said, and let him pull her closer.

His lips were moist against hers and as they moved Clara waited for the thrill, but it never came. Hope filled Michael's eyes, and she felt a rush of warmth for this kind young man. She smiled at him and gave him one last peck on the lips.

"See you next week?"

"Yes, please," he said.

In bed that night, Clara played the kiss over in her mind. Michael seemed happy with it, and she supposed no kiss could be as exciting as your first. A lump of guilt sat in her stomach, but she pushed it away. Jimmy had said he would write but had broken his promise. She owed him nothing. He had left, Michael was here.

Chapter 52

December, 1913

As the season raced towards its close, the herring girls' talk turned to winter plans and family reunions. Clara stayed quiet during these moments. She wanted to return home to the island, but there had been no word since she left, and she couldn't just turn up. What if they sent her away again?

Kitty offered her the chance to go home with her, and right now it appeared it might be Clara's only option. She could winter in the Highlands and join the herring girls again the following spring. She lay listening to her friends' chatter, feeling the uncertainty of life's path gnawing away at her.

Michael called for her the following Sunday, and wrapping up warm they headed off for their usual stroll. Clara was quiet and distracted, and he stopped to take her arm.

"Clara love, tell me what's on your mind."

"Home," she replied.

"Do you mean the island?"

"Yes, and no. I have to leave soon, and I want to return home, but may not be welcome. Kitty has offered to take me home with her. I suppose I'm trying to decide where home is for me now."

A look of devastation filled Michael's face as she spoke. "But I thought your home was here with me?"

Clara had not considered Michael in her plans. "I'm sorry," she said, stroking his face. "I can't stay here, though. The season is nearly over and there'll be no work for me soon."

Without warning, Michael got down on one knee, clasping her hand in his. "Marry me," he said, hope and longing mingling in his eyes.

"I... I..."

"Think about it, Clara, it would solve all your problems. We could wed, and you'd come and live with us. I love you, Clara."

Without returning his sentiment, she snatched her hand from his and turned on her heel, running back across the beach until the biting wind became too much and she huddled down in the shelter of an upturned boat. She should be grateful that a man like Michael wished to marry her, but to say yes would mean turning her back on dreams of returning home, dreams of Jimmy.

Clara pummelled the sand beneath her with balled fists and cursed the girl who had said she wouldn't wait, wouldn't leave the island to be with him. She had ended up away from Jimmy, away from her island and with the possibility that she might never return. Anyone downwind would've taken her for a drunken vagabond; her hair had escaped its pins and strands stuck to tears on her cheeks, and the wind carried words not befitting a young lady.

"Damn you, Jimmy. Damn you, Da. Damn you, damn you, damn you," she screamed into the wind.

The thought of Michael softened her heart a little. His ready smile and kind face, the way he looked at her, a heart so big it could hurt no one, least of all her. "What a fool I am," she said out loud. She stood up and shrugged off the self-loathing and self-pity that had cloaked her just moments before.

Clara strode back to where they had parted, but found Michael gone. Panic gripped her. What if she had just thrown away her chance at a good life, at happiness? She sped through the town's streets until she reached Michael's terrace. Her pace slowed and her cheeks burned with the memory of how she had behaved. She took a deep breath and marched up and knocked on the door. Ted opened it, unsmiling.

"Hello, Clara. I suppose you'll be wanting Michael?"

"Aye, please," said Clara, struggling to look the old man in the eye.

"Michael," he called over his shoulder. There was no answer. "Michael! Clara's here."

Footsteps sounded above them, and Michael appeared on the stairs. His eyes were red and Clara wondered if it was from the wind or from tears. Ted moved through to the kitchen, and Michael joined Clara on the doorstep.

"Can we walk?" she asked him. He nodded, grabbing his coat and closing the door.

"I'm sorry, Michael, I was so rude. I didn't mean to run. I just got so sad at the thought of never returning home."

"But I'd take you home," he said. "I want to meet your family, Clara. I want to know everything about you."

Clara sighed. "Michael, that's not what I mean. I mean that I'd never be able to live on the island again. I'd be joining your life, your family, leaving mine behind. It's a big decision."

"Yes, it is," he said, looking forlorn. "You know, when I've saved enough for my boat, we can go back to your island, make our life there."

A rational mind would have questioned the sincerity of his promise, but Clara was in no rational state. "Do you mean it?"

"Yes," he said, wanting to believe the lie as much as she did.

"Ask me again," she said. "Michael, ask me again."

He stared at the ground, unsure about risking his heart for the second time in a day. Eventually, he got down on one knee. "Clara, will you marry me?"

"Aye," she said. Michael jumped up, grabbing hold of her until her feet were no longer touching the floor. After much whooping, he set her down, and she leant against him to steady herself from the dizziness she was experiencing.

"Can we tell my family?" Clara nodded, and he skipped along the street, dancing her along, not caring who saw. As they neared the house, he pulled her round to face him. "Clara, are you sure?"

"Aye," she lied, and he scooped her up in his arms and carried her over the threshold.

Ted and Betty welcomed the news with delight. They had had their children late in life and worried they might not live to see their youngest son marry. They each took Clara into their arms. She noticed both had tears in their eyes, and the warmth of her new family salved her fears.

Chapter 53

December, 1913

It was to be a hasty wedding, for Clara was insistent they should marry before her friends departed for Scotland. She woke on the morning of her wedding in the dorm she had shared for the past three months. An end of an era in so many ways. The girls pushed away the sadness of farewells and focussed on the day ahead.

As soon as Clara was awake, Kitty worked on her hair, curling it up and pinning it to her head. There was no need for makeup; working outdoors for months had given Clara's flawless skin a ruddy glow, and her plump pink lips needed no rouge. She had hung her one smart dress the previous night and now pulled it on. Over it, she wore her mam's jacket... her something old. Kitty had lent a smart pair of low-heeled shoes... something borrowed. She slipped a small piece of navy yarn into her hair pins... something blue. The simple engagement band from Michael, her something new. Silver, to remind her of her time with the silver darlings.

"I think you're ready," said Kitty, spinning Clara around to check every detail was in place.

Clara took deep breaths to push back tears.

"You alright, lass?" Cassie asked.

"Aye, I will be."

This wasn't how she had pictured her wedding all those years ago in the island church when she'd watched Sally wed Robert. There was no petting stone, no toll at the gate, no arch of guns, no Mam and Da, no Jimmy.

Thoughts of her past life pushed from her head, she smiled at her friends. "I'm ready," she said, and headed to the door.

The wedding was a simple affair held in the town hall. Aside from her friends, the only other guests were Michael's family and his crew mates from the lugger. When she met him at the front of the room, he mouthed a silent, "You look beautiful".

Clara smiled at him. His round face filled with joy, eyes shining, big hands wringing together in excitement. She reached down and stroked Michael's hand with her fingers. He flushed with pleasure.

The ceremony was over in a blur, and later Clara struggled to recall the words spoken. All she remembered was the contentment of belonging to a family once more.

The newlyweds walked past their friends to cheers and clapping, all wishing the couple well in their new life. The wedding party walked through the wintry streets to Michael's family home, where Betty had laid on quite the spread. It was a job fitting everyone in, but all were used to being in close quarters and no one minded having to squeeze past each other to refill their plate or glass.

Soon the herring girls were leading the singing, the lads from Michael's crew joining in with their hearty baritones. It wouldn't have surprised Clara if there were a few kisses that night, but she would never know, for mid-afternoon it was time to leave for their one night of honeymoon.

As a wedding present, Ted and Betty had bought them a night at the Swan Hotel in Southwold and the entire party gathered outside to wave the newlyweds off. Alone for the first time that day, Clara snuggled into Michael, the last-minute jitters of the morning banished from her mind. She felt safe, loved, and there wasn't much more you could ask.

It took some time before the carriage pulled into the deserted Southwold streets. The village that had been humming with activity for the past few months now lay quiet.

The grand entrance of the hotel was silent, other than the ticking of a grandfather clock. Michael pushed the brass bell on the reception desk and an elderly lady in a smart black uniform appeared, her heels clicking on the tiled floor.

"Mr and Mrs Mason?" she asked, opening a large ledger with an almost blank page.

"Yes, ma'am, that's us," said Michael, his chest puffed at being called Mr and Mrs.

"You're in room seven," said the lady, handing over a key with a ceramic swan hanging from it.

"Thank you," said Michael, picking up their two small bags and following the directions to the room.

The grandeur of the room reminded Clara of her grandparents' home, and she wondered if they had received her letter informing them of her nuptials. She was sorry that in her haste she had not allowed enough time for them to be there. But she couldn't imagine them walking the Lowestoft streets and wasn't sure they would approve of her choice of husband.

They set their bags down and walked through the room, taking in the fine furnishings and immaculate bathroom facilities. Both knew the expectations of a wedding night, and tension hung in the air. Clara had received a raft of advice from her fellow herring girls, but the act they described sounded so crude that she had been dreading this moment ever since. An uncomfortable silence descended, and Michael suggested they go to bed.

Clara turned the lights off and they each undressed. In the darkness, Clara slipped a thin old blanket over the fine hotel linen, one piece of advice from her friends she now welcomed. The newlyweds climbed into the large four-poster bed and lay side by side, corpse-like, neither sure what should happen next.

"Should we turn to face each other?" asked Michael. They turned to lie on their sides. He kissed Clara with more force than usual. She pulled away, gasping for breath, rubbing her skin scratched by wiry stubble.

"Are you alright?" he asked, and Clara nodded, leaning over to kiss her husband. She found it was more pleasurable when she led proceedings but whipped back in shock as Michael's hand found its way to her small breast.

"Michael, what are you doing?"

Even in the darkness, she could tell he was blushing. "The lads told me this is what's done on these occasions."

"Oh," she said, lying back down. She replaced his hand on her breast and stifled a giggle as he squeezed in a manner reminiscent of a cow being milked.

They continued kissing and squeezing, more squeezing, more kissing until Clara found her mind drifting off to mundane issues, such as whether they could fit a double bed in Michael's small room at his parents' house.

He pushed her onto her back and climbed on top of her, fumbling beneath the bedsheets for quite some time. Clara felt his hand brushing against parts of her that had, until this moment, remained hidden. She gasped as a shard of pain ripped through the lower part of her body. Filled by a foreign object, it brought shots of pain each time it returned.

"Are you alright?" said Michael, panting.

"Aye," lied Clara, turning her head to the side and squeezing her eyes tight shut.

Michael's movement increased its pace while Clara lay dead still beneath him. The pain eased, but the sensation that replaced it was some way off the pleasure Clara had been expecting. She worried that people might hear the creaking bed frame and pulled it with her hand to lessen the noise. Michael's breathing was heavy and frantic. With a final shudder, he collapsed back onto the bed, and Clara assumed it must be over. Mortified by the dampness between her legs, she gathered the old blanket around her.

"That was lovely, thank you," said Michael, and Clara could hear the smile in his voice.

"Aye," she lied again. "I'm just going to use the facilities." She fumbled in her bag until she found a spare nightie, undergarments and the rags she used for her monthlies. In the bathroom's privacy, she began cleaning the mess that the act had caused. She felt bruised and her stomach ached. Once refreshed, she bundled her soiled garments into the old blanket and returned to the room.

Michael was snoring, but stirred as she climbed into the bed. He rolled over and wrapped an arm around her. Clara nestled into his chest, feeling his heart beating and considering how much more pleasant a cuddle was than the act which had preceded it. Despite the dull ache deep inside her, she slept soundly.

Chapter 54

April, 1914

Clara woke long before dawn to the clicking of a stray branch on glass and the low rumble of snores. Her body bristled with cold and she hugged her legs to her chest, squeezing her feet in her palms to return some feeling.

These small hours were her enemy, when the rational security of daylight couldn't protect her. Her mind was free to delve into its darkest depths. She had learned it was better to stay awake, for if she fell back to dreams now, they would take her to the island.

On some occasions she roamed her beloved shores, watching light dance on water, or sitting with her mam beside the fire. Sometimes she saw the broken face of her da, sending her away. Either way, she knew she would wake to a pillow soaked in tears and Michael's anxious face. She could never explain her dreams to him, for he was of a different world. He could never know the longing she felt for home and her community, despite its flaws. All he wanted was for his wife to be happy and she loved him for it, but not in the way he loved her, of that she was now sure.

Clara suppressed a sigh, careful not to wake her husband, who had a long day's fishing ahead. Her disturbed nights were evident in her sallow complexion and ever thinning frame. She noticed the concern in the eyes of those around her but insisted she was fine, reassuring them it was only a matter of time before sleep would return in wonderful fullness.

In the darkness, Clara mulled over the choices she had made. Since setting foot on the mainland, she belonged nowhere. For the first days of marriage, she believed Michael might come home with her. But he was as close to his family as she had once been to hers, and she doubted he would ever abandon his elderly parents for a small piece of land jutting out into the North Sea. Her butterfly mind was most active in these dark hours, flitting from thoughts of the brother she had never met, to the love she had lost.

She could still taste the salty longing of Jimmy's lips and had not yet discovered that same burning desire with Michael. Night after night, he climbed onto her and began his thrusting expression of love. In recent weeks there had been an urgency to his movements, spurred on by the fact that she was growing thinner, not fatter.

As lack of sleep stole her energy, she would see him watching her, wondering if it were a sign of life growing inside her. But despite her discreetness, he noticed the bloodied rags that appeared month after month.

In the comfort of daylight, with the distractions of keeping house, mending nets, or cooking for her in-laws, Clara found brief moments of solace. Kindness typified the family, and the home she had joined was a happy one. If she could only remove the longing in her heart, she would be alright.

The blackness of the room was turning grey, and in the cold growing light, Michael stirred. He stretched out his arms, yawning, and saw his wife was awake.

"Can't you sleep, dear?" he asked, turning over and putting an arm across her.

"No."

Clara tried to keep her voice level, but her nightly awakenings were chipping away at her patience and she knew she was becoming difficult.

"You'll settle in soon," he promised, kissing her on the cheek.

Clara brushed the kiss from her face. She sighed and waited for the comfort of daylight. Michael heaved himself out of the warm bed and pulled on his clothes.

*

If Michael were struggling to become a father, the same could not be said for his brother. Susan begged Clara to be at the birth, but the trauma of Anna's death still haunted her. Sitting together on the south beach, Clara explained her reasons for declining. Susan pulled her head onto her shoulder and stroked her hair.

"You'll make an excellent mam," said Clara.

Susan laughed. "Come on, let's go before this jumping baby explodes my bladder."

Two days later, Clara answered the door to an anxious-looking Joe. "Get Ma, please, Clara. Tell her to hurry, the baby's coming."

In the hours that followed, Clara wished she had put aside her fears to be with Susan, for waiting at home was worse. She paced the small house, jumping at footsteps on the pavement outside. Twelve hours later, an exhausted Betty returned home.

"Put the kettle on, Clara love," she called as she came through the front door.

"How is she?"

"Oh, she did so well. Her and the babies are all grand."

"That's wonderful," said Clara. "Hold on, did you say babies?"

Betty sighed. "Yes, I might have been home quicker if I hadn't been helping with two births. A boy and a girl."

Tears of happiness for her friend sprang to Clara's eyes. "Can I see them?"

"Not yet, dear. It's late and Susan is exhausted. Go first thing tomorrow. She'd love for the babies to meet their Aunty Clara."

Susan was still in bed when Clara arrived, but Joe said she was fine to go up. She beamed as she saw Clara, her face more beautiful than ever.

"How on earth did you fit two bairns in that tiny waist of yours?" said Clara, sitting on the edge of the bed.

"I must be hollow inside," laughed Susan. A baby lay each side of her in the crook of her arms.

"They're beautiful," said Clara, stroking a soft pink cheek. "Which one is this?"

"Lizzie, and this here is Edward."

Clara stayed admiring the babies until one cried and she took this as her cue to leave.

"Your turn next," called Susan as Clara let herself out of the room.

Chapter 55

July, 1914

Clara was hanging washing on the line when Michael appeared in the yard.

"I thought you were at sea," said Clara, surprised. Her husband wasn't due home for another few days. Pale-faced, he sat down on a step, head in his hands. Clara rushed over to him. She sat beside him and put her arm across his broad shoulders.

"Michael? Are you sick?" she asked, face full of concern. Michael shook his head but didn't respond. Clara persisted. "What's happened? Has there been an accident?"

Michael shook his head and put it in his hands. "We were out fishing when boats came and turned us back. Clara, there's going to be war."

Clara stared ahead of her, vision blurred. Rumours had been circulating for months, but now it seemed the one thing they all feared was to become a reality.

"We heard gunfire while we were out there, saw a vessel being chased by two British warships. Shells were landing not a mile from us. The fishing grounds have been closed."

"Oh, Michael, what will we do?" If Michael didn't fish, there would be no money for food.

"I've talked to Joe, talked of nothing else, in fact," said Michael with a wry laugh that held no joy. "He's going to stay on the boat. It's likely they'll be needed in the war effort. There's talk of using steam trawlers for mine-sweeping. Clara..." he said, taking her hands, "I'm going to join up."

"No. No, no, no!" she begged. Michael wouldn't meet her eye.

"It's decided, Clara. If both me and Joe are out on the boat and something happens, Mum and Dad would never recover. It's better this way. Better odds, at least one of us will come home."

"Please, Michael," said Clara. "Please don't go."

"Clara, I'm young and strong and that's what our country needs right now. Besides, I'm only third mate and if something happens to me on the boat, you'll all be penniless. Joe will be alright as skipper, the Admiralty will take care of Susan and the babies if he... if he....." Michael buried his head in his hands once more.

On hearing voices, Betty and Ted came outside and Michael told them the news. Betty's reaction was even stronger than Clara's. She sank to the ground, kneeling in front of Michael, gripping his legs and begging him not to go. Ted was resolute, clapping Michael on the back and telling his son he was proud of him. But his face contorted in anguish despite the calm of his actions.

In the evening, Joe, Susan and the twins came round and the solemn party sat in the kitchen. Joe was ready to serve. If sweeping for mines was what the Admiralty needed, sweeping mines was what he'd do. Michael planned to go the following morning to sign up. Events were moving at such a pace that Clara's mind struggled to keep up. In a single day, war was ripping through the centre of their family. Clara hoped it wouldn't last long.

Sooner than she feared, Michael received the news that he was being called up. That night in bed, Clara laid her head down on Michael's wide chest. For the first time in their marriage, instead of resenting the uncomfortable act of lovemaking, she welcomed the closeness it brought. She let Michael move in his familiar ways, pulling him close to her, feeling the dampness of tears on his cheeks as his head rested beside hers. When it was over, she cuddled close to him, her hand playing with the soft dark hairs that covered his chest.

"Clara, I hope I've left you with child this time," he said, the first time he had mentioned her barrenness aloud.

"Aye, maybe," she said, more to console him than out of any belief of its truth.

Clara didn't want a child. The circumstance of Anna's death still haunted her dreams at night, and she never wanted to experience such agony or live with such false hope. Having built such a fragile, imperfect happiness, she could not bear for it to be torn down. But she kept her thoughts sealed away, for if Michael knew, it would break his heart.

She had been spared pregnancy up till now and didn't consider it a coincidence that she came from a line of only children. Michael reached down and stroked Clara's firm stomach. Already her stomach twinged with monthly cramps, but she hoped the bleeding would wait till he had left. If she could send him away with some hope, it might make all the difference.

Morning came too soon, and the family gathered to wave Michael off. Unlike the silent fat tears that rolled down Clara's cheeks, Betty was inconsolable, large volcanic sobs shaking her entire body as Ted held his wife upright.

Many others from their street were heading to war, and all the neighbours gathered to see off their young men. There was a false air of celebration, cheers and shouts from well-wishers, as if the men were heading off on an exciting expedition, soon to return home.

Michael turned before setting off and gave them a salute. The family huddled together, arms around each other, willing him to be safe and return to them soon.

Chapter 56

November, 1914

War felt a distant threat, but one cold, cloudless morning in early November, the family woke to the sound of guns and the house shuddering. Clara met Ted coming out of his bedroom. "I'm off to see what's afoot," he said.

"I'll come with you."

Ted protested, but Clara rushed downstairs and threw on her coat and boots before he could stop her. He shook his head in frustration at the stubborn girl.

"Let's go," she said.

They hurried through the streets toward the cliffs. A crowd gathered and men were pointing out to sea, their faces full of rage. Clara followed their line of sight to the unmistakable flash of guns. Huge pillars of water flung into the air as shells dropped into the sea, and fear for Joe twisted in Clara's stomach. Ted put his arm round her shoulders and pulled her close. She breathed in his comforting smell of tobacco and fish.

"Is Joe out there?"

"I hope not," Ted whispered.

Even from a distance, they could see the target of the shells was an impressive gunboat flanked by two destroyers.

"Come on, boys," said Ted. "Get yourselves out of this mess and quick."

Someone must have heard Ted's prayers, for as he spoke, the firing stopped. Smoke rose from the gunboat's funnels, but she remained floating on the surface of the water.

"She must make for harbour," shouted a fisherman, and the crowd dispersed, many heading to await the vessel's arrival.

"Let's get Betty," said Ted, and Clara followed him back to the house. On their way they called at Joe's, relieved to find him safe and well, eating a bowl of porridge.

"You had me worried, boy," said Ted, pulling his startled son into a tight embrace.

"Get on with you," laughed Joe. "Ma will have your guts for garters if you don't return soon."

The thought of his wife's wrath was enough to stir Ted, and he said his goodbyes to his son. Betty was pacing around the kitchen, nursing a cold cup of tea.

"Where have you been?" she scolded. "I heard gunfire, then you disappeared and I've been worried sick."

Ted apologised and explained what they had seen. "Want to come to the harbour with us?" he asked.

"I'm not letting you out of my sight again, so I suppose I must," said Betty. Though she huffed and puffed, Clara knew she was as excited to see the gunship as they were.

The family pushed their way through the throng to get a view of the HMS Halcyon as the damaged ship made her way into the harbour. A tremendous cheer filled the air as she moored up alongside the quay. Relief mingled with pride as news spread that this great ship had survived an attack by a German flotilla. It was only as the family arrived home that the true meaning of the day's events hit them. The enemy was near. They had reached their town. They had reached their home.

*

Clara wiped a duster over the surfaces of the living room for the third time that morning. It was three months since she had had any word from Michael, and anxiety was gnawing away at her. A rap on the door made her jump, and she knocked over one of Betty's favourite vases, causing it to splinter into tiny pieces. She picked her way over the shards and rushed to open the door. The postman stood on the doorstep, shifting his weight between his feet.

"Morning, miss," he said.

When he looked up, his eyes were full of pity. He handed Clara an official-looking envelope. She took it from him with trembling hands, muttered her thanks and closed the door. With the letter clutched to her chest, she leaned against the door, needing to delay its news for a few moments longer. She slid down against the wood, hugged her knees to her chest, and tore the envelope's brown seal. *Missing, presumed dead.*

When Ted and Betty returned home, Clara's weight still blocked the door. She shuffled away and pulled herself up by the banister. Her in-laws saw the letter in her hands before they saw her. Ted ripped it from her and stormed through to the kitchen. Betty rushed after him, begging her husband to share the news. Clara watched as the letter slipped from Ted's hand and Betty fell into his arms.

Witness to an intimate moment of grief, Clara went to her bedroom to allow them some privacy. On their bed, she stroked her hand across Michael's side of the quilt. Sadness cloaked her; for Michael, Ted and Betty rather than herself. Anna's death had splintered her heart in two. Now, each new heartbreak just chipped away at a small corner, taking out a chink, leaving a fault line. This time there was no surge of grief, no tidal wave of tears, just a dull hollowness at yet another loss.

*

Michael proved harder to grieve for than Clara expected. She had seen Anna's cold, still body laid out, proving she had gone. But Michael's body had never been found. The army had told them the grim circumstances of his death, but with no body, no funeral, his death seemed unreal. Betty was cut to the core, crying herself to sleep at night, but Clara felt nothing.

She had grown used to Michael's absence and in her mind, he was still in some far-flung field fighting in the trenches. At night, Clara laid photographs of her husband across the bed, staring at his face, willing her heart to feel. Nothing. Blank. She pinched herself hard, in a vain attempt to draw tears from eyes that remained stubbornly dry.

For weeks after his death, self-loathing plagued her. What sort of wife doesn't mourn their husband's death? It was Susan who broke the spell.

"You all right?" she asked Clara one morning when they were alone in the kitchen.

"Aye."

"Come here."

Clara obeyed and stood in front of her friend. Susan gripped her wrists.

"Are you all right?" she asked again.

"I don't feel sad that Michael's gone. I don't cry, I don't miss him. I don't believe he's dead."

"Phew, that's a lot to be carrying in that head of yours. Sit down."

Clara pulled out a chair and sat opposite Susan.

"You know what you're feeling is normal, don't you?"

"It's not," said Clara. "I hear Betty crying at night, but no tears will come to me. If I was a proper wife, I'd be crying myself to sleep."

"Grief isn't the same for everyone. Did you ever see a body? Did you have a funeral?"

"No."

"Did you love him?"

Clara paused. She couldn't look Susan in the eye. "I loved him, but not in the way you love Joe."

"Clara, love isn't like they tell you in books. I was madly in love with a chap called Billy when I was fifteen. Did things with him no unmarried girl should do. He broke my heart. Do I love Joe like I loved Billy? No, of course not. It's a different love, but no less real. You made Michael happier than I ever saw him. Whether you cry that he's gone doesn't matter. What matters was the time you had together."

Clara moved to her friend and hugged her. "How did you get so wise?"

"Well, if you'd been to a school that stunk of pee, you might be wise too."

For the first time in weeks, Clara smiled. "Thank you."

"You can thank me by changing a nappy," Susan said, grinning.

Chapter 57

June, 1915

A loud shrieking filled the air, waking Clara from her already restless sleep. Behind the wall, Ted and Betty's footsteps pounded the floorboards.

"Clara!"

Clara rushed through to their room, entering without knocking. Betty and Ted stood at the window, staring out, gripping each other's arms.

"Come away from the window," said Clara. But they seemed frozen to the spot.

"Come away from the window." Her voice rose with panic, but the couple stood motionless, staring out at sea.

She crossed the room and pulled them away, just as a colossal explosion sounded nearby, rocking the house. Plumes of black smoke filled the sky. The explosion was only a few streets away.

"Quick, we have to get downstairs," she said, standing behind them, blocking their path back to the window.

Released from their trance, Ted and Betty hurried downstairs into the sitting room. Clara followed behind, gathering an armful of blankets. She found Ted and Betty huddled on the sofa, and wrapped blankets round their shivering bodies.

"I'll put the kettle on."

"Get me something stronger than tea, please," said Ted.

While the kettle bubbled, she poured them each a brandy. Clara had just handed out the drinks when a fist pummelled the door. Susan stood in the doorway, the twins balanced in her arms, a suitcase in one hand and a carpetbag in the other.

"The Zep's close to our house. The Crawleys two doors but one got hit."

Clara grabbed her bags and flung them into the sitting room, before taking a squirming Edward from Susan's arms. Betty's white face brightened at seeing her grandchildren, and she stretched out her arms. Clara handed Eddy to her and cradled Lizzie while Susan removed her coat and sat down. Her sister-in-law slumped into an armchair and cried.

"Joe," she sobbed. "Joe."

"Joe will be alright," said Clara, stroking her free hand up and down Susan's back.

"But he's out there," Susan whimpered, pointing in the sea's direction.

Clara didn't respond, for what was the point of false promises when they all knew the danger Joe faced.

"I should find out what's happening," she said.

"No," came three unanimous voices.

Clara sighed in frustration. "Very well, I shall just go into the yard, no further. I'll be back in a tick." She left the room before they could stop her.

Clara wasn't the only one outside. Families up and down the street peered into the smoke-filled gloom, trying to measure the peril they faced.

"What's going on?" she asked Maggie next door.

"A Zep over the town," shouted Maggie, above the hum of ominous engines. "They're at sea too. We must pray for our boys tonight."

Clara nodded and stared at the sky. Soon it would be the longest day; the sky never truly grew dark in June. *A perfect night for the Zep*, thought Clara.

"Stupid girl!" said Ted as she entered the sitting room. "You could've been killed going out there."

"Ted, you're as likely to die in here as I am out there. From what I can see, we're sitting ducks. The only weapon we have is prayer."

Clara never put much store in the power of prayer, but knew her in-laws did. In fact, Betty already had her eyes shut, whispering pleas of protection over the head of her grandson.

"Sorry," said Ted. "Stay here though, will you? At least if we're goners, we'll be goners together."

Clara nodded and patted his arm. "More tea?"

No one responded, so she settled herself in a chair. Her anxious fingers tapped against the chair arm and she picked up her knitting from a basket by the fire. The thought of death didn't frighten her, for when the moment came, Anna would be waiting. It was the twins she worried for, and Joe.

Her needles flew through patterns of her island and brought with them peace. The twins slept in the arms of mother and grandmother, blissfully unaware of the danger all around them.

*

Dawn had fully broken when the Zep's roars retreated from the town. For now, they were safe, but the same couldn't be said for the brave men out at sea.

"I want to check the house," said Susan.

"I don't think that's a good idea, love."

"Ted, the Zep's gone, we're safe, for now. I need to know if I have a home to go back to."

"Very well, I'll come with you."

"No, I'll take Clara, but thanks all the same."

Ted humphed, but let the matter drop. Clara understood Susan's need for female companionship amid disaster and grabbed her coat. She laid Lizzie down on Ted's lap and the two women let themselves out of the house. Worry etched itself across Susan's impish face.

"You all right?" Clara asked.

"I'm worried for Joe."

Clara tucked her arm in Susan's and led her through the streets. The rubble and glass that littered their path shocked both women. Wives and mothers hunched over, searching for precious keepsakes among the debris. Grave-faced men headed toward the beach.

On the corner of her street, Susan paused. Most houses were still standing, but windows were bare, their glass blown clean out. Others had large holes in the roofs.

"Come on," said Clara.

At Susan's house, they stopped and stared. The front of her terrace, and those on either side, had been blown clean off. A bed creaked as it seesawed on a half-torn landing. Papers and photographs fluttered among the rubble. Clara pulled Susan tight to her.

"I'm so glad ye came to us. I'm so pleased you're safe."

Susan broke free from Clara's embrace and retched into the rubble. "The twins," she said through coughs. "The twins...."

"The twins are safe," said Clara, holding her friend's hair from her face and stroking her back. Susan recovered herself and the two women sat on the pavement, clearing a space amongst the rubble. Clara looked up as Susan snorted.

"What on earth can be funny?" she asked.

"I always complained to Joe the house was damp and draughty.... Draughty," said Susan, waving at the wall-less house, exposed to all the elements. The pair dissolved into giggles, attracting glares from passers-by who felt this was no time for laughter. They wiped hysterical tears from their faces, but each time they tried to speak, laughter returned. Clara laughed till her stomach hurt, bending over to take big gulps of air.

She would often look back on that moment; it was strange what shock and loss could do to you. Once calm, Susan and Clara searched the rubble for any belongings they could save. Clara found a teddy bear, ears singed but still intact. Susan found a photograph album tucked beneath a lump of brick.

"There's no point staying here," said Susan. "It's only things. Let's get back to the twins. There might be news of Joe." Clara nodded, and they walked back to Betty's house. On the way, they agreed that Clara would give up her bedroom for Susan and the twins. Susan tried to refuse, but Clara insisted.

"I can sleep in the sitting room. It can't be worse than sharing a bunk with Heather," she said, and Susan smiled, despite the hopelessness of her situation.

Clara relayed the situation to Ted and Betty, who insisted Susan stay with them. Betty sprang into action, gathering any clothes her neighbours could spare for Susan and the babies. Ted headed to the beach to join the other men and search for news of Joe.

*

Out on his trawler, Joe watched as explosions tore through his town. Thunderous bangs brought vast plumes of smoke, which, as they cleared, revealed angry red flames. Even miles out to sea, the trawler rocked with each bomb dropped. The crew gathered on deck to watch the devastation they were powerless to prevent. Joe prayed that Susan and the twins were safe. Life would be meaningless without them. The Zep fled as quickly as it arrived, and the trawler bobbed on the water untouched.

Three weeks later, thirty miles from the coast the *Elizabeth* hit a mine. An almighty fireworks display played out in front of Joe's eyes before the world around him became dark and he collapsed on the burnt-out deck, screaming.

HOME

Chapter 58

April, 1924

Four years of war had taken a heavy toll on the community. In Clara's small corner, life had become coloured by a mundane bleakness, daily chores undertaken beneath a mist of sadness. Ted and Betty had aged since losing their son. Only their grandchildren could break through their grief, the innocent joy of youth patching up broken hearts.

Careful footsteps trod the stairs, the brushing of a hand on the banister signalling it was Joe.

"Morning, Joe," Clara called from the kitchen, as his stick clicked against skirting boards.

"Morning, Clara, didn't see you there."

Clara chuckled and watched him move around the room in admiration. He knew his way round by touch and set about pouring himself a glass of milk. His hand felt for a chair and he sat himself at the table.

"Up to much today?"

"Oh, the usual quiet day," said Clara. "I'm down at the Denes working the nets this morning, there's the Barnetts' laundry to do this afternoon, then I'm taking your mam to the doctor's at four for her check-up."

"Not much doing then," he said, smiling in her direction.

"Aye. How about you?"

"Work."

*

In the weeks following the explosion, Joe struggled to come to terms with his new life. The only survivor from the *Elizabeth's* crew, he felt more affected by the grim statistic than his injuries. His days in hospital were the worst. He refused visits from anyone but Susan. The pressure of caring for the twins and supporting her suffering husband took its toll.

After several weeks of rage and frustration, Joe retreated into himself, until just the shell of him remained. Only after returning home did glimpses of the man they loved appear. As with Ted and Betty, it had been the twins who offered a path to healing.

Unaware of the change in their father, they cuddled into him just as before, bouncing on his knee and giggling at his tickles. At these moments, the old Joe returned. Taking their cue from the children, the adults treated Joe as Joe, not Joe the blind man.

"Fetch me the twins' blanket," Susan would call.

"I can't!"

"Yes, you can. It's on the floor beside you."

"Can you get the door, please?" Clara would ask on hearing the postman knock. Joe would scowl, but do as she asked.

Slowly, his independence returned. The family was careful to keep everything in its place, for finding something moved caused him bouts of frustration. Betty had suggested they turn the sitting room into a bedroom, so Joe wouldn't need to negotiate the stairs. He refused, and give him his due, mastered not only the stairs, but his way around the entire house.

The biggest change came with his work. It caused a great commotion one morning when a shiny black motor car pulled into the street. A uniformed man stepped out, opening the door for an elegant middle-aged lady.

"Oh, my word," said Betty, ripping off her apron. "It's Lady Somerleyton!"

Lady Somerleyton's charitable works were the talk of the town, but Betty never expected they would receive a visit.

"Clara, tidy up, quick!"

Clara did as she was told and tidied the already tidy sitting room. She hung back as Betty answered the door.

"Good morning, Mrs Mason. Is your son Joseph at home?"

"Yes, ma'am," said a flushed Betty.

"Could I have a quick word with him?"

"Certainly, ma'am, would you like to come in?"

"I think that would be preferable to standing on the doorstep, don't you?" Lady Somerleyton smiled, a twinkle in her eye.

Betty showed Lady Somerleyton to a chair, and Clara made herself scarce. Joe came in, using his cane to find his way to a chair. Betty hovered in the doorway.

"I wonder if I could have a moment alone with your son?"

Betty nodded. "Would you like some tea?"

"That sounds lovely, thank you."

Betty scurried off to make the tea, desperate to catch any hint of the conversation. She was out of luck, for despite taking her time to set down the tea set, Joe and the lady paused their conversation, only resuming when Betty had left the room.

Clara and Susan lingered on the stairs, and Betty hovered outside the door. They heard the scrape of a chair, and Betty scampered through to the kitchen, Susan and Clara tiptoeing back upstairs. Only when Joe said his goodbyes did the family gather in the kitchen, desperate for a full account of the meeting.

"Well?" asked Betty.

"She's a lovely lady," said Joe.

"I know, I know, but what did she want with you?"

"She came to offer me a job."

Betty stared at him, open-mouthed. "A job?"

"Yes, Ma, a job making ropes. She wants to open her house to visitors, but they need rope to keep people away from the precious items."

"Oh, well, I always heard she was good with her charity work."

Joe's face darkened. "This isn't charity, Ma, it's kindness, yes, but not charity. I shall do a proper job, for proper money."

"Yes, I'm sorry. But... but..."

"Won't I need to see? No, I won't. I need to feel. I've hauled enough to know good rope when I hold it."

Betty patted her son's hands, and Ted clapped him on the back. "Well done, son."

Lady Somerleyton enjoyed Joe's company and became a regular visitor to the house. Betty swelled with pride, and took to greeting Lady Somerleyton on the street, to be sure the neighbours would see.

*

Clara was grateful to Lady Somerleyton, not just for her interest in Joe but for the light that shone from Betty's eyes after each visit.

Betty dealt with Michael's death by banning any mention of him in the home. Shelves and mantels housed empty spaces where Michael's photographs should have stood. Ted had burnt his clothes in an old tin bucket and his favourite mug lay buried in the yard.

Despite this, the 'out of sight, out of mind' strategy was an abject failure. Michael's absence filled the small home as much as the piles of Joe's ropes.

Chapter 59

May, 1924

The house was full to the rafters since Joe, Susan, and the children had moved in. Six years after the war ended, little had changed with their living arrangements. Perhaps if Joe hadn't lost his sight, he would have been keen for a place of his own. But with funds limited, and familiar surroundings a necessity, the family had stayed put. Clara kept her belongings in a kist and laid out a bed each night, packing it away before the family woke and needed to use the sitting room.

Since Michael's death, the ties that held her to the family had frayed. The extra money from her work on the nets was welcome, but Clara often felt like a stranger intruding on their grief. Ted and Betty never made her feel uncomfortable, but Clara wondered if her time in Lowestoft was drawing to a close.

A crossroads presented itself one morning when a letter arrived. The postmark was North Shields, and the address typed rather than handwritten. She carried the letter to the sitting room, closing the door behind her.

Clara read the letter with sadness and disbelief. In formal, unsympathetic prose, a gentleman named McClufferty informed her of her grandparents' death.

I regret to inform you... succumbed to influenza... a private funeral was held... Clara held her breath as she skimmed the remaining words...

only surviving family member... sole heir... They had left her everything. The house, business, assets; all hers.

The letter fell from Clara's hand and she sat cross-legged on the floor, head spinning from the news. Like a small rudderless boat at sea, she seemed unable to control her own path, buffeted back and forth by life's waves.

"Would you like a cup of tea, love?" Betty called from the kitchen.

"Aye, thank you."

Clara found Betty in the kitchen, pouring hot brown liquid from the pot into two china cups. She sat down in a chair and Betty glanced over.

"You alright, love?"

"No, not really," said Clara, smoothing the letter onto the table.

The teapot wobbled in her hands as Betty noticed the official-looking envelope. Tea pooled on the table below. "What's that you got there? Good news doesn't usually come in a brown envelope."

"Sorry, Betty, I didn't mean to alarm you. It's a letter about my grandparents. They're dead."

"Oh no. You poor love," said Betty, shuffling round the table and wrapping Clara in her arms.

Clara buried her head in Betty's shoulder. She felt she had no right to cry, having left her grandparents with no warning. But over the past few years, she had grown closer to her grandmother through their correspondence. Despite the gulf in their life experiences, she had hoped they would one day meet again. Clara lifted her head, and Betty moved to the chair opposite her.

"Do you mind me asking what the letter says? Tell me if you'd rather I didn't pry."

Clara smiled at her mother-in-law. "Betty, I don't think ye've ever pried in yer life. The letter tells me they died of influenza," she said. "The thing is, Betty, I'm the only person named in their will."

"Oh, well, that's something. It doesn't bring them back, I know, dear, but it will be nice for you to have a little money in your pocket."

Clara's cheeks turned pink. "Thing is, Betty, they weren't like the rest of my family. They were wealthy. Very wealthy."

"Oh."

Money was not something they ever discussed in the household, and Betty shuffled in her seat, turning her cup round and round on its saucer. "What are you going to do?"

"I want to go home."

"Then home you should go," said Betty, reaching across the table to pat Clara's hand.

"I'm sorry. I don't mean to sound ungrateful. I love you all and you've been so welcoming. It's just with Michael gone..."

Betty winced at the mention of her son's name. "Don't you worry about us, love. We'll miss you, but you must do what you need to do." Betty squeezed Clara's hand.

They sat in silence for a moment, then Clara made another rash decision. "Betty, I want you, Ted, Joe and Susan to have half of whatever they left me."

Betty pulled her hands away and frowned at Clara. "No, love. That money is yours and yours alone. We don't need charity, thank you very much."

Clara understood Betty's pride and was wise enough not to say that they were already surviving on charity and charity alone.

"Betty, I mean it. It isn't charity. Think of it as Michael's share, and payment for all you've done for me. You took me into your family when I had none. You gave me a home and for that I'll always be grateful."

Betty changed the subject to the weather, and they sat talking for some time. As Clara stood up to resume her chores, she looked across at Betty.

"What should I do now?"

Betty stirred the dregs of tea in her cup, pondering the question. "Well, I think the first thing you should do is go to a solicitor. You can't decide anything until you know the sum of money you're dealing with. Maybe your grandfather's business was in debt, or there is someone else contesting the will. That happened to Doreen's family when her father died. A right old fight broke out between her brothers. It turned out the old man had debts piled up. The whole thing was a poisoned chalice anyway!" She managed a small chuckle.

"You're right," said Clara. "I'll walk into town this afternoon and make an appointment. For now, let's pretend nothing's happened."

*

The solicitor's office was tucked away down a small street off London Road South. Clara rang the bell and a young girl in a smart two-piece met her at the door. She followed the click-clack of the girl's heels through a dark hallway and into a small waiting room.

"Sit here. Mr Heath will be with you shortly."

Clara obeyed and perched herself on an emerald green armchair. The room smelt of old books and Clara shrank against its formality, hoping Mr Heath wouldn't keep her waiting long.

A small wiry man poked his head around a heavy oak door. "Mrs Mason?" Clara nodded, "Good. Come with me."

He waved to a polished high-backed chair and Clara sat, her hands wringing in her lap. Mr Heath looked up and smiled, and Clara's hands stilled. He read through her letter and noted down Clara's circumstances in a businesslike fashion.

"I will need to correspond with the office in North Shields and should hear within a week. Make an appointment with Mavis and we can take things from there."

"Thank you," said Clara, shaking his hand.

When she returned the following week, Mr Heath informed her of an eye-watering inheritance.

"You look as if you could do with a brandy," he said, reaching in his desk drawer and pulling out a bottle and glass.

Clara took the glass with shaking hands. "Thank you."

"How do you wish to proceed?"

"I don't know."

"Well, the house is in a fine area. Would you consider relocating?"

"Not to North Shields. I mean, there's nothing wrong with the place, but I don't know anyone there and can't see myself playing lady of the manor."

"Hmm, no, well, there's also the business to deal with."

"Goodness, I don't have to become a shipbuilder, do I?"

Mr Heath laughed, "No, Clara, I don't think anyone expects that of you. I can instruct the firm in North Shields to sell both house and business if you wish."

"Aye, thank you."

"Well, I think that is all for now. Unless you have questions?"

"You're sure I'm the only person named in the will?"

"Yes, that's correct."

"Hmm."

"I can assure you no one is going to contest the will, if that is what's worrying you?"

"Oh no, it's not that. It's just their maid, Sibyl. Well, she was more family to them than I was. Could I arrange an allowance for her?"

"Yes, I suppose so. I'm sure the North Shields firm could arrange that for you. Is there anything else I can help you with?"

Clara considered her future. If she returned to the island, she couldn't live in her old cottage. Even if things had been right with her da, the memories of her mam would be too painful. She asked Mr Heath to write to Mrs Guthrey at the island post office. If anyone knew of homes for sale, it would be her. He would explain he was working on behalf of an islander, but not divulge Clara's name. She had no idea whether Bill would welcome her back and would rather deal with him in person than have him hearing about her return through village gossip.

Chapter 60

June, 1924

Clara walked along the beach where Michael had courted her all those years ago. She would miss the town, the family, Susan. Leaving her best friend would be the hardest thing of all. Why did life hold so many losses, so many goodbyes?

Susan headed towards her, a child in each hand. Clara waved and joined her. The twins busied themselves in the sand, and Clara stared out to sea.

"You're a million miles away," said Susan.

"Aye, I've got a lot on my mind."

Susan eyed Clara with curiosity. "Spill the beans."

"Susan, I've come into some money. I'm going to go home."

"Do you mean back to the island?"

Clara nodded.

"But why?"

"The thing is, I never wanted to leave in the first place, never would if it was up to me."

"Yes, your dad was unkind, that's for sure. Why now?"

"I was here for Michael. Now he's gone, there's nothing left." Susan looked hurt. "I don't mean you. You're my best friend. I wish I could stay with you, but this just doesn't feel like home anymore. I have a brother I've never met, a da I haven't seen in years."

Susan nodded her understanding. "Then you must go," she said.

Clara explained about the money, and as expected Susan tried to refuse.

"Susan, Michael would want me to take care of you all. *I* want to take care of you all. You will always be my family, and that's what families do for each other."

Susan remained unconvinced.

"Look," said Clara, "if you don't let me give it to you in the way I want, I'll bury it under this damn sand and send you a treasure map."

Susan laughed, and the women hugged.

"There is one condition to the money; you must bring the twins up to visit me." They watched the twins playing in the sand. "Susan, they would love it. You can take the train and have a proper holiday."

"That sounds like a good deal to me," said Susan.

*

The family sat round the kitchen table, looking nervous. Clara had asked them all to meet so she could talk about her plans. She didn't want to push anyone into a situation they were uncomfortable with, but Susan had agreed with Clara that it was the best option all round. Clara took a deep breath and addressed the family.

"As you know, I have come into an inheritance. It's a substantial sum and there's no way I could spend my way through it in one lifetime. You've been as kind to me as anyone I've known, and I want you to benefit from my good fortune. I intend to return to the island. I have a brother I've never met, and I'd like to resolve grievances with my da. What I propose is that I buy you a house, one large enough for you all to live in. The bairns could have a garden to play in, and Joe could have a workshop for his ropes. I want nothing in return except bringing some happiness to a family who deserves it."

When Clara finished speaking, the room was silent. Ted went to speak, then decided against it. She had made it clear to each individual on separate occasions that by helping them, she would not leave herself short. Ted stood up from his seat. He walked to Clara, bent down, and hugged her. "I'm off to the pub."

*

It was another two weeks before Mr Heath received a reply from the island's post office. He handed Clara the letter.

Dear Mr Heath,

In providing you with this information, I trust you are an honourable man, and are indeed acting on an islander's behalf. We don't want interlopers buying up all the homes here.

As it happens, The Manor House is for sale. If your client is looking for a modest family home, this will not be for them. It is a large building requiring substantial improvements, but with the right owner, it would make a fine hotel. Please be aware, to make the property habitable would require a LOT of capital and is not for the fainthearted.

Unfortunately, this is the only property on the market. There are smaller cottages available, but these are only lettings. I have enclosed two newspaper cuttings giving details of properties for let in case they interest your client. I have also enclosed the name and address of the vendor of The Manor House. Best of luck with your search, Mrs Guthrey.

Clara read the letter several times, along with the cuttings Mrs Guthrey had provided.

"What do you think I should do?"

Mr Heath frowned. "Hmm, that is not up to me. As I see it, you have two choices; either rent a small cottage and live off your inheritance, or invest it into the larger property. Neither is straightforward. With renting, there is always the chance the landlord may withdraw the property from the market. The Manor House offers more security, but only with a significant investment of time and money."

Clara weighed up her options.

"Would you be interested in Mrs Guthrey's suggestion of running The Manor House as a hotel?"

"I'm not sure. It's not something I've ever thought about."

"I see. You know, Clara, with the amount you have inherited, you need not work."

That decided it for Clara. She was still a young woman. Hard work was in her blood, she thrived on it.

"I'll buy The Manor House."

Mr Heath looked up from his papers. "Don't you think you should give it a little more thought? It's a significant commitment."

"No. I appreciate your advice, I really do, but if I spend too long thinking, I won't decide anything at all."

"Very well. I will arrange the purchase, but I will do nothing for two days, just in case you change your mind."

"I won't," Clara said. She shook his hand and said goodbye.

Chapter 61

July, 1924

Clara strolled up the wide, bustling London Road North and through the doors of one of its newest department stores. Chadds was the epitome of elegance. Across its vast floors lay polished counters of wood and glass. Here, you found anything your heart desired.

Clara knew it by reputation. Kitty and Cassie had been on a spree to buy Christmas presents before leaving the town, but she never ventured in herself. Despite her windfall, Clara had no intention of wasting her newfound wealth. But since the day she'd received the news of Michael, she'd wanted to replace the vase she had broken.

Past counters of perfume and makeup, Clara reached the women's fashion department. She pulled out a blood orange tea dress, held it up against her and swayed, closing her eyes, transporting herself to a dance. Muffled giggles reached her ears. She opened her eyes to see a gaggle of schoolgirls walking past. It was clear she was the source of their amusement. Well, there would be no need for pretty dresses where she was going. With a brief pause of regret, Clara placed the dress back on the rail.

She moved on to practical matters and found the homeware section. Try as she might, she could not find a vase resembling the one she broke. Instead, she found a vase of delicate china, painted a soft sky blue with colourful exotic birds dancing across it. She felt a pang at the memory it dredged up; a scared young woman standing in a grand room with exotic birds covering the walls. Certain Betty would like it, she carried it to the counter.

The shop assistant had her back turned and was busying herself with a stack of sweaters. Clara coughed, but the girl didn't respond. Annoyance rose in her. The young were so flighty these days. At twenty-nine Clara was still young herself, but didn't always feel it. For years she had been doing the work of a middle-aged woman, caring for an elderly couple who weren't her own blood. She coughed again, a brusque "Hu hum" that sent the shop girl spinning round. The girl's hair sat within a net, but wayward blonde curls spilled at its edges. Clara stared.

"Excuse me, miss, do you mind if I ask your name?"

"Marnie," the girl said.

The room spun, and Clara gripped the shop counter. Blood rushed to her head, and she staggered back a few paces. Marnie ran around the counter and took Clara in her arms, guiding her to a chair by the fitting room.

"Marnie?" Clara whispered once recovered. The girl nodded and stared at Clara, her mouth opening wide before she clapped a hand hard across it.

"Clara?"

A lady in a crisp uniform passed them by and glared at Marnie, who returned it with a smile. She squatted down beside Clara.

"Look, I'll get in trouble if I talk here, but I have my break in an hour. Come back then and we'll go for tea?"

Clara nodded and blundered back across the shop floor.

"Clara?" Marnie held the vase aloft. "Do ye still want it?"

Clara nodded, handing over the correct change and promising that she would be back in an hour. She walked through the town and found a bench. Sitting looking out to sea, she tried to calm herself. Marnie? In Lowestoft? Her head spun with both questions and memories. She saw the little girl hiding behind Jimmy all those years ago. Could this be the same Marnie? And Jimmy, where was he? Was he still alive?

Unable to settle her mind, Clara walked past the harbour, up along the promenade that stretched for miles along the golden sands. Betty would expect her back soon.

Her watch hand moved around its face, and Clara made her way to Chadds. Marnie was waiting in the doorway, glancing down the street, looking nervous. She spotted Clara and waved. Shyness lay between them. How many years had it been? Too many to count.

Marnie led Clara to a nearby café, and they waited for the waiter to take their order. Neither spoke till he returned with their drinks, set them down and retreated behind the counter.

"What are ye doing here?" they both asked, and laughing, the tension dissolved.

"You go first," said Marnie.

Clara told her tale, beginning at her grandparents' house, then to the herring girls, meeting Michael and all that happened since. At the mention of Michael, Marnie shifted in her seat.

"You married?" she asked, warmth gone from her voice.

"Aye," said Clara. "But now I'm widowed."

Marnie seemed unwilling to talk.

"Your turn," said Clara. "How did you end up so far from home?"

Marnie stared down at her cup, stirring the brown liquid round and round until it became a whirlpool.

"Marnie?"

Marnie looked up, straight into Clara's eyes. "I came here for Jimmy."

Clara's hands shook, spilling tea over the edges of her cup and into its saucer. She took a deep breath and began clearing up the mess with her napkin. "Jimmy's here?" she asked in a whisper.

"Aye, you didn't know? He told me he wrote to you many times, but you never replied." Her eyes took on a look of steel.

"He never wrote," said Clara, returning Marnie's cool look.

"Aye, he did. He wrote to you every month. You never got them?" There was a challenge in her voice.

"No." Clara's voice was hoarse, her throat dry. She took another sip of tea. "I don't understand. Where did he send the letters?"

"To the island. I told him you'd left for a while, but we both thought you would have gone back."

Clara moved to settle her cup down, but she couldn't see the table for the tears in her eyes. "I couldn't go back. They didn't want me." The tears broke free, tumbling down her cheeks. "Why didn't they forward the letters on?"

Marnie handed Clara her own napkin. "I don't know," she said. "Clara, can anyone in your house read?"

Clara looked up and dabbed her eyes. "Da read a little, but I don't think he knew how to write. How about Rachel?" Marnie shook her head in answer.

Sadness threatened to overwhelm Clara. "How is Jimmy?" she said. Had he married? Was he happy? She had to know, however much it might hurt.

"Aye, he's well... now."

"What do you mean?"

"He had a nasty accident a few years back. Mashed his leg good and proper. Hasn't been able to walk well since, but it turned good for him in the end."

"Oh?"

"He's a schoolmaster." As she spoke, Marnie's face filled with pride. Clara's mouth dropped open. Jimmy had done it. He had built the life he always wanted.

"He didn't wed," said Marnie in answer to Clara's unspoken question. "I think he was waiting for you." She gave Clara a long stare.

"Marnie, I didn't know he had written, I didn't know where he was, I thought he forgot me." She wrung her hands. "Is he happy?"

"Aye, I think he has a happiness of sorts. He loves his work and his pupils love him. He's a round peg in a round hole, as they say."

Clara smiled, pleased some good had come to him at last.

"I think he'd like to see you."

"Where is he?"

"His school is in a village nearby. We live in the schoolhouse together."

Clara struggled to take the information in. Jimmy, her Jimmy, living a few miles from her this whole time and she hadn't known.

"Can I have his address, please?"

"Aye," said Marnie and called the waiter over for a notebook and pencil. She sat writing the address down and looked up, noticing Clara's surprise.

Marnie chuckled. "Clara, you didn't think I'd be living with a schoolteacher and not learn to read and write?"

She laughed again, her eyes glinting in a way that reminded Clara of the child she had known all those years back.

Marnie handed her the note and stood up. “I have to get back to work, but write to him. It’s about time.” She winked. “Call at the shop again. My break is the same time each day. We’ve a lot more to catch up on.” She bent over to kiss Clara’s cheek before making her way out of the café.

Clara folded the paper and slipped it inside her bag. She ordered another cup of tea and sat for a while, trying to wrap her mind around all she now knew. Jimmy had been her best friend. She would give anything to have that friendship back again.

Chapter 62

July, 1924

When Marnie returned home that night, the light was off in Jimmy's room. She decided her news could wait till the morning. Though he loved his work, it exhausted him. The responsibility of it lay heavy on his shoulders.

Raymond had taught him well, and it had devastated both siblings when his heart gave out. For many months, they continued to share their small bedroom. By leaving it, Jimmy would have to acknowledge Raymond would not return, and it took a long time before he was ready to do so.

Jimmy's promotion to headmaster had been bittersweet. It was a remarkable achievement for someone of Jimmy's age and background, but he would give it up in a second if it meant Raymond could still be with them. Jimmy brushed off his success as luck, but Marnie knew it resulted from talent. Despite his firm hand, the pupils loved him. The board loved his confidence and steady nature, his colleagues loved his kindness and competence. There were times, though, when he would bury his head in his hands and complain that he no longer had his mentor to guide him.

They had been a family of sorts. Marnie had her suspicions why Raymond remained a bachelor. He loved Jimmy deeply, but he was never anything other than fatherly towards him. Marnie was certain

Raymond's final years were his happiest. His waifs and strays, as he referred to them, became the children he never had.

Marnie climbed into bed and lay thinking about her meeting with Clara. It had shaken her to see an island face, and a thin layer of homesickness shrouded her. Her thoughts turned to Tom, her young man, Jimmy called him. He had done a very successful job of banishing any homesickness when they met that evening. Marnie smiled, pulled her blanket closer and fell into a deep sleep.

*

Jimmy was up and making breakfast when Marnie appeared.

"Morning, sleepyhead."

"Morning," said Marnie, rubbing her eyes with the heels of her palms.

"How's your young man?" Jimmy asked and winked at his sister.

"Jimmy, you sound more like Raymond every day."

"Nae I dinna!" said Jimmy, reviving the accent he had all but buried beneath his King's English. Marnie laughed. Jimmy removed a hard-boiled egg from the pan with his spoon.

"I met Clara yesterday," she blurted out. As Jimmy's egg fell to the floor, shell smashing against wood, Marnie cursed her bluntness. "Sorry, I would've told you last night, but you were sound asleep."

Jimmy sat down at the table, buttering his toast, refusing to meet his sister's eye.

"Don't you want to know how she is?"

"No."

"Jimmy."

"No, Marnie."

They sat at the table, crunching toast the only sound. Marnie waited till her brother's mouth was full, then tried again. "She never got your letters."

Jimmy stopped chewing and looked up at his sister. "Really?"

"Aye, she never got them. She didn't forget you, Jimmy. She thought you forgot her."

Jimmy stood and scraped his chair against the floor. "I need to get ready for work."

Marnie stared at her brother's back as he retreated upstairs. She picked up the remains of his toast and took a bite. He was the same loveable Jimmy, but sometimes his eyes would darken as a memory crossed them. A section of his heart was closed off, of that she was sure. He would talk with fondness of his time on the *Star Gazer* in Seahouses, but if she asked about his time in Lowestoft, he clammed up. Marnie assumed it was because of the accident, but also wondered if something else had happened. She sighed and poured a cup of tea.

*

Jimmy stood staring into his wardrobe for a good five minutes. Instead of shirts and ties, he saw Clara. How stupid he had been, letting Alex in and common sense out. He could have spoken to her, held her. Tears broke into his eyes, but he rubbed them away and pulled on his jacket.

At the school gate, he welcomed the children as usual, but today his smile did not reach his eyes. He took his frustration out on his pupils, dishing out the dunce's hat for the first time in months. His dour mood caught the children off guard and left them unsettled. Their unhappiness added to Jimmy's own, and he was grateful when the day drew to a close.

Four days later, a letter arrived;

Dear Jimmy,

I'm sure Marnie will have told you by now, but we met each other last week. You can imagine my surprise at seeing her! I'm sorry I never replied to your letters, but I promise you, I never received them. Would you like to meet with me? I think we have a lot to catch up on. Please write to me at the above address with a date and time that would suit. I look forward to hearing from you, Clara.

Jimmy's hands shook as he read the letter. To hear from her own mouth that she had not forgotten him was quite something. He longed to meet her, but worried that his heart could not mend twice. What if he lost her again? If he had had more courage all those years ago at the dance, things might have turned out so differently.

Dear Clara,

Thank you for your letter. I must be honest from the off and tell you I knew you were in Lowestoft. I saw you once, many years ago, and will explain more in person. It would be wonderful to catch up after so long. My weekdays are very full, but a Sunday would suit me well. I shall wait by the docks next Sunday at midday. I very much hope you will join me, Jimmy.

Chapter 63

July, 1924

A thin shard of light bled through a gap in the curtains. Clara turned her head and looked at the clock on the wall. Five a.m. All night she had tossed and turned, heart fluttering and mind whirring each time she thought of the day ahead. She untangled her limbs from layers of blankets and pulled wide the curtains. It was a beautiful morning, and with nerves fizzing within her, there was no point trying to sleep. Clara dressed with care, spending more time on her hair than usual. She made herself a flask of tea and a sandwich, picked up her knitting and left the house.

Bar a few fishermen heading to the docks, the town was quiet. On London Road South, she passed tall terraces, her imagination straying to the lives within them. At the promenade, she jumped down from the seawall and settled herself on the straw-coloured sand, back against the smooth stone.

The sun slid up from the horizon, and Clara poured herself some tea. After one bite of her sandwich, she gave up on food, too nervous to eat. She picked up her knitting. Her body was jittery and her fingers needed occupying. Fuchsia light filled the vast sky, stretching out as far as Southwold in the distance. The sea was calm, but she'd been among fishermen long enough to know the sky, whilst beautiful, was ominous. She hoped the rain would hold off long enough for her to meet Jimmy.

Hours slipped past, and between knitting and people-watching, she had plenty to distract her. At half-past eleven, she made her way to the harbour. It was only a five-minute walk, but she would rather be early than late.

*

Trains were less regular on a Sunday, and as a result, Jimmy was in Lowestoft by ten. He wished he had come into town before, for facing his memories and Clara on one day felt overwhelming. With time to kill, he explored some of his old haunts, turning north from the station and ambling along the high street. He had recovered from the accident as well as he ever would. Although there was little movement in his leg, at least it no longer hurt.

He walked as far as Mariner's Score, then followed the path down the cliff. Rows of terraces stretched before him and in his mind's eye he saw Graham and the lads spilling out from the Rising Sun, Josie hanging washing on the line. He walked as far as the Denes before turning back towards the docks. Sand was no good for his leg, so he headed back down Whapload Road.

The Grit seemed to have lost some of its sparkle, and Jimmy heard the fishing had never since reached the great heights of 1913. He paused at Christchurch, slipping inside its walls to say a silent prayer of forgiveness, hope and love.

At the harbour, he spotted a woman standing on the far side of the docks. He recognised the straight-backed, fidgeting figure. She was early too. Clara hadn't seen him and he made his way around the harbour unobserved. As he turned the corner, he saw her shield her eyes and gaze in his direction. She gave a small wave, and amid jangling nerves, he worried he might throw up. His mind went blank and his body took control. With as much speed as he could muster, he rushed towards the girl he loved.

*

Clara shielded her eyes and squinted against the sunlight. The rain that threatened at dawn had not yet arrived, and the sea mirrored the sky in its blue. Along the harbour came a man, walking with the aid of a stick. She remembered Marnie's tale of the accident. It was only as he came closer that she was certain it was Jimmy. She raised a hand and waved.

Jimmy looked different. He was wearing a smart suit and wore polished leather shoes. His blond curls were cropped close to his head, and he had grown a beard. Something about his lopsided walk tugged at her heart and her breath caught. As he approached, his pace quickened until it was as close to a run as he could manage. Before he reached her, he flung his stick to the ground and spread his arms.

Clara rushed into his embrace. They said nothing, but stood in each other's arms, neither willing to break free. Clara buried her head into his broad chest and he stroked her hair. They didn't notice the man walking past to check on his boat, or the group of children throwing fishing lines into the water beside them. Jimmy pulled back and held Clara at arm's length.

"Hello," he said.

"Hello."

She looked away, shy, and Jimmy tilted her face back towards him. Where his confidence came from, he couldn't say. But with Clara in his arms, the years melted away. Gulls cried, the waves scattered pebbles on the shore, and they had the taste of salt on their tongues. They could be teenagers standing on the island's north shore.

"Shall we walk?" he asked.

"Aye," she said.

They walked south along the promenade, Clara keeping a careful distance from Jimmy, not trusting herself to get too close. Held in his arms, it was as if she had opened a box of feelings and sensations hidden under a bed for years. She wasn't sure she was ready to let them escape just yet.

Jimmy paused when they reached a refreshment stand. "Would you like a cup of tea?" he asked.

Clara tried to suppress a smirk.

"What's so funny?"

"Sorry," she said, "It's just... what's happened to your voice?"

"What do you mean?"

"What do you mean?" mimicked Clara. "You've lost your accent. You're speaking proper posh these days."

Jimmy smiled. "We've got a lot to catch up on, haven't we?"

Clara nodded, and he went to the counter, returning moments later with two cups of tea. She found a spot on the beach and laid out her shawl for them to sit on. Jimmy's hand brushed hers as he gave her the cup and she blushed, turning her face to the sea.

She reached down for her tea and noticed Jimmy staring at her wedding ring.

"I didn't forget you," he said.

"I know, Marnie explained. I thought you did, though." She looked at him, eyes pleading for him to understand.

"Was your husband a kind man?"

"Aye, he was. It was no great love affair, but we cared for each other deeply. His family took me in when I had nowhere else to go, and for that I will always be grateful."

"I saw you together once."

"What?" She spun her face round, searching his eyes.

"At a dance, I think it was the first time you met."

"Why didn't you come to me?"

Jimmy shrugged. "You looked happy. I thought you didn't care for me any longer."

"Oh, Jimmy," she said. "You could've... it could've..." Her voice trailed off. There was no point in regrets. What's done is done.

"Marnie told me what happened with Bill. I'm so sorry, Clara. I never knew."

"That's all in the past." Her face told him it wasn't.

"Marnie says he missed you, wanted you to come back."

"Then he should've told me," she said. Her face flushed with anger.

"Clara, Anna's death broke him. You have to forgive him one day."

"Aye, I know. I'm hoping to patch things up when I go home."

"You're going home?" he asked, unable to keep disappointment from his voice.

"Aye, seems like fate will keep us apart. Anyway, enough about me. How have you been? I see you've bashed in your leg somehow."

"Ha, yes. That's a long story. A moment of madness."

"And have you found yourself a nice Lowestoft lassie?"

Jimmy's face darkened, and he didn't meet her eye. "No."

"Marnie said you're teaching?"

"Yes," said Jimmy, the warmth returning to his eyes. "My accident was the best thing that ever happened to me. I met a man called Raymond in the hospital and it's thanks to him I am where I am."

"I'm pleased for you, Jimmy. I really am."

The sky darkened, and spots of rain fell on them.

"Let's find some shelter," said Clara. They moved off along the promenade, but the rain was quicker and soon large splodges of water were landing on the pavement.

"How about that shed?" asked Jimmy.

Coats held above their heads, they rushed towards a shed. It was unlocked, and they shook the rain from their hair as they walked through the door.

"Remember the spiders in your da's shed?"

Jimmy groaned. "I thought you may have forgotten about that by now."

"No chance."

They had to shout above the rain on the tin roof, but it didn't stop the flow of conversation. There were eleven years of life to catch up on, but they talked of their childhoods instead.

"It's funny," said Jimmy. "I only remember the bad times with Alex. Talking to you has reminded me of the good times we had, of a life beyond him."

"Enough to go back?"

"Maybe. One day perhaps, not yet."

"Well, that's better than never," said Clara.

They stayed in the shed waiting for the rain to stop, but its hammering continued, beating out a rhythm on rusty tin. Jimmy looked at his watch in alarm.

"I have to go or I'll miss the last train back. How long till you leave Lowestoft?"

"A month at least."

"Good. So we can do this again?"

"Hide out in a stinky fisherman's shed?"

"No," he laughed. "You know what I mean."

"Aye," said Clara. "I do, and yes, I'd like that."

"Same time next week?" he asked.

"Same time next week."

Jimmy leaned down and planted the lightest of kisses on Clara's cheek. She watched him walk back across the sand, already counting the minutes until she could see him again.

Chapter 64

August, 1924

Marnie caught Tom's eye across the table and smirked. Clara had spoken to both when she arrived, but it soon became apparent she and Jimmy were only interested in each other.

"Young love," mouthed Marnie to Tom, tilting her head in Jimmy's direction. Tom grinned.

"Anyone fancy a walk after lunch?" Tom asked.

Jimmy tore his eyes away from Clara. "That sounds like a splendid idea. Somerleyton Hall has opened its grounds to locals this weekend, so we could take a stroll there."

"Sounds lovely," said Clara.

Marnie cleared away the plates, and they headed outside. It was a fine day, and the village looked resplendent in the sunshine. Marnie and Tom hung back until Jimmy and Clara were a suitable distance away.

"They say absence makes the heart grow fonder," she said to Tom, as they noticed Jimmy take Clara's hand.

"I like her," said Tom.

"Aye, so do I. I just worry that her leaving will break his heart again."

Ahead of them, Clara and Jimmy walked side by side. She shivered in excitement as he took her hand in his.

"It's beautiful here," said Clara, gazing at the meadows and the hall in the distance.

"I know. I'm very lucky."

"I'd miss the sea, though. Do you?"

"Not at first. It was good to be free from reminders of the life I'd left. Now time has passed, I miss it. At least it's only a short train ride and I'm back by the waves again."

"Jimmy..."

"Clara, if you're going to ask me to come back to the island..."

"No," said Clara. "I wouldn't ask that of you. I know the memories are still too raw, and besides, how could I drag you away from this life you've built for yourself?"

Jimmy stopped walking, coughed, and scuffed his feet. He looked up at Clara from beneath his lashes. "I did write to the island school to see if there was a vacancy."

"You did what? Jimmy, you'd really do that for me?"

"I would, but unfortunately, the teacher who replaced Mrs McKinnon is well settled and showing no signs of wanting to leave."

"I can't believe you even tried. I know your feelings towards the place. If only I had met you before I bought the hotel..."

Jimmy took Clara's hands in his. "Clara, you're an islander through and through. You want to go home, you need to go home, there's no way I'd stand in the way of that."

"But to find you and lose you again..."

"You're not going to lose me though, are you? We might not be living in the same place, but that doesn't mean we can't see each other. And who knows what the future will bring?"

"Hmm. What do you make of Tom?"

"He's a pleasant fellow, from what I see. It won't surprise me if they're married within the year."

"They're lucky."

"Yes, they are. I sometimes wonder how life would have turned out if we hadn't lost touch."

"I do too, but we've followed our own paths and at least we've found each other now."

"If only there was longer before we're apart again."

"We'd better make the most of the little time we have then."

When Marnie and Tom turned a corner, they found Clara and Jimmy locked in an embrace.

"Let's leave them to it," said Marnie, and they crept away.

*

Leaving was every bit as hard as Clara expected. The last thing she wanted was a great fanfare at the station and she stood by the front door of the small terrace, ready to say goodbye.

"Write to me when you're in the new place. I want to hear all about it."

Betty rushed forward and took Clara in her arms. "You've been like a daughter to me, love. I'll be forever grateful for the love you showed Michael and all you have done for us."

"It's nothing compared to what you've done for me." She kissed Betty, Ted and Joe on the cheek, then bent down to speak to the twins. From her pocket, she pulled a small patchwork rabbit.

"Now, I only have one of these, so you'll have to share. Someone special made this for me, so I want you to take good care of it. Will you do that?" Both twins nodded. "She's an island rabbit, and she won't want to be away from home for too long, so you must bring her for a visit." The twins nodded again, and Clara pulled them into her arms. Not wanting to upset them, she swallowed back her tears. She hugged a tearful Susan and walked out of the door.

At the station, she paid for her ticket and made her way to the platform. Jimmy was waiting for her, despite the private goodbye they'd shared earlier that week.

"I told you not to come," she said as he pulled her into his arms.

"I love you, Clara."

"I love you too."

"I'll write."

"Aye, you'd better. I'll write too."

She broke free from his arms and straightened herself up. At the train door, she turned back and blew him a kiss. "I'll come back for Marnie's wedding," she called, and he smiled as she disappeared inside the carriage.

The whistle blew, and a large puff of smoke filled the platform. With a great squeal, the train pulled out of the station and headed north.

Chapter 65

April, 1946

"Where dee ye want this?" asked a tall handsome man holding a large box of squirming lobsters.

"On the counter, please."

"Nae bother," he said and retreated into the kitchen. He was the image of Bill as a young man, tall, broad shoulders, bear-like hands. These days Bill's beard was white, skin on his hands wrinkled, but salt water still hardened his leathery palms, and most days he was out on the boat.

"Anything else ye need?" called Ben from behind the swing door.

"Na. You got time for a cuppa?"

"Aye, why not, fishin's done fer the day."

"Grand, first guests don't arrive till four, so let's enjoy the freedom while we still have it."

Clara brought two teas outside to where her brother sat on a wooden bench. "I'll never tire of this view," she said, gazing out to the harbour.

"Thought ye'd be sick of it by now. How many years is it since ye've been back?"

"Twenty, give or take."

Ben whistled. "Time flies, doesn't it? I remember when ye turned up at the cottage, thought Da was gannin to pass oot."

Clara laughed, "Aye, in hindsight, it might have been better if I'd given him some warning."

"Na, dinna matter how ye came back, just that ye did. Da's been the happiest I've known him since ye've bin here."

Clara squeezed his hand. "Turns out having a little brother isn't as bad as they make out either."

Ben smiled. "Yer nae too bad yerself."

Embarrassed by the emotional turn the conversation was taking, Ben gulped back his tea and stood to leave.

"Oh, I almost forgot. Mam asked me to invite ye for tea. Ye coming?"

"Sounds good. Tell her I'll be over at six. The guests should be settled by then, and Olive can take care of the evening meals."

"Grand, see ye then."

Ben strode away. He opened the gate for the postman who had a pile of letters in his hand.

"Those for me?"

"Looks like it."

"Thanks," said Clara. She flicked through the pile of post, surprised by a Lowestoft postmark. Jimmy's next letter wasn't due for a week. She was desperate for news of his retirement plans, but their system of a letter a fortnight had served them well all these years and she didn't expect him to change it now.

Studying the envelope, she saw Susan's handwriting. Clara smiled as she read her friend would visit in a fortnight with Joe. Susan sent her apologies that the twins wouldn't be with them, but they couldn't take the time off work. Clara knew they would be as disappointed as she was. Over the years, they had grown to love the island almost as much as she did.

The gate creaked, signalling the first guests of the season had arrived. She greeted them with the warmth she knew would draw them back to her establishment time and again.

*

At six o'clock Clara called her goodbyes to her assistant, Olive, and headed out through the village. Crowds were milling around the main street, visiting for the Easter celebrations. In her youth, she'd sat on this street threading bait onto lines. Back then there was only a trickle of visitors, many being put off by the strong fishy smell and inaccessibility of the island's sands. Since the war ended, there had been a steady stream of visitors, folk wanting to escape the noise and destruction of cities and towns in increasing numbers.

Clara watched harried parents with young children coming out of the sweet shop and felt sympathy. Stylish couples strolled along the street arm in arm. The pilgrims, with their inquisitive faces and serious demeanours, left her bemused.

As she walked through the crowds, other, more familiar faces appeared; her mam, basket in one hand, small child in the other. Her hair was arranged on top of her head by a series of pins, in a style Clara never could replicate. Da was there too, spilling out of The Crown after a good day's catch, staggering up the street with Lobster Jim by his side. Old John stood leaning against a doorway, smoking the pipe that never left his lips.

"What ye deein' standing there starin'?"

Clara realised she was outside the door of her old cottage. Bill was staring at her, bemused by her faraway look.

"Sorry, Da, I was caught up in my memories."

"Well, if I were ye I'd stick to the here and now. Rachel's got a tasty fish pie waiting fer ye on the table."

Clara smiled and followed the old man into the cottage.

*

Jimmy shifted on the cushioned seat of his train carriage but couldn't settle. He ran his hands through his thick silver curls, one in a long line of reminders that his youth was long gone. The view from the window was becoming too familiar, wrenching him back to a time he would rather forget. He was grateful for the barrier of glass that separated him from the landscape, and turned his attention to his book. Its words, usually a comfort, now swam before his eyes. The ink blurred and images leapt from the page, a girl running towards him, skirts flying around her and hair escaping its pins like the dying embers of a fire.

Other images emerged, a man with his fist raised, a woman as wide as she was tall, scowling down at him. Jimmy snapped book and eyes shut, but the memories played against his closed lids like a moving picture at the theatre. Alex was gone. Things were different now. With a sigh of relief, he opened his eyes and turned back to the view.

Through the mist-like smoke of the train, he saw fields rolling down to a glistening sea and could just make out the land protruding from the body of water. Jimmy held his breath as the train sped on, the island coming clearer into view. His heart raced and his chest tightened as he thought of the life he should have led, the life he was returning to.

As the island slipped out from the window's picture frame, he thought of his girl with the wild hair, roaming her island, free as the birds that swooped above its shores. Jimmy took out his handkerchief and wiped away the tears dampening his cheeks.

*

Clara sat herself on the tall stool behind the reception desk. Her feet cried out with exhaustion and it was a relief to take the weight off them. It had been a long day. The hotel was almost full and guests seemed more demanding with each passing year. The clock in the lobby struck five, and she wished the last guest would hurry and arrive.

She regretted offering to cook for her da and Rachel. She would be dead on her feet by then. With Ben away at sea, and Rachel's arthritis playing up, it left her with no choice but to help. Five past, ten past. If the guest didn't arrive soon, Clara would be late.

The large front door gave its loud creak, and a smart gentleman appeared. He crossed the lobby with the aid of a stick and leaned against the desk. Clara stared, open-mouthed, and he smiled.

"Excuse me, madam. I believe I am booked into the room with a sea view."

Clara recovered herself. "That's correct, sir. How long will you be staying?"

The man tugged at his beard. "Hmm, that depends."

"Oh? Depends on what?"

"Well, I suppose it depends on the level of service I receive."

Clara grinned. The years melted away and her feet no longer hurt. She rushed around the desk and flung herself into Jimmy's arms.

About the Author

Author and musician LK (Laura) Wilde was born in Norwich, but spent her teenage years living on a Northumbrian island. She left the island to study Music, and after a few years of wandering settled in Cornwall, where she raises her two crazy, delightful boys.

To keep in touch with Laura and receive a 'bonus bundle' of material, join her monthly Readers' Club newsletter at-

www.lkwilde.com

Or find her on social media- @lkwildeauthor

Finally, if you enjoyed *Silver Darlings*, please consider leaving a review or rating on Amazon. Reviews are so important to indie authors as they're the best way to help more people discover the book!

Acknowledgements

Writing a novel during a pandemic was not without its challenges. Enormous thanks are due to my family, who gave me time and encouragement to write, in between lockdowns, when my brain suddenly kicked back into gear. With travel restricted and museums and archives closed, descriptions of places often relied on my memory, and as a result some details may have been changed or exaggerated due to the passage of time.

Researching this book was a joy, in part thanks to the wonderful books I read – *The Grit,* by Dean Parkin and Jack Rose which offers a fascinating window into Lowestoft's past, *Shiels to Shields* by Danny Lawrence, *Herring Drifters and the Prunier Trophy* by Malcolm R. White, *The Lifeboat Service in England* (The North East Coast Station by Station) by Nicholas Leach. The internet also proved a valuable resource, particularly the research by the Peregrini Lindisfarne Landscape Partnership and the Aladdin's cave that is the British Newspaper Archive.

Thanks are also due to my Lowestoft family for sharing knowledge and encouragement; my Nan's memories of her fisherman grandfather are retold as Joe's story.

I'm extremely grateful to my proofreader, Julia Gibbs. Not only does her knowledge of grammar and punctuation amaze me, her grasp of historical sayings and phrases is a huge help in making a book authentic to the time it is set.

Lastly, thank you to everyone who is picking up this book and reading it, I hope you enjoy reading it as much as I enjoyed writing it.

Also By LK Wilde

People say you get one life, but I've lived three.

I was born Ellen Hardy in 1900, dragged up in Queen Caroline's Yard, Norwich. There was nothing royal about our yard, and Mum was no queen.

At six years old Mum sold me. I became Nellie Westrop, roaming the country in a showman's wagon, learning the art of the fair.

And I've been the infamous Queenie of Norwich, moving up in the world by any means, legal or not.

I've been heart broken, abandoned, bought and sold, but I've never, ever given up. After all, it's not where you start that's important, but where you end up.

Based on a true story, *Queenie of Norwich* is the compelling tale of one remarkable girl's journey to womanhood. Spanning the first half of the 20th century, Queenie's story is one of heartbreak and triumph, love and loss and the power of family. It is a story of redemption, and how, with grit and determination, anything is possible.

1840, Cornwall. The victim, the accused, and the wives left behind. Welcome to the trial of the century...

Based on a true story.

When merchant Nevell Norway is murdered, suspicion soon falls on the Lightfoot brothers. The trial of the century begins, and two women's lives change forever.

Sarah Norway must fight for the future of her children. Battling against her inner demons, can Sarah unlock the strength she needs to move on without Nevell?

Maria Lightfoot's future looks bleak, but she's a fighter. Determined to rebuild her life, an unexpected friendship offers a glimmer of hope...

With their lives in turmoil, can Maria and Sarah overcome the fate of their husbands? Or will they forever remain the wives left behind?

Book 1 in the Cornish feel-good *The House of Many Lives* series

Kate is stuck in a rut, She works a dead end job, lives in a grotty bedsit and still pines for the man who broke her heart.

When Kate inherits a house in a small Cornish town, she jumps at the chance of a fresh start. A surprise letter from her grandmother persuades Kate to open her home and her heart to strangers.

But with friends harbouring secrets, demanding house guests, and her past catching up with her- can Kate really move on? And will her broken heart finally find a home?

Made in United States
North Haven, CT
12 April 2024

51246300R00211